EVERGREEN
CLASSIC SHORT STORIES

EVERGREEN CLASSIC SHORT STORIES

CLASSICS FOR THE AGES

HarperCollins*Children's Books*

First published in 2023 by HarperCollins *Children's Books*
This hardback edition published in 2024 by HarperCollins *Children's Books*
An imprint of HarperCollins *Publishers* India
Building No 10, Tower A, 4th Floor, DLF Cyber City, Phase II,
Gurugram – 122002

2 4 6 8 10 9 7 5 3 1

P-ISBN: 978-93-5699-672-4
E-ISBN: 978-93-5699-740-0

To the best of our knowledge, all works included in this collection are out of copyright and available in the public domain. To give a true sense of the classic genre, we have tried to retain the original form of the stories.

This is a work of fiction and all characters and incidents described in this book are the product of the author's imagination. Any resemblance to actual persons, living or dead, is entirely coincidental.

Typeset in 11.5 on 15.2 / Garamond
Manipal Technologies Limited, Manipal

Printed and bound at
Thomson Press (India) Ltd

FSC www.fsc.org MIX Paper | Supporting responsible forestry FSC® C010615

This book is produced from independently certified FSC® paper to ensure responsible forest management.

CONTENTS

The Mystery of Hunter's Lodge

Agatha Christie

"After all," murmured Poirot, "it is possible that I shall not die this time."

Coming from a convalescent influenza patient, I hailed the remark as showing a beneficial optimism. I myself had been the first sufferer from the disease. Poirot in his turn had gone down. He was now sitting up in bed, propped up with pillows, his head muffled in a woollen shawl, and was slowly sipping a particularly noxious tisane which I had prepared according to his directions. His eye rested with pleasure upon a neatly graduated row of medicine bottles which adorned the mantelpiece.

"Yes, yes," my little friend continued. "Once more shall I be myself again, the great Hercule Poirot, the terror of evil-doers!

Figure to yourself, mon ami, that I have a little paragraph to myself in Society Gossip. But yes! Here it is! 'Go it—criminals—all out! Hercule Poirot—and believe me, girls, he's some Hercules!—our own pet society detective can't get a grip on you. 'Cause why? 'Cause he's got la grippe himself'!"

I laughed.

"Good for you, Poirot. You are becoming quite a public character. And fortunately you haven't missed anything of particular interest during this time."

"That is true. The few cases I have had to decline did not fill me with any regret."

Our landlady stuck her head in at the door.

"There's a gentleman downstairs. Says he must see Monsieur Poirot or you, Captain. Seeing as he was in a great to-do—and with all that quite the gentleman—I brought up 'is card."

She handed me the bit of pasteboard. "Mr Roger Havering," I read.

Poirot motioned with his head towards the bookcase, and I obediently pulled forth "Who's Who". Poirot took it from me and scanned the pages rapidly.

"Second son of fifth Baron Windsor. Married 1913 Zoe, fourth daughter of William Crabb."

"H'm!" I said. "I rather fancy that's the girl who used to act at the Frivolity—only she called herself Zoe Carrisbrook. I remember she married some young man about town just before the War."

"Would it interest you, Hastings, to go down and hear what our visitor's particular little trouble is? Make him all my excuses."

Roger Havering was a man of about forty, well set up and of smart appearance. His face, however, was haggard, and he was evidently labouring under great agitation.

"Captain Hastings? You are Monsieur Poirot's partner, I understand. It is imperative that he should come with me to Derbyshire to-day."

"I'm afraid that's impossible," I replied. "Poirot is ill in bed—influenza."

His face fell.

"Dear me, that is a great blow to me."

"The matter on which you want to consult him is serious?"

"My God, yes! My uncle, the best friend I have in the world, was foully murdered last night."

"Here in London?"

"No, in Derbyshire. I was in town and received a telegram from my wife this morning. Immediately upon its receipt I determined to come round and beg Monsieur Poirot to undertake the case."

"If you will excuse me a minute," I said, struck by a sudden idea.

I rushed upstairs, and in a few brief words acquainted Poirot with the situation. He took any further words out of my mouth.

"I see. I see. You want to go yourself, is it not so? Well, why not? You should know my methods by now. All I ask is that you should report to me fully every day, and follow implicitly any instructions I may wire you."

To this I willingly agreed.

• • •

An hour later I was sitting opposite Mr Havering in a first-class carriage on the Midland Railway, speeding rapidly away from London.

"To begin with, Captain Hastings, you must understand that Hunter's Lodge, where we are going, and where the tragedy took place, is only a small shooting-box in the heart of the Derbyshire moors. Our real home is near Newmarket, and we usually rent a flat in town for the season. Hunter's Lodge is looked after by a housekeeper who is quite capable of doing all we need when we run down for an occasional week-end. Of course, during the shooting season, we take down some of our own servants from Newmarket. My uncle, Mr Harrington Pace (as you may know, my mother was a Miss Pace of New York), has, for the last three years, made his home with us. He never got on well with my father, or my elder brother, and I suspect that my being somewhat of a prodigal son myself rather increased than diminished his affection towards me. Of course I am a poor man, and my uncle was a rich one—in other words, he paid the piper! But, though exacting in many ways, he was not really hard to get on with, and we all three lived very harmoniously together. Two days ago my uncle, rather wearied with some recent gaieties of ours in town, suggested that we should run down to Derbyshire for a day or two. My wife telegraphed to Mrs Middleton, the housekeeper, and we went down that same afternoon. Yesterday evening I was forced to return to town, but my wife and my uncle remained on. This morning I received this telegram." He handed it over to me:

"Come at once uncle Harrington murdered last night bring good detective if you can but do come—Zoe."

"Then, as yet you know no details?"

"No, I suppose it will be in the evening papers. Without doubt the police are in charge."

It was about three o'clock when we arrived at the little station of Elmer's Dale. From there a five-mile drive brought us to a small grey stone building in the midst of the rugged moors.

"A lonely place," I observed with a shiver.

Havering nodded.

"I shall try and get rid of it. I could never live here again."

We unlatched the gate and were walking up the narrow path to the oak door when a familiar figure emerged and came to meet us.

"Japp!" I ejaculated.

The Scotland Yard inspector grinned at me in a friendly fashion before addressing my companion.

"Mr Havering, I think? I've been sent down from London to take charge of this case, and I'd like a word with you, if I may, sir."

"My wife—"

"I've seen your good lady, sir—and the housekeeper. I won't keep you a moment, but I'm anxious to get back to the village now that I've seen all there is to see here."

"I know nothing as yet as to what—"

"Ex-actly," said Japp soothingly. "But there are just one or two little points I'd like your opinion about all the same. Captain Hastings here, he knows me, and he'll go on up to the house and tell them you're coming. What have you done with the little man, by the way, Captain Hastings?"

"He's ill in bed with influenza."

"Is he now? I'm sorry to hear that. Rather the case of the cart without the horse, your being here without him, isn't it?"

And on his rather ill-timed jest I went on to the house. I rang the bell, as Japp had closed the door behind him. After some moments it was opened to me by a middle-aged woman in black.

"Mr Havering will be here in a moment," I explained. "He has been detained by the inspector. I have come down with him from London to look into the case. Perhaps you can tell me briefly what occurred last night."

"Come inside, sir." She closed the door behind me, and we stood in the dimly-lighted hall. "It was after dinner last night, sir, that the man came. He asked to see Mr Pace, sir, and, seeing that he spoke the same way, I thought it was an American gentleman friend of Mr Pace's and I showed him into the gun-room, and then went to tell Mr Pace. He wouldn't give any name, which, of course, was a bit odd, now I come to think of it. I told Mr Pace, and he seemed puzzled like, but he said to the mistress: 'Excuse me, Zoe, while I just see what this fellow wants.' He went off to the gun-room, and I went back to the kitchen, but after a while I heard loud voices, as if they were quarrelling, and I came out into the hall. At the same time, the mistress she comes out too, and just then there was a shot and then a dreadful silence. We both ran to the gun-room door, but it was locked and we had to go round to the window. It was open, and there inside was Mr Pace, all shot and bleeding."

"What became of the man?"

"He must have got away through the window, sir, before we got to it."

"And then?"

"Mrs Havering sent me to fetch the police. Five miles to walk it was. They came back with me, and the constable he stayed all night, and this morning the police gentleman from London arrived."

"What was this man like who called to see Mr Pace?"

The housekeeper reflected.

"He had a black beard, sir, and was about middle-aged, and had on a light overcoat. Beyond the fact that he spoke like an American I didn't notice much about him."

"I see. Now I wonder if I can see Mrs Havering?"

"She's upstairs, sir. Shall I tell her?"

"If you please. Tell her that Mr Havering is outside with Inspector Japp, and that the gentleman he has brought back with him from London is anxious to speak to her as soon as possible."

"Very good, sir."

I was in a fever of impatience to get at all the facts. Japp had two or three hours' start on me, and his anxiety to be gone made me keen to be close at his heels.

Mrs Havering did not keep me waiting long. In a few minutes I heard a light step descending the stairs, and looked up to see a very handsome young woman coming towards me. She wore a flame-coloured jumper, that set off the slender boyishness of her figure. On her dark head was a little hat of flame-coloured leather. Even the present tragedy could not dim the vitality of her personality.

I introduced myself, and she nodded in quick comprehension.

"Of course I have often heard of you and your colleague, Monsieur Poirot. You have done some wonderful things together, haven't you? It was very clever of my husband to get you so promptly. Now will you ask me questions? That is the easiest way, isn't it, of getting to know all you want to about this dreadful affair?"

"Thank you, Mrs Havering. Now what time was it that this man arrived?"

"It must have been just before nine o'clock. We had finished dinner, and were sitting over our coffee and cigarettes."

"Your husband had already left for London?"

"Yes, he went up by the 6.15."

"Did he go by car to the station, or did he walk?"

"Our own car isn't down here. One came out from the garage in Elmer's Dale to fetch him in time for the train."

"Was Mr Pace quite his usual self?"

"Absolutely. Most normal in every way."

"Now, can you describe this visitor at all?"

"I'm afraid not. I didn't see him. Mrs Middleton showed him straight into the gun-room and then came to tell my uncle."

"What did your uncle say?"

"He seemed rather annoyed, but went off at once. It was about five minutes later that I heard the sound of raised voices. I ran out into the hall and almost collided with Mrs Middleton. Then we heard the shot. The gun-room door was locked on the inside, and we had to go right round the house to the window. Of course that took some time, and the murderer had been able to get well away. My poor uncle"—her voice faltered—"had been shot through the head. I saw at once that he was dead. I sent Mrs Middleton for the police. I was careful to touch nothing in the room but to leave it exactly as I found it."

I nodded approval.

"Now, as to the weapon?"

"Well, I can make a guess at it, Captain Hastings. A pair of revolvers of my husband's were mounted upon the wall. One of them is missing. I pointed this out to the police, and they took the other one away with them. When they have extracted the bullet, I suppose they will know for certain."

"May I go to the gun-room?"

"Certainly. The police have finished with it. But the body has been removed."

She accompanied me to the scene of the crime. At that moment Havering entered the hall, and with a quick apology his wife ran to him. I was left to undertake my investigations alone.

I may as well confess at once that they were rather disappointing. In detective novels clues abound, but here I could find nothing that struck me as out of the ordinary except a large bloodstain on the carpet where I judged the dead man had fallen. I examined everything with painstaking care and took a couple of pictures of the room with my little camera which I had brought with me. I also examined the ground outside the window, but it appeared to have been so heavily trampled underfoot that I judged it was useless to waste time over it. No, I had seen all that Hunter's Lodge had to show me. I must go back to Elmer's Dale and get into touch with Japp. Accordingly I took leave of the Haverings, and was driven off in the car that had brought us up from the station.

I found Japp at the Matlock Arms and he took me forthwith to see the body. Harrington Pace was a small, spare clean-shaven man, typically American in appearance. He had been shot through the back of the head, and the revolver had been discharged at close quarters.

"Turned away for a moment," remarked Japp, "and the other fellow snatched up a revolver and shot him. The one Mrs Havering handed over to us was fully loaded and I suppose the other one was also. Curious what darn fool things people do. Fancy keeping two loaded revolvers hanging up on your wall."

"What do you think of the case?" I asked, as we left the gruesome chamber behind us.

"Well, I'd got my eye on Havering to begin with. Oh, yes!" noting my exclamation of astonishment. "Havering has one or two shady incidents in his past. When he was a boy at Oxford there was some funny business about the signature on one of his father's cheques. All hushed up of course. Then, he's pretty heavily in debt now, and they're the kind of debts he wouldn't like to go to his uncle about, whereas you may be sure the uncle's will would be in his favour. Yes, I'd got my eye on him, and that's why I wanted to speak to him before he saw his wife, but their statements dovetail all right, and I've been to the station and there's no doubt whatever that he left by the 6.15. That gets up to London about 10.30. He went straight to his club, he says, and if that's confirmed all right—why, he couldn't have been shooting his uncle here at nine o'clock in a black beard!"

"Ah, yes, I was going to ask you what you thought about that beard?"

Japp winked.

"I think it grew pretty fast—grew in the five miles from Elmer's Dale to Hunter's Lodge. Americans that I've met are mostly clean-shaven. Yes, it's amongst Mr Pace's American associates that we'll have to look for the murderer. I questioned the housekeeper first, and then her mistress, and their stories agree all right, but I'm sorry Mrs Havering didn't get a look at the fellow. She's a smart woman, and she might have noticed something that would set us on the track."

I sat down and wrote a minute and lengthy account to Poirot. I was able to add various further items of information before I posted the letter.

The bullet had been extracted and was proved to have been fired from a revolver identical with the one held by the police. Furthermore, Mr Havering's movements on the night in question had been checked and verified, and it was proved beyond doubt that he had actually arrived in London by the train in question. And, thirdly, a sensational development had occurred. A city gentleman, living at Ealing, on crossing Haven Green to get to the District Railway Station that morning, had observed a brown-paper parcel stuck between the railings. Opening it, he found that it contained a revolver. He handed the parcel over to the local police station, and before night it was proved to be the one we were in search of, the fellow to that given us by Mrs Havering. One bullet had been fired from it.

All this I added to my report. A wire from Poirot arrived whilst I was at breakfast the following morning:

"Of course black bearded man was not Havering only you or Japp would have such an idea wire me description of housekeeper and what clothes she wore this morning same of Mrs Havering do not waste time taking photographs of interiors they are underexposed and not in the least artistic."

It seemed to me that Poirot's style was unnecessarily facetious. I also fancied he was a shade jealous of my position on the spot with full facilities for handling the case. His request for a description of the clothes worn by the two women appeared to me to be simply ridiculous, but I complied as well as I, a mere man, was able to.

At eleven a reply wire came from Poirot:

"Advise Japp arrest housekeeper before it is too late."

Dumbfounded, I took the wire to Japp. He swore softly under his breath.

"He's the goods, Monsieur Poirot! If he says so, there's something in it. And I hardly noticed the woman. I don't know that I can go so far as arresting her, but I'll have her watched. We'll go up right away, and take another look at her."

But it was too late. Mrs Middleton, that quiet middle-aged woman, who had appeared so normal and respectable, had vanished into thin air. Her box had been left behind. It contained only ordinary wearing apparel. There was no clue in it to her identity, or as to her whereabouts.

From Mrs Havering we elicited all the facts we could:

"I engaged her about three weeks ago when Mrs Emery, our former housekeeper, left. She came to me from Mrs Selbourne's Agency in Mount Street—a very well-known place. I get all my servants from there. They sent several women to see me, but this Mrs Middleton seemed much the nicest, and had splendid references. I engaged her on the spot, and notified the Agency of the fact. I can't believe that there was anything wrong with her. She was such a nice quiet woman."

The thing was certainly a mystery. Whilst it was clear that the woman herself could not have committed the crime, since at the moment the shot was fired Mrs Havering was with her in the hall, nevertheless she must have some connection with the murder, or why should she suddenly take to her heels and bolt? I wired the latest development to Poirot and suggested returning to London and making inquiries at Selbourne's Agency.

Poirot's reply was prompt:

"Useless to inquire at agency they will never have heard of her find out what vehicle took her up to hunters lodge when she first arrived there."

Though mystified, I was obedient. The means of transport in Elmer's Dale were limited. The local garage had two battered Ford cars, and there were two station flies. None of these had been requisitioned on the date in question. Questioned, Mrs Havering explained that she had given the woman the money for her fare down to Derbyshire and sufficient to hire a car or fly to take her up to Hunter's Lodge. There was usually one of the Fords at the station on the chance of its being required. Taking into consideration the further fact that nobody at the station had noticed the arrival of a stranger, black-bearded or otherwise, on the fatal evening, everything seemed to point to the conclusion that the murderer had come to the spot in a car, which had been waiting near at hand to aid his escape, and that the same car had brought the mysterious housekeeper to her new post. I may mention that inquiries at the Agency in London bore out Poirot's prognostication. No such woman as "Mrs Middleton" had ever been on their books. They had received the Hon. Mrs Havering's application for a housekeeper, and had sent her various applicants for the post. When she sent them the engagement fee, she omitted to mention which woman she had selected.

Somewhat crestfallen, I returned to London. I found Poirot established in an arm-chair by the fire in a garish, silk dressing-gown. He greeted me with much affection.

"Mon ami Hastings! But how glad I am to see you. Veritably I have for you a great affection. And you have enjoyed yourself? You have run to and fro with the good Japp? You have interrogated and investigated to your heart's content?"

"Poirot," I cried, "the thing's a dark mystery! It will never be solved."

"It is true that we are not likely to cover ourselves with glory over it."

"No, indeed. It's a hard nut to crack."

"Oh, as far as that goes, I am very good at cracking the nuts! A veritable squirrel! It is not that which embarrasses me. I know well enough who killed Mr Harrington Pace."

"You know? How did you find out?"

"Your illuminating answers to my wires supplied me with the truth. See here, Hastings, let us examine the facts methodically and in order. Mr Harrington Pace is a man with a considerable fortune which at his death will doubtless pass to his nephew. Point No. 1. His nephew is known to be desperately hard up. Point No. 2. His nephew is also known to be—shall we say a man of rather loose moral fibre? Point No. 3."

"But Roger Havering is proved to have journeyed straight up to London."

"Précisément—and therefore, as Mr Havering left Elmer's Dale at 6.15, and since Mr Pace cannot have been killed before he left, or the doctor would have spotted the time of the crime as being given wrongly when he examined the body, we conclude quite rightly, that Mr Havering did not shoot his uncle. But there is a Mrs Havering, Hastings."

"Impossible! The housekeeper was with her when the shot was fired."

"Ah, yes, the housekeeper. But she has disappeared."

"She will be found."

"I think not. There is something peculiarly elusive about that housekeeper, don't you think so, Hastings? It struck me at once."

"She played her part, I suppose, and then got out in the nick of time."

"And what was her part?"

"Well, presumably to admit her confederate, the black-bearded man."

"Oh, no, that was not her part! Her part was what you have just mentioned, to provide an alibi for Mrs Havering at the moment the shot was fired. And no one will ever find her, mon ami, because she does not exist! 'There's no sech person,' as your so great Shakespeare says."

"It was Dickens," I murmured, unable to suppress a smile. "But what do you mean, Poirot?"

"I mean that Zoe Havering was an actress before her marriage, that you and Japp only saw the housekeeper in a dark hall, a dim middle-aged figure in black with a faint subdued voice, and finally that neither you nor Japp, nor the local police whom the housekeeper fetched, ever saw Mrs Middleton and her mistress at one and the same time. It was child's play for that clever and daring woman. On the pretext of summoning her mistress, she runs upstairs, slips on a bright jumper and a hat with black curls attached which she jams down over the grey transformation. A few deft touches, and the make-up is removed, a slight dusting of rouge, and the brilliant Zoe Havering comes down with her clear ringing voice. Nobody looks particularly at the housekeeper. Why should they? There is nothing to connect her with the crime. She, too, has an alibi."

"But the revolver that was found at Ealing? Mrs Havering could not have placed it there?"

"No, that was Roger Havering's job—but it was a mistake on their part. It put me on the right track. A man who has committed a murder with a revolver which he found on the spot would fling it away at once, he would not carry it up to London with him. No, the motive was clear, the criminals wished to focus the interest of the police on a spot far removed from Derbyshire they were anxious to get the police away as soon as possible from the vicinity of Hunter's Lodge. Of course the revolver found at Ealing was not the one with which Mr Pace was shot. Roger Havering discharged one shot from it, brought it up to London, went straight to his club to establish his alibi, then went quickly out to Ealing by the district, a matter of about twenty minutes only, placed the parcel where it was found and so back to town. That charming creature, his wife, quietly shoots Mr Pace after dinner—you remember he was shot from behind? Another significant point, that!—reloads the revolver and puts it back in its place, and then starts off with her desperate little comedy."

"It's incredible," I murmured, fascinated, "and yet—"

"And yet it is true. Bien sur, my friend, it is true. But to bring that precious pair to justice, that is another matter. Well, Japp must do what he can—I have written him fully—but I very much fear, Hastings, that we shall be obliged to leave them to Fate, or le bon Dieu, whichever you prefer."

"The wicked flourish like a green bay tree," I reminded him.

"But at a price, Hastings, always at a price, croyez-moi!"

Poirot's forebodings were confirmed. Japp, though convinced of the truth of his theory, was unable to get together the necessary evidence to ensure a conviction.

Mr Pace's huge fortune passed into the hands of his murderers. Nevertheless, Nemesis did overtake them, and when I read in the paper that the Hon. Roger and Mrs Havering were amongst those killed in the crashing of the Air Mail to Paris I knew that Justice was satisfied.

~

Agatha Christie (1890–1976) is known throughout the world as the Queen of Crime. Her books have sold over a billion copies. She is the author of eighty crime novels and short-story collections, nineteen plays and six novels written under the pseudonym Mary Westmacott.

THE HUNTSMAN

ANTON CHEKHOV

A sultry, stifling midday. Not a cloudlet in the sky... The sun-baked grass had a disconsolate, hopeless look: even if there were rain it could never be green again... The forest stood silent, motionless, as though it were looking at something with its tree-tops or expecting something.

At the edge of the clearing a tall, narrow-shouldered man of forty in a red shirt, in patched trousers that had been a gentleman's, and in high boots, was slouching along with a lazy, shambling step. He was sauntering along the road. On the right was the green of the clearing, on the left a golden sea of ripe rye stretched to the very horizon. He was red and perspiring, a white cap with a straight jockey peak, evidently a gift from some open-handed young gentleman, perched jauntily on his handsome flaxen head. Across his shoulder hung a game-bag with a blackcock lying in it. The man held a double-barrelled gun cocked in his hand, and screwed up his eyes in the direction of his lean old dog who was running on ahead sniffing the bushes. There was stillness all round, not a sound... everything living was hiding away from the heat.

"Yegor Vlassitch!" the huntsman suddenly heard a soft voice.

He started and, looking round, scowled. Beside him, as though she had sprung out of the earth, stood a pale-faced woman of thirty with a sickle in her hand. She was trying to look into his face, and was smiling diffidently.

"Oh, it is you, Pelagea!" said the huntsman, stopping and deliberately uncocking the gun. "H'm!... How have you come here?"

"The women from our village are working here, so I have come with them... As a labourer, Yegor Vlassitch."

"Oh..." growled Yegor Vlassitch, and slowly walked on.

Pelagea followed him. They walked in silence for twenty paces.

"I have not seen you for a long time, Yegor Vlassitch..." said Pelagea looking tenderly at the huntsman's moving shoulders. "I have not seen you since you came into our hut at Easter for a drink of water... you came in at Easter for a minute and then God knows how... drunk... you scolded and beat me and went away... I have been waiting and waiting... I've tired my eyes out looking for you. Ah, Yegor Vlassitch, Yegor Vlassitch! you might look in just once!"

"What is there for me to do there?"

"Of course there is nothing for you to do... though to be sure... there is the place to look after... To see how things are going... You are the master... I say, you have shot a blackcock, Yegor Vlassitch! You ought to sit down and rest!"

As she said all this Pelagea laughed like a silly girl and looked up at Yegor's face. Her face was simply radiant with happiness.

"Sit down? If you like..." said Yegor in a tone of indifference, and he chose a spot between two fir-trees. "Why are you standing? You sit down too."

Pelagea sat a little way off in the sun and, ashamed of her joy, put her hand over her smiling mouth. Two minutes passed in silence.

"You might come for once," said Pelagea.

"What for?" sighed Yegor, taking off his cap and wiping his red forehead with his hand. "There is no object in my coming. To go for an hour or two is only waste of time, it's simply upsetting you, and to live continually in the village my soul could not endure... You know yourself I am a pampered man... I want a bed to sleep in, good tea to drink, and refined conversation... I want all the niceties, while you live in poverty and dirt in the village... I couldn't stand it for a day. Suppose there were an edict that I must live with you, I should either set fire to the hut or lay hands on myself. From a boy I've had this love for ease; there is no help for it."

"Where are you living now?"

"With the gentleman here, Dmitry Ivanitch, as a huntsman. I furnish his table with game, but he keeps me... more for his pleasure than anything."

"That's not proper work you're doing, Yegor Vlassitch... For other people it's a pastime, but with you it's like a trade... like real work."

"You don't understand, you silly," said Yegor, gazing gloomily at the sky. "You have never understood, and as long as you live you will never understand what sort of man I am... You think of me as a foolish man, gone to the bad, but to anyone who understands I am the best shot there is in the whole district. The gentry feel that, and they have even printed things about me in a magazine. There isn't a man to be compared with me as a sportsman... And it is not because I am pampered and proud that I look down upon your village work. From my childhood, you know, I have never had any calling apart from guns and dogs. If they took away my gun, I used to go out with the fishing-hook, if they took the hook I caught things with my hands. And I went in for horse-dealing too, I used to go to the fairs when I had the money, and you know that if a peasant goes in for being a sportsman, or a horse-dealer, it's good-bye to the plough. Once the spirit of freedom has taken a man you will never root it out of him. In the same way, if a gentleman goes in for being an actor or for any other art, he will never make an official or a landowner. You are a woman, and you do not understand, but one must understand that."

"I understand, Yegor Vlassitch."

"You don't understand if you are going to cry..."

"I... I'm not crying," said Pelagea, turning away. "It's a sin, Yegor Vlassitch! You might stay a day with luckless me, anyway. It's twelve years since I was married to you, and... and... there has never once been love between us!... I... I am not crying."

"Love..." muttered Yegor, scratching his hand. "There can't be any love. It's only in name we are husband and wife; we aren't really. In your eyes I am a wild man, and in mine you are a simple peasant woman with no understanding. Are we well matched? I am a free, pampered, profligate man, while you are a working woman, going in bark shoes and never straightening your back. The way I think of myself is that I am the foremost man in every kind of sport, and you look at me with pity... Is that being well matched?"

"But we are married, you know, Yegor Vlassitch," sobbed Pelagea.

"Not married of our free will... Have you forgotten? You have to thank Count Sergey Paylovitch and yourself. Out of envy, because I shot better than he did, the Count kept giving me wine for a whole month, and when a man's drunk you could make him change his religion, let alone getting married. To pay me out he married me to you when I was drunk... A huntsman to a herd-girl! You saw I was drunk, why did you marry me? You were not a serf, you know; you could have resisted. Of course it was a bit of luck for a herd-girl to marry a huntsman, but you ought to have thought about it. Well, now be miserable, cry. It's a joke for the Count, but a crying matter for you... Beat yourself against the wall."

A silence followed. Three wild ducks flew over the clearing. Yegor followed them with his eyes till, transformed into three scarcely visible dots, they sank down far beyond the forest.

"How do you live?" he asked, moving his eyes from the ducks to Pelagea.

"Now I am going out to work, and in the winter I take a child from the Foundling Hospital and bring it up on the bottle. They give me a rouble and a half a month."

"Oh..."

Again a silence. From the strip that had been reaped floated a soft song which broke off at the very beginning. It was too hot to sing.

"They say you have put up a new hut for Akulina," said Pelagea.

Yegor did not speak.

"So she is dear to you..."

"It's your luck, it's fate!" said the huntsman, stretching. "You must put up with it, poor thing. But good-bye, I've been chattering long enough... I must be at Boltovo by the evening."

Yegor rose, stretched himself, and slung his gun over his shoulder; Pelagea got up.

"And when are you coming to the village?" she asked softly.

"I have no reason to, I shall never come sober, and you have little to gain from me drunk; I am spiteful when I am drunk. Good-bye!"

"Good-bye, Yegor Vlassitch."

Yegor put his cap on the back of his head and, clicking to his dog, went on his way. Pelagea stood still looking after him... She saw his moving shoulder-blades, his jaunty cap, his lazy, careless step, and her eyes were full of sadness and tender affection... Her gaze flitted over her husband's tall, lean figure and caressed and fondled it... He, as though he felt that gaze, stopped and looked round... He did not speak, but from his face, from his shrugged shoulders, Pelagea could see that he wanted to say something to her. She went up to him timidly and looked at him with imploring eyes.

"Take it," he said, turning round.

He gave her a crumpled rouble note and walked quickly away.

"Good-bye, Yegor Vlassitch," she said, mechanically taking the rouble.

He walked by a long road, straight as a taut strap. She, pale and motionless as a statue, stood, her eyes seizing every step he took. But the red of his shirt melted into the dark colour of his trousers, his step could not be seen, and the dog could not be distinguished from the boots. Nothing could be seen but the cap, and... suddenly Yegor turned off sharply into the clearing and the cap vanished in the greenness.

"Good-bye, Yegor Vlassitch," whispered Pelagea, and she stood on tiptoe to see the white cap once more.

~

Anton Chekhov (1860–1904) was a Russian writer who is considered a master of the short story form. He also wrote plays such as *The Cherry Orchard*, *Uncle Vanya* and *The Seagull.* He once famously said that when writing a story, every detail included must be essential: if a gun appears in the first chapter, it must eventually be fired. This principle is now known as Chekhov's Gun.

A Scandal In Bohemia

Sir Arthur Conan Doyle

I.

To Sherlock Holmes she is always *the* woman. I have seldom heard him mention her under any other name. In his eyes she eclipses and predominates the whole of her sex. It was not that he felt any emotion akin to love for Irene Adler. All emotions, and that one particularly, were abhorrent to his cold, precise but admirably balanced mind. He was, I take it, the most perfect reasoning and observing machine that the world has seen, but as a lover he would have placed himself in a false position. He never spoke of the softer passions, save with a gibe and a sneer. They were admirable things for the observer—excellent for drawing the veil from men's motives and actions. But for the trained reasoner to admit such intrusions into his own delicate and finely adjusted temperament was to introduce a distracting factor which might throw a doubt upon all his mental results. Grit in a sensitive instrument, or a crack in one of his own high-power lenses, would not be more disturbing than a strong emotion in a nature such as his. And yet there was but one woman to him, and that woman was the late Irene Adler, of dubious and questionable memory.

I had seen little of Holmes lately. My marriage had drifted us away from each other. My own complete happiness, and the home-centred interests which rise up around the man who first finds himself master of his own establishment, were sufficient to absorb all my attention, while Holmes, who loathed every form of society with his whole Bohemian soul, remained in our lodgings in Baker Street, buried among his old books, and alternating from week to week between cocaine and ambition, the drowsiness of the drug, and the fierce energy of his own keen nature. He was still, as ever, deeply attracted by the study of crime, and occupied his immense faculties and extraordinary powers of observation in following out those clues, and clearing up those mysteries which had been abandoned as hopeless by the official police. From time to time I heard some vague account of his doings: of his summons to Odessa in the case of the Trepoff murder, of his clearing up of the singular tragedy of the Atkinson brothers at Trincomalee, and finally of the mission which he had accomplished so delicately and successfully for the reigning family of Holland. Beyond these signs of his activity, however, which I merely shared with all the readers of the daily press, I knew little of my former friend and companion.

One night—it was on the twentieth of March, 1888—I was returning from a journey to a patient (for I had now returned to civil practice), when my way led me through Baker Street. As I passed the well-remembered door, which must always be associated in my mind with my wooing, and with the dark incidents of the Study in Scarlet, I was seized with a keen desire to see Holmes again, and to know how he was employing his extraordinary powers. His rooms were brilliantly lit, and, even as I looked up, I saw his tall, spare figure pass twice in a dark silhouette against the blind. He was pacing the room swiftly, eagerly, with his head sunk upon his chest and his hands clasped behind him. To me, who knew his every mood and habit, his attitude and manner told their own story. He was at work again. He had risen out of his drug-created dreams and was hot upon the scent of some new problem. I rang the bell and was shown up to the chamber which had formerly been in part my own.

His manner was not effusive. It seldom was; but he was glad, I think, to see me. With hardly a word spoken, but with a kindly eye, he waved me to an armchair, threw across his case of cigars, and indicated a spirit case and a gasogene in the corner. Then he stood before the fire and looked me over in his singular introspective fashion.

"Wedlock suits you," he remarked. "I think, Watson, that you have put on seven and a half pounds since I saw you."

"Seven!" I answered.

"Indeed, I should have thought a little more. Just a trifle more, I fancy, Watson. And in practice again, I observe. You did not tell me that you intended to go into harness."

"Then, how do you know?"

"I see it, I deduce it. How do I know that you have been getting yourself very wet lately, and that you have a most clumsy and careless servant girl?"

"My dear Holmes," said I, "this is too much. You would certainly have been burned, had you lived a few centuries ago. It is true that I had a country walk on Thursday and came home in a dreadful mess, but as I have changed my clothes I can't imagine how you deduce it. As to Mary Jane, she is incorrigible, and my wife has given her notice, but there, again, I fail to see how you work it out."

He chuckled to himself and rubbed his long, nervous hands together.

"It is simplicity itself," said he; "my eyes tell me that on the inside of your left shoe, just where the firelight strikes it, the leather is scored by six almost parallel cuts. Obviously they have been caused by someone who has very carelessly scraped round the edges of the sole in order to remove crusted mud from it. Hence, you see, my double deduction that you had been out in vile weather, and that you had a particularly malignant boot-slitting specimen of the London slavey. As to your practice, if a gentleman walks into my rooms smelling of iodoform, with a black mark of nitrate of silver upon his right forefinger, and a bulge on the right side of his top-hat to show where he has secreted his stethoscope, I must be dull, indeed, if I do not pronounce him to be an active member of the medical profession."

I could not help laughing at the ease with which he explained his process of deduction. "When I hear you give your reasons," I remarked, "the thing always appears to me to be so ridiculously simple that I could easily do it myself, though at each successive instance of your reasoning I am baffled until you explain your process. And yet I believe that my eyes are as good as yours."

"Quite so," he answered, lighting a cigarette, and throwing himself down into an armchair. "You see, but you do not observe. The distinction is clear. For example, you have frequently seen the steps which lead up from the hall to this room."

"Frequently."

"How often?"

"Well, some hundreds of times."

"Then how many are there?"

"How many? I don't know."

"Quite so! You have not observed. And yet you have seen. That is just my point. Now, I know that there are seventeen steps, because I have both seen and observed. By the way, since you are interested in these little problems, and since you are good enough to chronicle one or two of my trifling experiences, you may be interested in this." He threw over a sheet of thick, pink-tinted notepaper which had been lying open upon the table. "It came by the last post," said he. "Read it aloud."

The note was undated, and without either signature or address.

"There will call upon you to-night, at a quarter to eight o'clock," it said, "a gentleman who desires to consult you upon a matter of the very deepest moment. Your recent services to one of the royal houses of Europe have shown that you are one who may safely be trusted with matters which are of an importance which can hardly be exaggerated. This account of you we have from all quarters received. Be in your chamber then at that hour, and do not take it amiss if your visitor wear a mask."

"This is indeed a mystery," I remarked. "What do you imagine that it means?"

"I have no data yet. It is a capital mistake to theorise before one has data. Insensibly one begins to twist facts to suit theories, instead of theories to suit facts. But the note itself. What do you deduce from it?"

I carefully examined the writing, and the paper upon which it was written.

"The man who wrote it was presumably well to do," I remarked, endeavouring to imitate my companion's processes. "Such paper could not be bought under half a crown a packet. It is peculiarly strong and stiff."

"Peculiar—that is the very word," said Holmes. "It is not an English paper at all. Hold it up to the light."

I did so, and saw a large "E" with a small "g," a "P," and a large "G" with a small "t" woven into the texture of the paper.

"What do you make of that?" asked Holmes.

"The name of the maker, no doubt; or his monogram, rather."

"Not at all. The 'G' with the small 't' stands for 'Gesellschaft,' which is the German for 'Company.' It is a customary contraction like our 'Co.' 'P,' of course, stands for 'Papier.' Now for the 'Eg.' Let us glance at our Continental Gazetteer." He took down a heavy brown volume from his shelves. "Eglow, Eglonitz—here we are, Egria. It is in a German-speaking country—in Bohemia, not far from Carlsbad. 'Remarkable as being the scene of the death of Wallenstein, and for its numerous glass-factories and paper-mills.' Ha, ha, my boy, what do you make of that?" His eyes sparkled, and he sent up a great blue triumphant cloud from his cigarette.

"The paper was made in Bohemia," I said.

"Precisely. And the man who wrote the note is a German. Do you note the peculiar construction of the sentence—'This account of you we have from all quarters received.' A Frenchman or Russian could not have written that. It is the German who is so uncourteous to his verbs. It only remains, therefore, to discover what is wanted by this German who writes upon Bohemian paper and prefers wearing a mask to showing his face. And here he comes, if I am not mistaken, to resolve all our doubts."

As he spoke there was the sharp sound of horses' hoofs and grating wheels against the curb, followed by a sharp pull at the bell. Holmes whistled.

"A pair, by the sound," said he. "Yes," he continued, glancing out of the window. "A nice little brougham and a pair of beauties. A hundred and fifty guineas apiece. There's money in this case, Watson, if there is nothing else."

"I think that I had better go, Holmes."

"Not a bit, Doctor. Stay where you are. I am lost without my Boswell. And this promises to be interesting. It would be a pity to miss it."

"But your client—"

"Never mind him. I may want your help, and so may he. Here he comes. Sit down in that armchair, Doctor, and give us your best attention."

A slow and heavy step, which had been heard upon the stairs and in the passage, paused immediately outside the door. Then there was a loud and authoritative tap.

"Come in!" said Holmes.

A man entered who could hardly have been less than six feet six inches in height, with the chest and limbs of a Hercules. His dress was rich with a richness which would, in England, be looked upon as akin to bad taste. Heavy bands of astrakhan were slashed across the sleeves and fronts of his double-breasted coat, while the deep blue cloak which was thrown over his shoulders was lined with flame-coloured silk and secured at the neck with a brooch which consisted of a single flaming beryl. Boots which extended halfway up his calves, and which were trimmed at the tops with rich brown fur, completed the impression of barbaric opulence which was suggested by his whole appearance. He carried a broad-brimmed hat in his hand, while he wore across the upper part of his face, extending down past the cheekbones, a black vizard mask, which he had apparently adjusted that very moment, for his hand was still raised to it as he entered. From the lower part of the face he appeared to be a man of strong character, with a thick, hanging lip, and a long, straight chin suggestive of resolution pushed to the length of obstinacy.

"You had my note?" he asked with a deep harsh voice and a strongly marked German accent. "I told you that I would call."

He looked from one to the other of us, as if uncertain which to address.

"Pray take a seat," said Holmes. "This is my friend and colleague, Dr Watson, who is occasionally good enough to help me in my cases. Whom have I the honour to address?"

"You may address me as the Count Von Kramm, a Bohemian nobleman. I understand that this gentleman, your friend, is a man of honour and discretion, whom I may trust with a matter of the most extreme importance. If not, I should much prefer to communicate with you alone."

I rose to go, but Holmes caught me by the wrist and pushed me back into my chair. "It is both, or none," said he. "You may say before this gentleman anything which you may say to me."

The Count shrugged his broad shoulders. "Then I must begin," said he, "by binding you both to absolute secrecy for two years; at the end of that time the matter will be of no importance. At present it is not too much to say that it is of such weight it may have an influence upon European history."

"I promise," said Holmes.

"And I."

"You will excuse this mask," continued our strange visitor. "The august person who employs me wishes his agent to be unknown to you, and I may confess at once that the title by which I have just called myself is not exactly my own."

"I was aware of it," said Holmes dryly.

"The circumstances are of great delicacy, and every precaution has to be taken to quench what might grow to be an immense scandal and seriously compromise one of the reigning families of Europe. To speak plainly, the matter implicates the great House of Ormstein, hereditary kings of Bohemia."

"I was also aware of that," murmured Holmes, settling himself down in his armchair and closing his eyes.

Our visitor glanced with some apparent surprise at the languid, lounging figure of the man who had been no doubt depicted to him as the most incisive reasoner and most energetic agent in Europe. Holmes slowly reopened his eyes and looked impatiently at his gigantic client.

"If your Majesty would condescend to state your case," he remarked, "I should be better able to advise you."

The man sprang from his chair and paced up and down the room in uncontrollable agitation. Then, with a gesture of desperation, he tore the mask from his face and hurled it upon the ground. "You are right," he cried; "I am the King. Why should I attempt to conceal it?"

"Why, indeed?" murmured Holmes. "Your Majesty had not spoken before I was aware that I was addressing Wilhelm Gottsreich Sigismond von Ormstein, Grand Duke of Cassel-Felstein, and hereditary King of Bohemia."

"But you can understand," said our strange visitor, sitting down once more and passing his hand over his high white forehead, "you can understand that I am not accustomed to doing such business in my own person. Yet the matter was so delicate that I could not confide it to an agent without putting myself in his power. I have come *incognito* from Prague for the purpose of consulting you."

"Then, pray consult," said Holmes, shutting his eyes once more.

"The facts are briefly these: Some five years ago, during a lengthy visit to Warsaw, I made the acquaintance of the well-known adventuress, Irene Adler. The name is no doubt familiar to you."

"Kindly look her up in my index, Doctor," murmured Holmes without opening his eyes. For many years he had adopted a system of docketing all paragraphs concerning men and things, so that it was difficult to name a subject or a person on which he could not at once furnish information. In this case I found her biography sandwiched in between that of a Hebrew rabbi and that of a staff-commander who had written a monograph upon the deep-sea fishes.

"Let me see!" said Holmes. "Hum! Born in New Jersey in the year 1858. Contralto—hum! La Scala, hum! Prima donna Imperial Opera of Warsaw—yes! Retired from operatic stage—ha! Living in London—quite so! Your Majesty, as I understand, became entangled with this young person, wrote her some compromising letters, and is now desirous of getting those letters back."

"Precisely so. But how—"

"Was there a secret marriage?"

"None."

"No legal papers or certificates?"

"None."

"Then I fail to follow your Majesty. If this young person should produce her letters for blackmailing or other purposes, how is she to prove their authenticity?"

"There is the writing."

"Pooh, pooh! Forgery."

"My private note-paper."

"Stolen."

"My own seal."

"Imitated."

"My photograph."

"Bought."

"We were both in the photograph."

"Oh, dear! That is very bad! Your Majesty has indeed committed an indiscretion."

"I was mad—insane."

"You have compromised yourself seriously."

"I was only Crown Prince then. I was young. I am but thirty now."

"It must be recovered."

"We have tried and failed."

"Your Majesty must pay. It must be bought."

"She will not sell."

"Stolen, then."

"Five attempts have been made. Twice burglars in my pay ransacked her house. Once we diverted her luggage when she travelled. Twice she has been waylaid. There has been no result."

"No sign of it?"

"Absolutely none."

Holmes laughed. "It is quite a pretty little problem," said he.

"But a very serious one to me," returned the King reproachfully.

"Very, indeed. And what does she propose to do with the photograph?"

"To ruin me."

"But how?"

"I am about to be married."

"So I have heard."

"To Clotilde Lothman von Saxe-Meningen, second daughter of the King of Scandinavia. You may know the strict principles of her family. She is herself the very soul of delicacy. A shadow of a doubt as to my conduct would bring the matter to an end."

"And Irene Adler?"

"Threatens to send them the photograph. And she will do it. I know that she will do it. You do not know her, but she has a soul of steel. She has the face of the most beautiful of women, and the mind of the most resolute of men. Rather than I should marry another woman, there are no lengths to which she would not go—none."

"You are sure that she has not sent it yet?"

"I am sure."

"And why?"

"Because she has said that she would send it on the day when the betrothal was publicly proclaimed. That will be next Monday."

"Oh, then we have three days yet," said Holmes with a yawn. "That is very fortunate, as I have one or two matters of importance to look into just at present. Your Majesty will, of course, stay in London for the present?"

"Certainly. You will find me at the Langham under the name of the Count Von Kramm."

"Then I shall drop you a line to let you know how we progress."

"Pray do so. I shall be all anxiety."

"Then, as to money?"

"You have *carte blanche*."

"Absolutely?"

"I tell you that I would give one of the provinces of my kingdom to have that photograph."

"And for present expenses?"

The King took a heavy chamois leather bag from under his cloak and laid it on the table.

"There are three hundred pounds in gold and seven hundred in notes," he said.

Holmes scribbled a receipt upon a sheet of his note-book and handed it to him.

"And Mademoiselle's address?" he asked.

"Is Briony Lodge, Serpentine Avenue, St. John's Wood."

Holmes took a note of it. "One other question," said he. "Was the photograph a cabinet?"

"It was."

"Then, good-night, your Majesty, and I trust that we shall soon have some good news for you. And good-night, Watson," he added, as the wheels of the royal brougham rolled down the street. "If you will be good enough to call to-morrow afternoon at three o'clock I should like to chat this little matter over with you."

II.

At three o'clock precisely I was at Baker Street, but Holmes had not yet returned. The landlady informed me that he had left the house shortly after eight o'clock in the morning. I sat down beside the fire, however, with the intention of awaiting him, however long he might be. I was already deeply interested in his inquiry, for, though it was surrounded by none of the grim and strange features which were associated with the two crimes which I have already recorded, still, the nature of the case and the exalted station of his client gave it a character of its own. Indeed, apart from the nature of the investigation which my friend had on hand, there was something in his masterly grasp of a situation, and his keen, incisive reasoning, which made it a pleasure to me to study his system of work, and to follow the quick, subtle methods by which he disentangled the most inextricable mysteries. So accustomed was I to his invariable success that the very possibility of his failing had ceased to enter into my head.

It was close upon four before the door opened, and a drunken-looking groom, ill-kempt and side-whiskered, with an inflamed face and disreputable clothes, walked into the room. Accustomed as I was to my friend's amazing powers in the use of disguises, I had to look three times before I was certain that it was indeed he. With a nod he vanished into the bedroom, whence he emerged in five minutes tweed-suited and respectable, as of old. Putting his hands into his pockets, he stretched out his legs in front of the fire and laughed heartily for some minutes.

"Well, really!" he cried, and then he choked and laughed again until he was obliged to lie back, limp and helpless, in the chair.

"What is it?"

"It's quite too funny. I am sure you could never guess how I employed my morning, or what I ended by doing."

"I can't imagine. I suppose that you have been watching the habits, and perhaps the house, of Miss Irene Adler."

"Quite so; but the sequel was rather unusual. I will tell you, however. I left the house a little after eight o'clock this morning in the character of a groom out of work. There is a wonderful sympathy and freemasonry among horsey men. Be one of them, and you will know all that there is to know. I soon found Briony Lodge. It is a *bijou* villa, with a garden at the back, but built out in front right up to the road, two stories. Chubb lock to the door. Large sitting-room on the right side, well furnished, with long windows almost to the floor, and those preposterous English window fasteners which a child could open. Behind there was nothing remarkable, save that the passage window could be reached from the top of the coach-house. I walked round it and examined it closely from every point of view, but without noting anything else of interest.

"I then lounged down the street and found, as I expected, that there was a mews in a lane which runs down by one wall of the garden. I lent the ostlers a hand in rubbing down their horses, and received in exchange twopence, a glass of half-and-half, two fills of shag tobacco, and as much information as I could desire about Miss Adler, to say nothing of half a dozen other people in the neighbourhood in whom I was not in the least interested, but whose biographies I was compelled to listen to."

"And what of Irene Adler?" I asked.

"Oh, she has turned all the men's heads down in that part. She is the daintiest thing under a bonnet on this planet. So say the Serpentine-mews, to a man. She lives quietly, sings at concerts, drives out at five every day, and returns at seven sharp for dinner. Seldom goes out at other times, except when she sings. Has only one male visitor, but a good deal of him. He is dark, handsome, and dashing, never calls less than once a day, and often twice. He is a Mr Godfrey Norton, of the Inner Temple. See the advantages of a cabman as a confidant. They had driven him home a dozen times from Serpentine-mews, and knew all about him. When I had listened to all they had to tell, I began to walk up and down near Briony Lodge once more, and to think over my plan of campaign.

"This Godfrey Norton was evidently an important factor in the matter. He was a lawyer. That sounded ominous. What was the relation between them, and what the object of his repeated visits? Was she his client, his friend, or his mistress? If the former, she had probably transferred the photograph to his keeping. If the latter, it was less likely. On the issue of this question depended whether I should continue my work at Briony Lodge, or turn my attention to the gentleman's chambers in the Temple. It was a delicate point, and it widened the field of my inquiry. I fear that I bore you with these details, but I have to let you see my little difficulties, if you are to understand the situation."

"I am following you closely," I answered.

"I was still balancing the matter in my mind when a hansom cab drove up to Briony Lodge, and a gentleman sprang out. He was a remarkably handsome man, dark, aquiline, and moustached—evidently the man of whom I had heard. He appeared to be in a great hurry, shouted to the cabman to wait, and brushed past the maid who opened the door with the air of a man who was thoroughly at home.

"He was in the house about half an hour, and I could catch glimpses of him in the windows of the sitting-room, pacing up and down, talking excitedly, and waving his arms. Of her I could see nothing. Presently he emerged, looking even more flurried than before. As he stepped up to the cab, he pulled a gold watch from his pocket and looked at it earnestly, 'Drive like the devil,' he shouted, 'first to Gross & Hankey's in Regent Street, and then to the Church of St. Monica in the Edgeware Road. Half a guinea if you do it in twenty minutes!'

"Away they went, and I was just wondering whether I should not do well to follow them when up the lane came a neat little landau, the coachman with his coat only half-buttoned, and his tie under his ear, while all the tags of his harness were sticking out of the buckles. It hadn't pulled up before she shot out of the hall door and into it. I only caught a glimpse of her at the moment, but she was a lovely woman, with a face that a man might die for.

"'The Church of St. Monica, John,' she cried, 'and half a sovereign if you reach it in twenty minutes.'

"This was quite too good to lose, Watson. I was just balancing whether I should run for it, or whether I should perch behind her landau when a cab came through the street. The driver looked twice at such a shabby fare, but I jumped in before he could object. 'The Church of St. Monica,' said I, 'and half a sovereign if you reach it in twenty minutes.' It was twenty-five minutes to twelve, and of course it was clear enough what was in the wind.

"My cabby drove fast. I don't think I ever drove faster, but the others were there before us. The cab and the landau with their steaming horses were in front of the door when I arrived. I paid the man and hurried into the church. There was not a soul there save the two whom I had followed and a surpliced clergyman, who seemed to be expostulating with them. They were all three standing in a knot in front of the altar. I lounged up the side aisle like any other idler who has dropped into a church. Suddenly, to my surprise, the three at the altar faced round to me, and Godfrey Norton came running as hard as he could towards me.

"'Thank God,' he cried. 'You'll do. Come! Come!'

"'What then?' I asked.

"'Come, man, come, only three minutes, or it won't be legal.'

"I was half-dragged up to the altar, and before I knew where I was I found myself mumbling responses which were whispered in my ear, and vouching for things of which I knew nothing, and generally assisting in the secure tying up of Irene Adler, spinster, to Godfrey Norton, bachelor. It was all done in an instant, and there was the gentleman thanking me on the one side and the lady on the other, while the clergyman beamed on me in front. It was the most preposterous position in which I ever found myself in my life, and it was the thought of it that started me laughing just now. It seems that there had been some informality about their license, that the clergyman absolutely refused to marry them without a witness of some sort, and that my lucky appearance saved the bridegroom from having to sally out into the streets in search of a best man. The bride gave me a sovereign, and I mean to wear it on my watch chain in memory of the occasion."

"This is a very unexpected turn of affairs," said I; "and what then?"

"Well, I found my plans very seriously menaced. It looked as if the pair might take an immediate departure, and so necessitate very prompt and energetic measures on my part. At the church door, however, they separated, he driving back to the Temple, and she to her own house. 'I shall drive out in the park at five as usual,' she said as she left him. I heard no more. They drove away in different directions, and I went off to make my own arrangements."

"Which are?"

"Some cold beef and a glass of beer," he answered, ringing the bell. "I have been too busy to think of food, and I am likely to be busier still this evening. By the way, Doctor, I shall want your co-operation."

"I shall be delighted."

"You don't mind breaking the law?"

"Not in the least."

"Nor running a chance of arrest?"

"Not in a good cause."

"Oh, the cause is excellent!"

"Then I am your man."

"I was sure that I might rely on you."

"But what is it you wish?"

"When Mrs Turner has brought in the tray I will make it clear to you. Now," he said as he turned hungrily on the simple fare that our landlady had provided, "I must discuss it while I eat, for I have not much time. It is nearly five now. In two hours we must be on the scene of action. Miss Irene, or Madame, rather, returns from her drive at seven. We must be at Briony Lodge to meet her."

"And what then?"

"You must leave that to me. I have already arranged what is to occur. There is only one point on which I must insist. You must not interfere, come what may. You understand?"

"I am to be neutral?"

"To do nothing whatever. There will probably be some small unpleasantness. Do not join in it. It will end in my being conveyed into the house. Four or five minutes afterwards the sitting-room window will open. You are to station yourself close to that open window."

"Yes."

"You are to watch me, for I will be visible to you."

"Yes."

"And when I raise my hand—so—you will throw into the room what I give you to throw, and will, at the same time, raise the cry of fire. You quite follow me?"

"Entirely."

"It is nothing very formidable," he said, taking a long cigar-shaped roll from his pocket. "It is an ordinary plumber's smoke-rocket, fitted with a cap at either end to make it self-lighting. Your task is confined to that. When you raise your cry of fire, it will be taken up by quite a number of people. You may then walk to the end of the street, and I will rejoin you in ten minutes. I hope that I have made myself clear?"

"I am to remain neutral, to get near the window, to watch you, and at the signal to throw in this object, then to raise the cry of fire, and to wait you at the corner of the street."

"Precisely."

"Then you may entirely rely on me."

"That is excellent. I think, perhaps, it is almost time that I prepare for the new role I have to play."

He disappeared into his bedroom and returned in a few minutes in the character of an amiable and simple-minded Nonconformist clergyman. His broad black hat, his baggy trousers, his white tie, his sympathetic smile, and general look of peering and benevolent curiosity were such as Mr John Hare alone could have equalled. It was not merely that Holmes changed his costume. His expression, his manner, his very soul seemed to vary with every fresh part that he assumed. The stage lost a fine actor, even as science lost an acute reasoner, when he became a specialist in crime.

It was a quarter past six when we left Baker Street, and it still wanted ten minutes to the hour when we found ourselves in Serpentine Avenue. It was already dusk, and the lamps were just being lighted as we paced up and down in front of Briony Lodge, waiting for the coming of its occupant. The house was just such as I had pictured it from Sherlock Holmes' succinct description, but the locality appeared to be less private than I expected. On the contrary, for a small street in a quiet neighbourhood, it was remarkably animated. There was a group of shabbily dressed men smoking and laughing in a corner, a scissors-grinder with his wheel, two guardsmen who were flirting with a nurse-girl, and several well-dressed young men who were lounging up and down with cigars in their mouths.

"You see," remarked Holmes, as we paced to and fro in front of the house, "this marriage rather simplifies matters. The photograph becomes a double-edged weapon now. The chances are that she would be as averse to its being seen by Mr Godfrey Norton, as our client is to its coming to the eyes of his princess. Now the question is, Where are we to find the photograph?"

"Where, indeed?"

"It is most unlikely that she carries it about with her. It is cabinet size. Too large for easy concealment about a woman's dress. She knows that the King is capable of having her waylaid and searched. Two attempts of the sort have already been made. We may take it, then, that she does not carry it about with her."

"Where, then?"

"Her banker or her lawyer. There is that double possibility. But I am inclined to think neither. Women are naturally secretive, and they like to do their own secreting. Why should she hand it over to anyone else? She could trust her own guardianship, but she could not tell what indirect or political influence might be brought to bear upon a business man. Besides, remember that she had resolved to use it within a few days. It must be where she can lay her hands upon it. It must be in her own house."

"But it has twice been burgled."

"Pshaw! They did not know how to look."

"But how will you look?"

"I will not look."

"What then?"

"I will get her to show me."

"But she will refuse."

"She will not be able to. But I hear the rumble of wheels. It is her carriage. Now carry out my orders to the letter."

As he spoke the gleam of the sidelights of a carriage came round the curve of the avenue. It was a smart little landau which rattled up to the door of Briony Lodge. As it pulled up, one of the loafing men at the corner dashed forward to open the door in the hope of earning a copper, but was elbowed away by another loafer, who had rushed up with the same intention. A fierce quarrel broke out, which was increased by the two guardsmen, who took sides with one of the loungers, and by the scissors-grinder, who was equally hot upon the other side. A blow was struck, and in an instant the lady, who had stepped from her carriage, was the centre of a little knot of flushed and struggling men, who struck savagely at each other with their fists and sticks. Holmes dashed into the crowd to protect the lady; but, just as he reached her, he gave a cry and dropped to the ground, with the blood running freely down his face. At his fall the guardsmen took to their heels in one direction and the loungers in the other, while a number of better dressed people, who had watched the scuffle without taking part in it, crowded in to help the lady and to attend to the injured man. Irene Adler, as I will still call her, had hurried up the steps; but she stood at the top with her superb figure outlined against the lights of the hall, looking back into the street.

"Is the poor gentleman much hurt?" she asked.

"He is dead," cried several voices.

"No, no, there's life in him!" shouted another. "But he'll be gone before you can get him to hospital."

"He's a brave fellow," said a woman. "They would have had the lady's purse and watch if it hadn't been for him. They were a gang, and a rough one, too. Ah, he's breathing now."

"He can't lie in the street. May we bring him in, marm?"

"Surely. Bring him into the sitting-room. There is a comfortable sofa. This way, please!"

Slowly and solemnly he was borne into Briony Lodge and laid out in the principal room, while I still observed the proceedings from my post by the window. The lamps had been lit, but the blinds had not been drawn, so that I could see Holmes as he lay upon the couch. I do not know whether he was seized with compunction at that moment for the part he was playing, but I know that I never felt more heartily ashamed of myself in my life than when I saw the beautiful creature against whom I was conspiring, or the grace and kindliness with which she waited upon the injured man. And yet it would be the blackest treachery to Holmes to draw back now from the part which he had intrusted to me. I hardened my heart, and took the smoke-rocket from under my ulster. After all, I thought, we are not injuring her. We are but preventing her from injuring another.

Holmes had sat up upon the couch, and I saw him motion like a man who is in need of air. A maid rushed across and threw open the window. At the same instant I saw him raise his hand and at the signal I tossed my rocket into the room with a cry of "Fire!" The word was no sooner out of my mouth than the whole crowd of spectators, well dressed and ill—gentlemen, ostlers, and servant maids—joined in a general shriek of "Fire!" Thick clouds of smoke curled through the room and out at the open window. I caught a glimpse of rushing figures, and a moment later the voice of Holmes from within assuring them that it was a false alarm. Slipping through the shouting crowd I made my way to the corner of the street, and in ten minutes was rejoiced to find my friend's arm in mine, and to get away from the scene of uproar. He walked swiftly and in silence for some few minutes until we had turned down one of the quiet streets which lead towards the Edgeware Road.

"You did it very nicely, Doctor," he remarked. "Nothing could have been better. It is all right."

"You have the photograph?"

"I know where it is."

"And how did you find out?"

"She showed me, as I told you she would."

"I am still in the dark."

"I do not wish to make a mystery," said he, laughing. "The matter was perfectly simple. You, of course, saw that everyone in the street was an accomplice. They were all engaged for the evening."

"I guessed as much."

"Then, when the row broke out, I had a little moist red paint in the palm of my hand. I rushed forward, fell down, clapped my hand to my face, and became a piteous spectacle. It is an old trick."

"That also I could fathom."

"Then they carried me in. She was bound to have me in. What else could she do? And into her sitting-room, which was the very room which I suspected. It lay between that and her bedroom, and I was determined to see which. They laid me on a couch, I motioned for air, they were compelled to open the window, and you had your chance."

"How did that help you?"

"It was all-important. When a woman thinks that her house is on fire, her instinct is at once to rush to the thing which she values most. It is a perfectly overpowering impulse, and I have more than once taken advantage of it. In the case of the Darlington Substitution Scandal it was of use to me, and also in the Arnsworth Castle business. A married woman grabs at her baby; an unmarried one reaches for her jewel-box. Now it was clear to me that our lady of to-day had nothing in the house more precious to her than what we are in quest of. She would rush to secure it. The alarm of fire was admirably done. The smoke and shouting were enough to shake nerves of steel. She responded beautifully. The photograph is in a recess behind a sliding panel just above the right bell-pull. She was there in an instant, and I caught a glimpse of it as she half drew it out. When I cried out that it was a false alarm, she replaced it, glanced at the rocket, rushed from the room, and I have not seen her since. I rose, and, making my excuses, escaped from the house. I hesitated whether to attempt to secure the photograph at once; but the coachman had come in, and as he was watching me narrowly, it seemed safer to wait. A little over-precipitance may ruin all."

"And now?" I asked.

"Our quest is practically finished. I shall call with the King to-morrow, and with you, if you care to come with us. We will be shown into the sitting-room to wait for the lady, but it is probable that when she comes she may find neither us nor the photograph. It might be a satisfaction to his Majesty to regain it with his own hands."

"And when will you call?"

"At eight in the morning. She will not be up, so that we shall have a clear field. Besides, we must be prompt, for this marriage may mean a complete change in her life and habits. I must wire to the King without delay."

We had reached Baker Street and had stopped at the door. He was searching his pockets for the key when someone passing said:

"Good-night, Mister Sherlock Holmes."

There were several people on the pavement at the time, but the greeting appeared to come from a slim youth in an ulster who had hurried by.

"I've heard that voice before," said Holmes, staring down the dimly lit street. "Now, I wonder who the deuce that could have been."

III.

I slept at Baker Street that night, and we were engaged upon our toast and coffee in the morning when the King of Bohemia rushed into the room.

"You have really got it!" he cried, grasping Sherlock Holmes by either shoulder and looking eagerly into his face.

"Not yet."

"But you have hopes?"

"I have hopes."

"Then, come. I am all impatience to be gone."

"We must have a cab."

"No, my brougham is waiting."

"Then that will simplify matters." We descended and started off once more for Briony Lodge.

"Irene Adler is married," remarked Holmes.

"Married! When?"

"Yesterday."

"But to whom?"

"To an English lawyer named Norton."

"But she could not love him."

"I am in hopes that she does."

"And why in hopes?"

"Because it would spare your Majesty all fear of future annoyance. If the lady loves her husband, she does not love your Majesty. If she does not love your Majesty, there is no reason why she should interfere with your Majesty's plan."

"It is true. And yet—! Well! I wish she had been of my own station! What a queen she would have made!" He relapsed into a moody silence, which was not broken until we drew up in Serpentine Avenue.

The door of Briony Lodge was open, and an elderly woman stood upon the steps. She watched us with a sardonic eye as we stepped from the brougham.

"Mr Sherlock Holmes, I believe?" said she.

"I am Mr Holmes," answered my companion, looking at her with a questioning and rather startled gaze.

"Indeed! My mistress told me that you were likely to call. She left this morning with her husband by the 5:15 train from Charing Cross for the Continent."

"What!" Sherlock Holmes staggered back, white with chagrin and surprise. "Do you mean that she has left England?"

"Never to return."

"And the papers?" asked the King hoarsely. "All is lost."

"We shall see." He pushed past the servant and rushed into the drawing-room, followed by the King and myself. The furniture was scattered about in every direction, with dismantled shelves and open drawers, as if the lady had hurriedly ransacked them before her flight. Holmes rushed at the bell-pull, tore back a small sliding shutter, and, plunging in his hand, pulled out a photograph and a letter. The photograph was of Irene Adler herself in evening dress, the letter was superscribed to "Sherlock Holmes, Esq. To be left till called for." My friend tore it open, and we all three read it together. It was dated at midnight of the preceding night and ran in this way:

"MY DEAR MR SHERLOCK HOLMES,—You really did it very well. You took me in completely. Until after the alarm of fire, I had not a suspicion. But then, when I found how I had betrayed myself, I began to think. I had been warned against you months ago. I had been told that, if the King employed an agent, it would certainly be you. And your address had been given me. Yet, with all this, you made me reveal what you wanted to know. Even after I became suspicious, I found it hard to think evil of such a dear, kind old clergyman. But, you know, I have been trained as an actress myself. Male costume is nothing new to me. I often take advantage of the freedom which it gives. I sent John, the coachman, to watch you, ran upstairs, got into my walking clothes, as I call them, and came down just as you departed.

"Well, I followed you to your door, and so made sure that I was really an object of interest to the celebrated Mr Sherlock Holmes. Then I, rather imprudently, wished you good-night, and started for the Temple to see my husband.

"We both thought the best resource was flight, when pursued by so formidable an antagonist; so you will find the nest empty when you call to-morrow. As to the photograph, your client may rest in peace. I love and am loved by a better man than he. The King may do what he will without hindrance from one whom he has cruelly wronged. I keep it only to safeguard myself, and to preserve a weapon which will always secure me from any steps which he might take in the future. I leave a photograph which he might care to possess; and I remain, dear Mr Sherlock Holmes,

"Very truly yours,

"IRENE NORTON, *née* ADLER."

"What a woman—oh, what a woman!" cried the King of Bohemia, when we had all three read this epistle. "Did I not tell you how quick and resolute she was? Would she not have made an admirable queen? Is it not a pity that she was not on my level?"

"From what I have seen of the lady, she seems, indeed, to be on a very different level to your Majesty," said Holmes coldly. "I am sorry that I have not been able to bring your Majesty's business to a more successful conclusion."

"On the contrary, my dear sir," cried the King; "nothing could be more successful. I know that her word is inviolate. The photograph is now as safe as if it were in the fire."

"I am glad to hear your Majesty say so."

"I am immensely indebted to you. Pray tell me in what way I can reward you. This ring—" He slipped an emerald snake ring from his finger and held it out upon the palm of his hand.

"Your Majesty has something which I should value even more highly," said Holmes.

"You have but to name it."

"This photograph!"

The King stared at him in amazement.

"Irene's photograph!" he cried. "Certainly, if you wish it."

"I thank your Majesty. Then there is no more to be done in the matter. I have the honour to wish you a very good morning." He bowed, and, turning away without observing the hand which the King had stretched out to him, he set off in my company for his chambers.

And that was how a great scandal threatened to affect the kingdom of Bohemia, and how the best plans of Mr Sherlock Holmes were beaten by a woman's wit. He used to make merry over the cleverness of women, but I have not heard him do it of late. And when he speaks of Irene Adler, or when he refers to her photograph, it is always under the honourable title of *the* woman.

~

Sir Arthur Conan Doyle (1859–1930) is the creator of Sherlock Holmes, possibly the best-known detective character in English literature. He also wrote historical and fantasy stories and had a career as a medical doctor. The Sherlock Holmes stories continue to be adapted into books and TV shows and are regarded as classics of crime fiction.

From Dracula

Bram Stoker

Jonathan Harker's Journal

5 *May.*—I must have been asleep, for certainly if I had been fully awake I must have noticed the approach of such a remarkable place. In the gloom the courtyard looked of considerable size, and as several dark ways led from it under great round arches, it perhaps seemed bigger than it really is. I have not yet been able to see it by daylight.

When the calèche stopped, the driver jumped down and held out his hand to assist me to alight. Again I could not but notice his prodigious strength. His hand actually seemed like a steel vice that could have crushed mine if he had chosen. Then he took out my traps, and placed them on the ground beside me as I stood close to a great door, old and studded with large iron nails, and set in a projecting doorway of massive stone. I could see even in the dim light that the stone was massively carved, but that the carving had been much worn by time and weather. As I stood, the driver jumped again into his seat and shook the reins; the horses started forward, and trap and all disappeared down one of the dark openings.

I stood in silence where I was, for I did not know what to do. Of bell or knocker there was no sign; through these frowning walls and dark window openings it was not likely that my voice could penetrate. The time I waited seemed endless, and I felt doubts and fears crowding upon me. What sort of place had I come to, and among what kind of people? What sort of grim adventure was it on which I had embarked? Was this a customary incident in the life of a solicitor's clerk sent out to explain the purchase of a London estate to a foreigner? Solicitor's clerk! Mina would not like that. Solicitor—for just before leaving London I got word that my examination was successful; and I am now a full-blown solicitor! I began to rub my eyes and pinch myself to see if I were awake. It all seemed like a horrible nightmare to me, and I expected that I should suddenly awake, and find myself at home, with the dawn struggling in through the windows, as I had now and again felt in the morning after a day of overwork. But my flesh answered the pinching test, and my eyes were not to be deceived. I was indeed awake and among the Carpathians. All I could do now was to be patient, and to wait the coming of the morning.

Just as I had come to this conclusion I heard a heavy step approaching behind the great door, and saw through the chinks the gleam of a coming light. Then there was the sound of rattling chains and the clanking of massive bolts drawn back. A key was turned with the loud grating noise of long disuse, and the great door swung back.

Within, stood a tall old man, clean shaven save for a long white moustache, and clad in black from head to foot, without a single speck of colour about him anywhere. He held in his hand an antique silver lamp, in which the flame burned without chimney or globe of any kind, throwing long quivering shadows as it flickered in the draught of the open door. The old man motioned me in with his right hand with a courtly gesture, saying in excellent English, but with a strange intonation:—

"Welcome to my house! Enter freely and of your own will!" He made no motion of stepping to meet me, but stood like a statue, as though his gesture of welcome had fixed him into stone. The instant, however, that I had stepped over the threshold, he moved impulsively forward, and holding out his hand grasped mine with a strength which made me wince, an effect which was not lessened by the fact that it seemed as cold as ice—more like the hand of a dead than a living man. Again he said:—

"Welcome to my house. Come freely. Go safely; and leave something of the happiness you bring!" The strength of the handshake was so much akin to that which I had noticed in the driver, whose face I had not seen, that for a moment I doubted if it were not the same person to whom I was speaking; so to make sure, I said interrogatively:—

"Count Dracula?" He bowed in a courtly way as he replied:—

"I am Dracula; and I bid you welcome, Mr Harker, to my house. Come in; the night air is chill, and you must need to eat and rest." As he was speaking, he put the lamp on a bracket on the wall, and stepping out, took my luggage; he had carried it in before I could forestall him. I protested but he insisted:—

"Nay, sir, you are my guest. It is late, and my people are not available. Let me see to your comfort myself." He insisted on carrying my traps along the passage, and then up a great winding stair, and along another great passage, on whose stone floor our steps rang heavily. At the end of this he threw open a heavy door, and I rejoiced to see within a well-lit room in which a table was spread for supper, and on whose mighty hearth a great fire of logs, freshly replenished, flamed and flared.

The Count halted, putting down my bags, closed the door, and crossing the room, opened another door, which led into a small octagonal room lit by a single lamp, and seemingly without a window of any sort. Passing through this, he opened another door, and motioned me to enter. It was a welcome sight; for here was a great bedroom well lighted and warmed with another log fire,—also added to but lately, for the top logs were fresh—which sent a hollow roar up the wide chimney. The Count himself left my luggage inside and withdrew, saying, before he closed the door:—

"You will need, after your journey, to refresh yourself by making your toilet. I trust you will find all you wish. When you are ready, come into the other room, where you will find your supper prepared."

The light and warmth and the Count's courteous welcome seemed to have dissipated all my doubts and fears. Having then reached my normal state, I discovered that I was half famished with hunger; so making a hasty toilet, I went into the other room.

I found supper already laid out. My host, who stood on one side of the great fireplace, leaning against the stonework, made a graceful wave of his hand to the table, and said:—

"I pray you, be seated and sup how you please. You will, I trust, excuse me that I do not join you; but I have dined already, and I do not sup."

I handed to him the sealed letter which Mr Hawkins had entrusted to me. He opened it and read it gravely; then, with a charming smile, he handed it to me to read. One passage of it, at least, gave me a thrill of pleasure.

"I must regret that an attack of gout, from which malady I am a constant sufferer, forbids absolutely any travelling on my part for some time to come; but I am happy to say I can send a sufficient substitute, one in whom I have every possible confidence. He is a young man, full of energy and talent in his own way, and of a very faithful disposition. He is discreet and silent, and has grown into manhood in my service. He shall be ready to attend on you when you will during his stay, and shall take your instructions in all matters."

The Count himself came forward and took off the cover of a dish, and I fell to at once on an excellent roast chicken. This, with some cheese and a salad and a bottle of old Tokay, of which I had two glasses, was my supper. During the time I was eating it the Count asked me many questions as to my journey, and I told him by degrees all I had experienced.

By this time I had finished my supper, and by my host's desire had drawn up a chair by the fire and begun to smoke a cigar which he offered me, at the same time excusing himself that he did not smoke. I had now an opportunity of observing him, and found him of a very marked physiognomy.

His face was a strong—a very strong—aquiline, with high bridge of the thin nose and peculiarly arched nostrils; with lofty domed forehead, and hair growing scantily round the temples but profusely elsewhere. His eyebrows were very massive, almost meeting over the nose, and with bushy hair that seemed to curl in its own profusion. The mouth, so far as I could see it under the heavy moustache, was fixed and rather cruel-looking, with peculiarly sharp white teeth; these protruded over the lips, whose remarkable ruddiness showed astonishing vitality in a man of his years. For the rest, his ears were pale, and at the tops extremely pointed; the chin was broad and strong, and the cheeks firm though thin. The general effect was one of extraordinary pallor.

Hitherto I had noticed the backs of his hands as they lay on his knees in the firelight, and they had seemed rather white and fine; but seeing them now close to me, I could not but notice that they were rather coarse—broad, with squat fingers. Strange to say, there were hairs in the centre of the palm. The nails were long and fine, and cut to a sharp point. As the Count leaned over me and his hands touched me, I could not repress a shudder. It may have been that his breath was rank, but a horrible feeling of nausea came over me, which, do what I would, I could not conceal. The Count, evidently noticing it, drew back; and with a grim sort of smile, which showed more than he had yet done his protuberant teeth, sat himself down again on his own side of the fireplace. We were both silent for a while; and as I looked towards the window I saw the first dim streak of the coming dawn. There seemed a strange stillness over everything; but as I listened I heard as if from down below in the valley the howling of many wolves. The Count's eyes gleamed, and he said:—

"Listen to them—the children of the night. What music they make!" Seeing, I suppose, some expression in my face strange to him, he added:—

"Ah, sir, you dwellers in the city cannot enter into the feelings of the hunter." Then he rose and said:—

"But you must be tired. Your bedroom is all ready, and to-morrow you shall sleep as late as you will. I have to be away till the afternoon; so sleep well and dream well!" With a courteous bow, he opened for me himself the door to the octagonal room, and I entered my bedroom...

I am all in a sea of wonders. I doubt; I fear; I think strange things, which I dare not confess to my own soul. God keep me, if only for the sake of those dear to me!

7 May.—It is again early morning, but I have rested and enjoyed the last twenty-four hours. I slept till late in the day, and awoke of my own accord. When I had dressed myself I went into the room where we had supped, and found a cold breakfast laid out, with coffee kept hot by the pot being placed on the hearth. There was a card on the table, on which was written:—

"I have to be absent for a while. Do not wait for me.—D." I set to and enjoyed a hearty meal. When I had done, I looked for a bell, so that I might let the servants know I had finished; but I could not find one. There are certainly odd deficiencies in the house, considering the extraordinary evidences of wealth which are round me. The table service is of gold, and so beautifully wrought that it must be of immense value. The curtains and upholstery of the chairs and sofas and the hangings of my bed are of the costliest and most beautiful fabrics, and must have been of fabulous value when they were made, for they are centuries old, though in excellent order. I saw something like them in Hampton Court, but there they were worn and frayed and moth-eaten. But still in none of the rooms is there a mirror. There is not even a toilet glass on my table, and I had to get the little shaving glass from my bag before I could either shave or brush my hair. I have not yet seen a servant anywhere, or heard a sound near the castle except the howling of wolves. Some time after I had finished my meal—I do not know whether to call it breakfast or dinner, for it was between five and six o'clock when I had it—I looked about for something to read, for I did not like to go about the castle until I had asked the Count's permission. There was absolutely nothing in the room, book, newspaper, or even writing materials; so I opened another door in the room and found a sort of library. The door opposite mine I tried, but found it locked.

In the library I found, to my great delight, a vast number of English books, whole shelves full of them, and bound volumes of magazines and newspapers. A table in the centre was littered with English magazines and newspapers, though none of them were of very recent date. The books were of the most varied kind—history, geography, politics, political economy, botany, geology, law—all relating to England and English life and customs and manners. There were even such books of reference as the London Directory, the "Red" and "Blue" books, Whitaker's Almanac, the Army and Navy Lists, and—it somehow gladdened my heart to see it—the Law List.

Whilst I was looking at the books, the door opened, and the Count entered. He saluted me in a hearty way, and hoped that I had had a good night's rest. Then he went on:—

"I am glad you found your way in here, for I am sure there is much that will interest you. These companions"—and he laid his hand on some of the books—"have been good friends to me, and for some years past, ever since I had the idea of going to London, have given me many, many hours of pleasure. Through them I have come to know your great England; and to know her is to love her. I long to go through the crowded streets of your mighty London, to be in the midst of the whirl and rush of humanity, to share its life, its change, its death, and all that makes it what it is. But alas! as yet I only know your tongue through books. To you, my friend, I look that I know it to speak."

"But, Count," I said, "you know and speak English thoroughly!" He bowed gravely.

"I thank you, my friend, for your all too-flattering estimate, but yet I fear that I am but a little way on the road I would travel. True, I know the grammar and the words, but yet I know not how to speak them."

"Indeed," I said, "you speak excellently."

"Not so," he answered. "Well, I know that, did I move and speak in your London, none there are who would not know me for a stranger. That is not enough for me. Here I am noble; I am *boyar*; the common people know me, and I am master. But a stranger in a strange land, he is no one; men know him not—and to know not is to care not for. I am content if I am like the rest, so that no man stops if he see me, or pause in his speaking if he hear my words, 'Ha, ha! a stranger!' I have been so long master that I would be master still—or at least that none other should be master of me. You come to me not alone as agent of my friend Peter Hawkins, of Exeter, to tell me all about my new estate in London. You shall, I trust, rest here with me awhile, so that by our talking I may learn the English intonation; and I would that you tell me when I make error, even of the smallest, in my speaking. I am sorry that I had to be away so long to-day; but you will, I know, forgive one who has so many important affairs in hand."

Of course I said all I could about being willing, and asked if I might come into that room when I chose. He answered: "Yes, certainly," and added:—

"You may go anywhere you wish in the castle, except where the doors are locked, where of course you will not wish to go. There is reason that all things are as they are, and did you see with my eyes and know with my knowledge, you would perhaps better understand." I said I was sure of this, and then he went on:—

"We are in Transylvania; and Transylvania is not England. Our ways are not your ways, and there shall be to you many strange things. Nay, from what you have told me of your experiences already, you know something of what strange things there may be."

This led to much conversation; and as it was evident that he wanted to talk, if only for talking's sake, I asked him many questions regarding things that had already happened to me or come within my notice. Sometimes he sheered off the subject, or turned the conversation by pretending not to understand; but generally he answered all I asked most frankly. Then as time went on, and I had got somewhat bolder, I asked him of some of the strange things of the preceding night, as, for instance, why the coachman went to the places where he had seen the blue flames. He then explained to me that it was commonly believed that on a certain night of the year—last night, in fact, when all evil spirits are supposed to have unchecked sway—a blue flame is seen over any place where treasure has been concealed. "That treasure has been hidden," he went on, "in the region through which you came last night, there can be but little doubt; for it was the ground fought over for centuries by the Wallachian, the Saxon, and the Turk. Why, there is hardly a foot of soil in all this region that has not been enriched by the blood of men, patriots or invaders. In old days there were stirring times, when the Austrian and the Hungarian came up in hordes, and the patriots went out to meet them—men and women, the aged and the children too—and waited their coming on the rocks above the passes, that they might sweep destruction on them with their artificial avalanches. When the invader was triumphant he found but little, for whatever there was had been sheltered in the friendly soil."

"But how," said I, "can it have remained so long undiscovered, when there is a sure index to it if men will but take the trouble to look?" The Count smiled, and as his lips ran back over his gums, the long, sharp, canine teeth showed out strangely; he answered:—

"Because your peasant is at heart a coward and a fool! Those flames only appear on one night; and on that night no man of this land will, if he can help it, stir without his doors. And, dear sir, even if he did he would not know what to do. Why, even the peasant that you tell me of who marked the place of the flame would not know where to look in daylight even for his own work. Even you would not, I dare be sworn, be able to find these places again?"

"There you are right," I said. "I know no more than the dead where even to look for them." Then we drifted into other matters.

"Come," he said at last, "tell me of London and of the house which you have procured for me." With an apology for my remissness, I went into my own room to get the papers from my bag. Whilst I was placing them in order I heard a rattling of china and silver in the next room, and as I passed through, noticed that the table had been cleared and the lamp lit, for it was by this time deep into the dark. The lamps were also lit in the study or library, and I found the Count lying on the sofa, reading, of all things in the world, an English Bradshaw's Guide. When I came in he cleared the books and papers from the table; and with him I went into plans and deeds and figures of all sorts. He was interested in everything, and asked me a myriad questions about the place and its surroundings. He clearly had studied beforehand all he could get on the subject of the neighbourhood, for he evidently at the end knew very much more than I did. When I remarked this, he answered:—

"Well, but, my friend, is it not needful that I should? When I go there I shall be all alone, and my friend Harker Jonathan—nay, pardon me, I fall into my country's habit of putting your patronymic first—my friend Jonathan Harker will not be by my side to correct and aid me. He will be in Exeter, miles away, probably working at papers of the law with my other friend, Peter Hawkins. So!"

We went thoroughly into the business of the purchase of the estate at Purfleet. When I had told him the facts and got his signature to the necessary papers, and had written a letter with them ready to post to Mr Hawkins, he began to ask me how

I had come across so suitable a place. I read to him the notes which I had made at the time, and which I inscribe here:—

"At Purfleet, on a by-road, I came across just such a place as seemed to be required, and where was displayed a dilapidated notice that the place was for sale. It is surrounded by a high wall, of ancient structure, built of heavy stones, and has not been repaired for a large number of years. The closed gates are of heavy old oak and iron, all eaten with rust.

"The estate is called Carfax, no doubt a corruption of the old *Quatre Face*, as the house is four-sided, agreeing with the cardinal points of the compass. It contains in all some twenty acres, quite surrounded by the solid stone wall above mentioned. There are many trees on it, which make it in places gloomy, and there is a deep, dark-looking pond or small lake, evidently fed by some springs, as the water is clear and flows away in a fair-sized stream. The house is very large and of all periods back, I should say, to mediæval times, for one part is of stone immensely thick, with only a few windows high up and heavily barred with iron. It looks like part of a keep, and is close to an old chapel or church. I could not enter it, as I had not the key of the door leading to it from the house, but I have taken with my kodak views of it from various points. The house has been added to, but in a very straggling way, and I can only guess at the amount of ground it covers, which must be very great. There are but few houses close at hand, one being a very large house only recently added to and formed into a private lunatic asylum. It is not, however, visible from the grounds."

When I had finished, he said:—

"I am glad that it is old and big. I myself am of an old family, and to live in a new house would kill me. A house cannot be made habitable in a day; and, after all, how few days go to make up a century. I rejoice also that there is a chapel of old times.

We Transylvanian nobles love not to think that our bones may lie amongst the common dead. I seek not gaiety nor mirth, not the bright voluptuousness of much sunshine and sparkling waters which please the young and gay. I am no longer young; and my heart, through weary years of mourning over the dead, is not attuned to mirth. Moreover, the walls of my castle are broken; the shadows are many, and the wind breathes cold through the broken battlements and casements. I love the shade and the shadow, and would be alone with my thoughts when I may." Somehow his words and his look did not seem to accord, or else it was that his cast of face made his smile look malignant and saturnine.

Presently, with an excuse, he left me, asking me to put all my papers together. He was some little time away, and I began to look at some of the books around me. One was an atlas, which I found opened naturally at England, as if that map had been much used. On looking at it I found in certain places little rings marked, and on examining these I noticed that one was near London on the east side, manifestly where his new estate was situated; the other two were Exeter, and Whitby on the Yorkshire coast.

It was the better part of an hour when the Count returned. "Aha!" he said; "still at your books? Good! But you must not work always. Come; I am informed that your supper is ready." He took my arm, and we went into the next room, where I found an excellent supper ready on the table. The Count again excused himself, as he had dined out on his being away from home. But he sat as on the previous night, and chatted whilst I ate. After supper I smoked, as on the last evening, and the Count stayed with me, chatting and asking questions on every conceivable subject, hour after hour. I felt that it was getting very late indeed, but I did not say anything, for I felt under obligation to meet my host's wishes in every way. I was not sleepy, as the long sleep yesterday had fortified me; but I could not help experiencing that chill which comes over one at the coming of the dawn, which is like, in its way, the turn of the tide. They say that people who are near death die generally at the change to the dawn or at the turn of the tide; any one who has when tired, and tied as it were to his post, experienced this change in the atmosphere can well believe it. All at once we heard the crow of a cock coming up with preternatural shrillness through the clear morning air; Count Dracula, jumping to his feet, said:—

"Why, there is the morning again! How remiss I am to let you stay up so long. You must make your conversation regarding my dear new country of England less interesting, so that I may not forget how time flies by us," and, with a courtly bow, he quickly left me.

I went into my own room and drew the curtains, but there was little to notice; my window opened into the courtyard, all I could see was the warm grey of quickening sky. So I pulled the curtains again, and have written of this day.

8 May.—I began to fear as I wrote in this book that I was getting too diffuse; but now I am glad that I went into detail from the first, for there is something so strange about this place and all in it that I cannot but feel uneasy. I wish I were safe out of it, or that I had never come. It may be that this strange night-existence is telling on me; but would that that were all! If there were any one to talk to I could bear it, but there is no one. I have only the Count to speak with, and he!—I fear I am myself the only living soul within the place. Let me be prosaic so far as facts can be; it will help me to bear up, and imagination must not run riot with me. If it does I am lost. Let me say at once how I stand—or seem to.

I only slept a few hours when I went to bed, and feeling that I could not sleep any more, got up. I had hung my shaving glass by the window, and was just beginning to shave. Suddenly I felt a hand on my shoulder, and heard the Count's voice saying to me, "Good-morning." I started, for it amazed me that I had not seen him, since the reflection of the glass covered the whole room behind me. In starting I had cut myself slightly, but did not notice it at the moment. Having answered the Count's salutation, I turned to the glass again to see how I had been mistaken. This time there could be no error, for the man was close to me, and I could see him over my shoulder. But there was no reflection of him in the mirror! The whole room behind me was displayed; but there was no sign of a man in it, except myself. This was startling, and, coming on the top of so many strange things, was beginning to increase that vague feeling of uneasiness which I always have when the Count is near; but at the instant I saw that the cut had bled a little, and the blood was trickling over my chin. I laid down the razor, turning as I did so half round to look for some sticking plaster. When the Count saw my face, his eyes blazed with a sort of demoniac fury, and he suddenly made a grab at my throat. I drew away, and his hand touched the string of beads which held the crucifix. It made an instant change in him, for the fury passed so quickly that I could hardly believe that it was ever there.

"Take care," he said, "take care how you cut yourself. It is more dangerous than you think in this country." Then seizing the shaving glass, he went on: "And this is the wretched thing that has done the mischief. It is a foul bauble of man's vanity. Away with it!" and opening the heavy window with one wrench of his terrible hand, he flung out the glass, which was shattered into a thousand pieces on the stones of the courtyard far below. Then he withdrew without a word. It is very annoying, for I do not see how I am to shave, unless in my watch-case or the bottom of the shaving-pot, which is fortunately of metal.

When I went into the dining-room, breakfast was prepared; but I could not find the Count anywhere. So I breakfasted alone. It is strange that as yet I have not seen the Count eat or drink. He must be a very peculiar man! After breakfast I did a little exploring in the castle. I went out on the stairs, and found a room looking towards the South. The view was magnificent, and from where I stood there was every opportunity of seeing it. The castle is on the very edge of a terrible precipice. A stone falling from the window would fall a thousand feet without touching anything! As far as the eye can reach is a sea of green tree tops, with occasionally a deep rift where there is a chasm. Here and there are silver threads where the rivers wind in deep gorges through the forests.

But I am not in heart to describe beauty, for when I had seen the view I explored further; doors, doors, doors everywhere, and all locked and bolted. In no place save from the windows in the castle walls is there an available exit.

The castle is a veritable prison, and I am a prisoner!

~

Abraham "Bram" Stoker (1847–1912) was an Irish author whose most famous work is the vampire novel *Dracula*. The novel uses an epistolary style, which means it is put together as a series of diary entries, letters and newspaper articles.

The Tempest

William Shakespeare, Retold by Charles and Mary Lamb

There was a certain island in the sea, the only inhabitants of which were an old man, whose name was Prospero, and his daughter Miranda, a very beautiful young lady. She came to this island so young that she had no memory of having seen any other human face than her father's.

They lived in a cave or cell, made out of a rock; it was divided into several apartments, one of which Prospero called his study; there he kept his books, which chiefly treated of magic, a study at that time much affected by all learned men: and the knowledge of this art he found very useful to him; for being thrown by a strange chance upon this island, which had been enchanted by a witch called Sycorax, who died there a short time before his arrival, Prospero, by virtue of his art, released many good spirits that Sycorax had imprisoned in the bodies of large trees, because they had refused to execute her wicked commands. These gentle spirits were ever after obedient to the will of Prospero. Of these Ariel was the chief.

The lively little sprite Ariel had nothing mischievous in his nature, except that he took rather too much pleasure in tormenting an ugly monster called Caliban, for be owed him a grudge because he was the son of his old enemy Sycorax. This Caliban, Prospero found in the woods, a strange misshapen thing, far less human in form than an ape: he took him home to his cell, and taught him to speak; and Prospero would have been very kind to him, but the bad nature which Caliban inherited from his mother, Sycorax, would not let him learn anything good or useful: therefore he was employed like a slave, to fetch wood and do the most laborious offices; and Ariel had the charge of compelling him to these services.

When Caliban was lazy and neglected his work, Ariel (who was invisible to all eyes but Prospero's) would come slyly and pinch him, and sometimes tumble him down in the mire; and then Ariel, in the likeness of an ape, would make mouths at him. Then swiftly changing his shape, in the likeness of a hedgehog, he would lie tumbling in Caliban's way, who feared the hedgehog's sharp quills would prick his bare feet. With a variety of such-like vexatious tricks Ariel would often torment him, whenever Caliban neglected the work which Prospero commanded him to do.

Having these powerful spirits obedient to his will, Prospero could by their means command the winds, and the waves of the sea. By his orders they raised a violent storm, in the midst of which, and struggling with the wild sea-waves that every moment,threatened to swallow it up, he showed his daughter a fine large ship, which he told her was full of living beings like themselves. "O my dear father," said she, "if by your art you have raised this dreadful storm, have pity on their sad distress. See! the vessel will be dashed to pieces. Poor souls! they will all perish. If I had power I would sink the sea beneath the earth, rather than the good ship should be destroyed, with all the precious souls within her."

"Be not amazed, daughter Miranda," said Prospero; "there. is no harm done. I have so ordered it, that no person in the ship shall receive any hurt. What I have done has been in care of you, my dear child. You are ignorant who you are, or where you came from, and you know no more of me, but that I am your father and live in this poor cave. Can you remember a time before you came to this cell? I think you cannot, for you were not then three years of age."

"Certainly I can, sir," replied Miranda.

"By what?" asked Prospero; "by any other house or person? Tell me what you can remember, my child."

Miranda said: "It seems to me like the recollection of a dream. But had I not once four or five women who attended upon me?" Prospero answered: "You had, and more. How is it that this still lives in your mind? Do you remember how you came here?" "No, sir," said Miranda, "I remember nothing more."

"Twelve years ago, Miranda," continued Prospero, "I was Duke of Milan, and you were a princess, and my only heir. had a younger brother, whose name was Antonio, to whom I trusted everything; and as I was fond of retirement and deep study I commonly left the management of my state affairs to your uncle, my false brother (for so indeed he proved). 1, neglecting all worldly ends, buried among my books, did dedicate whole time to the bettering of my mind. My brother Antonio, being thus in possession of my power, began to think himself the duke indeed. The opportunity I gave him of making himself popular among my subjects awakened in his bad nature a proud ambition to deprive me of my dukedom; this he soon effected with the aid of the King of Naples, a powerful prince, who was my enemy."

"Wherefore," said Miranda, "did they not that hour destroy us?"

"My child," answered her father, "they durst not, so dear was the love that my people bore me. Antonio carried us on board a ship, and when we were some leagues out at sea, he forced us into a small boat, without either tackle, sail, or mast; there he left us, as he thought, to perish. But a kind lord of my court, one Gonzalo, who loved me, had privately placed in the boat water, provisions, apparel, and some books which I prize above my dukedom."

"O my father," said Miranda, "what a trouble must I have been to you then!"

"No, my love," said Prospero, "you were a little cherub that did preserve me. Your innocent smiles made me bear up against my misfortunes. Our food lasted till we landed on this desert island, since when my chief delight has been in teaching you, Miranda, and well have you profited by my instructions."

"Heaven thank you, my dear father," said Miranda. "Now pray tell me, sir, your reason for raising this sea-storm?"

"Know then," said her father, "that by means of this storm, my enemies, the King of Naples and my cruel brother, are cast ashore upon this island."

Having so said, Prospero gently touched his daughter with his magic wand, and she fell fast asleep; for the spirit Ariel just then presented himself before his master, to give an account of the tempest, and how he had disposed of the ship's company, and though the spirits were always invisible to Miranda, Prospero did not choose she should hear him holding converse (as would seem to her) with the empty air.

"Well, my brave spirit," said Prospero to Ariel, "how have you performed your task?"

Ariel gave a lively description of the storm, and of the terrors of the mariners, and how the king's son, Ferdinand, was the first who leaped into the sea; and his father thought he saw his dear son swallowed up by the waves and lost. "But he is safe," said Ariel, "in a corner of the isle, sitting with his arms folded, sadly lamenting the loss of the king, his father, whom he concludes drowned. Not a hair of his head is injured, and his princely garments, though drenched in the sea-waves, look fresher than before."

"That's my delicate Ariel," said Prospero. "Bring him hither: my daughter must see this young prince. Where is the king, and my brother?"

"I left them," answered Ariel, "searching for Ferdinand, whom they have little hopes of finding, thinking they saw him perish. Of the ship's crew not one is missing; though each one thinks himself the only one saved; and the ship, though invisible to them, is safe in the harbor."

"Ariel," said Prospero, "thy charge is faithfully performed; but there is more work yet."

"Is there more work?" said Ariel. "Let me remind you, master, you have promised me my liberty. I pray, remember, , I have done you worthy service, told you no lies, made no mistakes, served you without grudge or grumbling."

"How now!" said Prospero. "You do not recollect what a torment I freed you from. Have you forgot the wicked witch Sycorax, who with age and envy was almost bent double? Where was she born? Speak; tell me."

"Sir, in Algiers," said Ariel.

"Oh, was she so?" said Prospero. "I must recount what you have been, which I find you do not remember. This bad witch,

Sycorax, for her witchcrafts, too terrible to enter human hearing, was banished from Algiers, and here left by the sailors-; and because you were a spirit too delicate to execute her wicked commands, she shut you up in a tree, where I found you howling. This torment, remember, I did free you from."

"Pardon me, dear master," said Ariel, ashamed to seem ungrateful; "I will obey your commands."

"Do so," said Prospero, "and I will set you free." He then gave orders what further he would have him do; and away went Ariel, first to where he had left Ferdinand, and found him still sitting on the grass in the same melancholy posture.

"Oh, my young gentleman," said Ariel, when he saw him, "I will soon move you. You must be brought, I find, for the Lady Miranda to have a sight of your pretty person. Come, sir, follow me." He then began singing:

"Full fathom five thy father lies;
Of his bones are coral made;
Those are pearls that were his eyes:
Nothing of him that doth fade,
But doth suffer a sea-change
Into something rich and strange.
Sea-nymphs hourly ring his knell:
Hark! now I hear them—Ding-dong, bell."

This strange news of his lost father soon roused the prince from the stupid fit into which he had fallen. He followed in amazement the sound of Ariel's voice, till it led him to Prospero and Miranda, who were sitting under the shade of a large tree. Now Miranda had never seen a man before, except her own father.

"Miranda," said Prospero, "tell me what you are looking at yonder."

"Oh, father," said Miranda, in a strange surprise, "surely that is a spirit. Lord! how it looks about! Believe me, sir, it is a beautiful creature. Is it not a spirit?"

"No, girl," answered her father; "it eats, and sleeps, and has senses such as we have. This young man you see was in the ship. He is somewhat altered by grief, or you might call him a handsome person. He has lost his companions, and is wandering about to find them."

Miranda, who thought all men had grave faces and gray beards like her father, was delighted with the appearance of this beautiful young prince; and Ferdinand, seeing such a lovely lady in this desert place, and from the strange sounds he had heard, expecting nothing but wonders, thought be was upon an enchanted island, and that Miranda was the goddess of the place, and as such he began to address her.

She timidly answered, she was no goddess, but a simple maid and was going to give him an account of herself, when Prospero interrupted her. He was well pleased to find they admired each other, for he plainly perceived they had (as we say) fallen in love at first sight: but to try Ferdinand's constancy, he resolved to throw some difficulties in their way: therefore, advancing forward, be addressed the prince with a stern air, telling him, he came to the island as a spy, to take it from him who was the lord of it. "Follow me," said be. "I will tie your neck and feet together. You shall drink sea-water; shell-fish, withered roots, and husks of acorns shall be your food."

"No," said Ferdinand, "I will resist such entertainment till I see a more powerful enemy," and drew his sword; but Prospero, waving his magic wand, fixed him to the spot where he stood, so that he had no power to move.

Miranda hung upon her father, saying: "Why are you so ungentle? Have pity, I will be his surety. This is the second man I ever saw, and to me he seems a true one."

"Silence!" said the father. "One word more will make me chide you, girl! What! an advocate for an impostor! You think there are no more such fine men, having seen only him and Caliban. I tell you, foolish girl, most men as far excel this as he does Calliban." This he said to prove his daughter's constancy; and she replied:

"My affections are most humble. I have no wish to see a goodlier man."

"Come on, young man," said Prospero to the prince; "you have no power to disobey me."

"I have not indeed," answered Ferdinand; and not knowing that it was by magic he was deprived of all power of resistance, he was astonished to kind himself so strangely compelled to follow Prospero: looking back on Miranda as long as he could see her, he said, as he went after Prospero into the cave: "My spirits are all bound up as if I were in a dream; but this man's threats, and the weakness which I feel, would seem light to me if from my prison I might once a day behold this fair maid."

Prospero kept Ferdinand not long confined within the cell: he soon brought out his prisoner, and set him a severe task to perform, taking care to let his daughter know the hard labour he had imposed on him, and then pretending to go into his study, he secretly watched them both.

Prospero had commanded Ferdinand to pile up some heavy logs of wood. Kings' sons not being much used to laborious work, Miranda soon after found her lover almost dying with fatigue. "Alas!" said she, "do not work so hard; my father is at his studies, he is safe for these three hours; pray rest yourself."

"O my dear lady," said Ferdinand, "I dare not. I must finish my task before I take my rest."

"If you will sit down," said Miranda, "I will carry your logs the while." But this Ferdinand would by no means agree to. Instead of a help Miranda became a hindrance, for they began a long conversation, so that the business of log-carrying went on very slowly.

Prospero, who had enjoined Ferdinand this task merely as a trial of his love, was not at his books, as his daughter supposed, but was standing by them invisible, to overhear what they said.

Ferdinand inquired her name, which she told, saying it was against her father's express command she did so.

Prospero only smiled at this first instance of his daughter's disobedience, for having by his magic art caused his daughter to fall in love so suddenly, he was not angry that she showed her love by forgetting to obey his commands. And he listened well pleased to a long speech of Ferdinand's, in which he professed to love her above all the ladies he ever saw.

In answer to his praises of her beauty, which he said exceeded all the women in the world, she replied: "I do not remember the face of any woman, nor have I seen any more men than you, my good friend, and my dear father. How features are abroad, I know not: but, believe me, sir, I would not wish any companion in the world but you, nor can my imagination form any shape but yours that I could like. But, sir, I fear I talk to you too freely, and my father's precepts I forget."

At this Prospero smiled, and nodded his head, as much as to say: "This goes on exactly as I could wish; my girl will be queen of Naples."

And then Ferdinand, in another fine long speech (for young princes speak in courtly phrases), told the innocent Miranda he was heir to the crown of Naples, and that she should be his queen.

"Ah! sir," said she, "I am a fool to weep at what I am glad of. I will answer you in plain and holy innocence. I am your wife if you will marry me."

Prospero prevented Ferdinand's thanks by appearing visible before them.

"Fear nothing, my child," said he; "I have overheard, and approve of all you have said. And, Ferdinand, if I have too severely used you, I will make you rich amends, by giving you my daughter. All your vexations were but trials of your love, and you have nobly stood the test. Then as my gift, which your true love has worthily purchased, take my daughter, and do not smile that I boast she is above all praise." He then, telling them that he had business which required his presence, desired they would sit down and talk together till he returned; and this command Miranda seemed not at all disposed to disobey.

When Prospero left them, he called his spirit Ariel, who quickly appeared before him, eager to relate what he had done with Prospero's brother and the king of Naples. Ariel said he had left them almost out of their senses with fear, at the strange things he had caused them to see and hear. When fatigued with wandering about, and famished for want of food, he had suddenly set before them a delicious banquet, and then, just as they were going to eat, he appeared visible before them in the shape of a harpy, a voracious monster with wings, and the feast vanished away. Then, to their utter amazement, this seeming harpy spoke to them, reminding them of their cruelty in driving Prospero from his dukedom, and leaving him and his infant daughter to perish in the sea, saying, that for this cause these terrors were suffered to afflict them.

The King of Naples, and Antonio the false brother, repented the injustice they had done to Prospero; and Ariel told his master he was certain their penitence was sincere, and that he, though a spirit, could not but pity them.

"Then bring them hither, Ariel," said Prospero: "if you, who are but a spirit, feel for their distress, shall not I, who am a human being like themselves, have compassion on them? Bring them quickly, my dainty Ariel."

Ariel soon returned with the king, Antonio, and old Gonzalo in their train, who had followed him, wondering at the wild music he played in the air to draw them on to his master's presence. This Gonzalo was the same who had so kindly provided Prospero formerly with books and provisions, when his wicked brother left him, as he thought, to perish in an open boat in the sea.

Grief and terror had so stupefied their senses that they did not know Prospero. He first discovered himself to the good old Gonzalo, calling him the preserver of his life; and then his brother and the king knew that he was the injured Prospero.

Antonio, with tears and sad words of sorrow and true repentance, implored his brother's forgiveness, and the king expressed his sincere remorse for having assisted Antonio to depose his brother: and Prospero forgave them; and, upon their engaging to restore his dukedom, he said to the King of Naples, "I have a gift in store for you, too"; and, opening a door, showed him his son Ferdinand playing at chess with Miranda.

Nothing could exceed the joy of the father and the son at this unexpected meeting, for they each thought the other drowned in the storm.

"Oh wonder!" said Miranda, "what noble creatures these are! It must surely be a brave world that has such people in it."

The King of Naples was almost as much astonished at the beauty and excellent graces of the young Miranda as his son had been. "Who is this maid?" said he; "she seems the goddess that has parted us, and brought us thus together."

"No, sir," answered Ferdinand, smiling to find his father had fallen into the same mistake that he had done when he first saw Miranda, "she is a mortal, but by immortal Providence she is mine; I chose her when I could not ask you, my father, for your consent, not thinking you were alive. She is the daughter this Prospero, who is the famous Duke of Milan, of whose renown I have heard so much, but never saw him till now: of him I have received a new life: he has made himself to me a second father, giving me this dear lady."

"Then I must be her father," said the king; "but, oh, how oddly will it sound, that I must ask my child forgiveness."

"No more of that," said Prospero: "let us not remember our troubles past, since they so happily have ended." And then Prospero embraced his brother, and again assured him of his forgiveness; and said that a wise overruling Providence had permitted that he should be driven from his poor dukedom of Milan, that his daughter might inherit the crown of Naples, for that by their meeting in this desert island it had happened that the king's son had loved Miranda.

These kind words which Prospero spoke, meaning to comfort his brother, so filled Antonio with shame and remorse that be wept and was unable to speak; and the kind old Gonzalo wept to see this joyful reconciliation, and prayed for blessings on the young couple.

Prospero now told them that their ship was safe in the harbor, and the sailors all on board her, and that he and his daughter would accompany them home the next morning. "In the mean time," says he, "partake of such refreshments as my poor cave affords; and for your evening's entertainment I will relate the history of my life from my first landing in this desert island." He then called for Caliban to prepare some food, and set the cave in order; and the company were astonished at the uncouth form and savage appearance of this ugly monster, who (Prospero said) was the only attendant he had to wait upon him.

Before Prospero left the island he dismissed Ariel from service, to the great joy of that lively little spirit, who, though he had been a faithful servant to his master, was always longing to enjoy his free liberty, to wander uncontrolled in the air, like a wild bird, under green trees, among pleasant fruits, and sweet-smelling flowers.

"My quaint Ariel," said Prospero to the little sprite when he made him free, "I shall miss you; yet you shall have your freedom."

"Thank you, my dear master," said Ariel; "but give me leave to attend your ship home with prosperous gales, before you bid farewell to the assistance of your faithful spirit; and then, master, when I am free, how merrily I shall live!" Here Ariel sang this pretty song:

"Where the bee sucks, there suck!;
In a cowslip's bell I lie:
There I crouch when owls do cry.
On the bat's back I do fly
After summer merrily.
Merrily, merrily shall I live now
Under the blossom that hangs on the bough."

Prospero then buried deep in the earth his magical books and wand, for he was resolved never more to make use of the magic art. And having thus overcome his enemies, and being reconciled to his brother and the King of Naples, nothing now remained to complete his happiness but to revisit his native land, to take possession of his dukedom, and to witness the happy nuptials of his daughter and Prince Ferdinand, which the king said should be instantly celebrated with great splendor on their return to Naples. At which place, under the safe convoy of the spirit Ariel they, after a pleasant voyage, soon arrived.

~

Charles Lamb (1775–1834) and his sister Mary (1764–1847) collaborated on *Tales from Shakespeare*, a collection of prose adaptations of Shakespeare's plays for young readers. This story is a retelling of *The Tempest*, one of Shakespeare's most memorable plays. The Lamb siblings were friends with poets such as William Wordsworth and Samuel Taylor Coleridge.

From Great Expectations

Charles Dickens

Mr Pumblechook's premises in the High Street of the market town, were of a peppercorny and farinaceous character, as the premises of a cornchandler and seedsman should be. It appeared to me that he must be a very happy man indeed, to have so many little drawers in his shop; and I wondered when I peeped into one or two on the lower tiers, and saw the tied-up brown paper packets inside, whether the flower-seeds and bulbs ever wanted of a fine day to break out of those jails, and bloom.

It was in the early morning after my arrival that I entertained this speculation. On the previous night, I had been sent straight to bed in an attic with a sloping roof, which was so low in the corner where the bedstead was, that I calculated the tiles as being within a foot of my eyebrows. In the same early morning, I discovered a singular affinity between seeds and corduroys. Mr Pumblechook wore corduroys, and so did his shopman; and somehow, there was a general air and flavor about the corduroys, so much in the nature of seeds, and a general air and flavor about the seeds, so much in the nature of corduroys, that I hardly knew which was which. The same opportunity served me for noticing that Mr Pumblechook appeared to conduct his business by looking across the street at the saddler, who appeared to transact his business by keeping his eye on the coachmaker, who appeared to get on in life by putting his hands in his pockets and contemplating the baker, who in his turn folded his arms and stared at the grocer, who stood at his door and yawned at the chemist. The watchmaker, always poring over a little desk with a magnifying-glass at his eye, and always inspected by a group of smock-frocks poring over him through the glass of his shop-window, seemed to be about the only person in the High Street whose trade engaged his attention.

Mr Pumblechook and I breakfasted at eight o'clock in the parlor behind the shop, while the shopman took his mug of tea and hunch of bread and butter on a sack of peas in the front premises. I considered Mr Pumblechook wretched company. Besides being possessed by my sister's idea that a mortifying and penitential character ought to be imparted to my diet,—besides giving me as much crumb as possible in combination with as little butter, and putting such a quantity of warm water into my milk that it would have been more candid to have left the milk out altogether,—his conversation consisted of nothing but arithmetic. On my politely bidding him Good morning, he said, pompously, "Seven times nine, boy?" And how should I be able to answer, dodged in that way, in a strange place, on an empty stomach! I was hungry, but before I had swallowed a morsel, he began a running sum that lasted all through the breakfast. "Seven?" "And four?" "And eight?" "And six?" "And two?" "And ten?" And so on. And after each figure was disposed of, it was as much as I could do to get a bite or a sup, before the next came; while he sat at his ease guessing nothing, and eating bacon and hot roll, in (if I may be allowed the expression) a gorging and gormandizing manner.

For such reasons, I was very glad when ten o'clock came and we started for Miss Havisham's; though I was not at all at my ease regarding the manner in which I should acquit myself under that lady's roof. Within a quarter of an hour we came to Miss Havisham's house, which was of old brick, and dismal, and had a great many iron bars to it. Some of the windows had been walled up; of those that remained, all the lower were rustily barred. There was a courtyard in front, and that was barred; so we had to wait, after ringing the bell, until some one should come to open it. While we waited at the gate, I peeped in (even then Mr Pumblechook said, "And fourteen?" but I pretended not to hear him), and saw that at the side of the house there was a large brewery. No brewing was going on in it, and none seemed to have gone on for a long long time.

A window was raised, and a clear voice demanded "What name?" To which my conductor replied, "Pumblechook." The voice returned, "Quite right," and the window was shut again, and a young lady came across the court-yard, with keys in her hand.

"This," said Mr Pumblechook, "is Pip."

"This is Pip, is it?" returned the young lady, who was very pretty and seemed very proud; "come in, Pip."

Mr Pumblechook was coming in also, when she stopped him with the gate.

"Oh!" she said. "Did you wish to see Miss Havisham?"

"If Miss Havisham wished to see me," returned Mr Pumblechook, discomfited.

"Ah!" said the girl; "but you see she don't."

She said it so finally, and in such an undiscussible way, that Mr Pumblechook, though in a condition of ruffled dignity, could not protest. But he eyed me severely,—as if I had done anything to him!—and departed with the words reproachfully delivered: "Boy! Let your behavior here be a credit unto them which brought you up by hand!" I was not free from apprehension that he would come back to propound through the gate, "And sixteen?" But he didn't.

My young conductress locked the gate, and we went across the courtyard. It was paved and clean, but grass was growing in every crevice. The brewery buildings had a little lane of communication with it, and the wooden gates of that lane stood open, and all the brewery beyond stood open, away to the high enclosing wall; and all was empty and disused. The cold wind seemed to blow colder there than outside the gate; and it made a shrill noise in howling in and out at the open sides of the brewery, like the noise of wind in the rigging of a ship at sea.

She saw me looking at it, and she said, "You could drink without hurt all the strong beer that's brewed there now, boy."

"I should think I could, miss," said I, in a shy way.

"Better not try to brew beer there now, or it would turn out sour, boy; don't you think so?"

"It looks like it, miss."

"Not that anybody means to try," she added, "for that's all done with, and the place will stand as idle as it is till it falls. As to strong beer, there's enough of it in the cellars already, to drown the Manor House."

"Is that the name of this house, miss?"

"One of its names, boy."

"It has more than one, then, miss?"

"One more. Its other name was Satis; which is Greek, or Latin, or Hebrew, or all three—or all one to me—for enough."

"Enough House," said I, "that's a curious name, miss."

"Yes," she replied; "but it meant more than it said. It meant, when it was given, that whoever had this house could want nothing else. They must have been easily satisfied in those days, I should think. But don't loiter, boy."

Though she called me "boy" so often, and with a carelessness that was far from complimentary, she was of about my own age. She seemed much older than I, of course, being a girl, and beautiful and self-possessed; and she was as scornful of me as if she had been one-and-twenty, and a queen.

We went into the house by a side door, the great front entrance had two chains across it outside,—and the first thing I noticed was, that the passages were all dark, and that she had left a candle burning there. She took it up, and we went through more passages and up a staircase, and still it was all dark, and only the candle lighted us.

At last we came to the door of a room, and she said, "Go in."

I answered, more in shyness than politeness, "After you, miss."

To this she returned: "Don't be ridiculous, boy; I am not going in." And scornfully walked away, and—what was worse—took the candle with her.

This was very uncomfortable, and I was half afraid. However, the only thing to be done being to knock at the door, I knocked, and was told from within to enter. I entered, therefore, and found myself in a pretty large room, well lighted with wax candles. No glimpse of daylight was to be seen in it. It was a dressing-room, as I supposed from the furniture, though much of it was of forms and uses then quite unknown to me. But prominent in it was a draped table with a gilded looking-glass, and that I made out at first sight to be a fine lady's dressing-table.

Whether I should have made out this object so soon if there had been no fine lady sitting at it, I cannot say. In an arm-chair, with an elbow resting on the table and her head leaning on that hand, sat the strangest lady I have ever seen, or shall ever see.

She was dressed in rich materials,—satins, and lace, and silks,—all of white. Her shoes were white. And she had a long white veil dependent from her hair, and she had bridal flowers in her hair, but her hair was white. Some bright jewels sparkled on her neck and on her hands, and some other jewels lay sparkling on the table. Dresses, less splendid than the dress she wore, and half-packed trunks, were scattered about. She had not quite finished dressing, for she had but one shoe on,—the other was on the table near her hand,—her veil was but half arranged, her watch and chain were not put on, and some lace for her bosom lay with those trinkets, and with her handkerchief, and gloves, and some flowers, and a Prayer-Book all confusedly heaped about the looking-glass.

It was not in the first few moments that I saw all these things, though I saw more of them in the first moments than might be supposed. But I saw that everything within my view which ought to be white, had been white long ago, and had lost its lustre and was faded and yellow. I saw that the bride within the bridal dress had withered like the dress, and like the flowers, and had no brightness left but the brightness of her sunken eyes. I saw that the dress had been put upon the rounded figure of a young woman, and that the figure upon which it now hung loose had shrunk to skin and bone. Once, I had been taken to see some ghastly waxwork at the Fair, representing I know not what impossible personage lying in state. Once, I had been taken to one of our old marsh churches to see a skeleton in the ashes of a rich dress that had been dug out of a vault under the church pavement. Now, waxwork and skeleton seemed to have dark eyes that moved and looked at me. I should have cried out, if I could.

"Who is it?" said the lady at the table.

"Pip, ma'am."

"Pip?"

"Mr Pumblechook's boy, ma'am. Come—to play."

"Come nearer; let me look at you. Come close."

It was when I stood before her, avoiding her eyes, that I took note of the surrounding objects in detail, and saw that her watch had stopped at twenty minutes to nine, and that a clock in the room had stopped at twenty minutes to nine.

"Look at me," said Miss Havisham. "You are not afraid of a woman who has never seen the sun since you were born?"

I regret to state that I was not afraid of telling the enormous lie comprehended in the answer "No."

"Do you know what I touch here?" she said, laying her hands, one upon the other, on her left side.

"Yes, ma'am." (It made me think of the young man.)

"What do I touch?"

"Your heart."

"Broken!"

She uttered the word with an eager look, and with strong emphasis, and with a weird smile that had a kind of boast in it. Afterwards she kept her hands there for a little while, and slowly took them away as if they were heavy.

"I am tired," said Miss Havisham. "I want diversion, and I have done with men and women. Play."

I think it will be conceded by my most disputatious reader, that she could hardly have directed an unfortunate boy to do anything in the wide world more difficult to be done under the circumstances.

"I sometimes have sick fancies," she went on, "and I have a sick fancy that I want to see some play. There, there!" with an impatient movement of the fingers of her right hand; "play, play, play!"

For a moment, with the fear of my sister's working me before my eyes, I had a desperate idea of starting round the room in the assumed character of Mr Pumblechook's chaise-cart. But I felt myself so unequal to the performance that I gave it up, and stood looking at Miss Havisham in what I suppose she took for a dogged manner, inasmuch as she said, when we had taken a good look at each other,—

"Are you sullen and obstinate?"

"No, ma'am, I am very sorry for you, and very sorry I can't play just now. If you complain of me I shall get into trouble with my sister, so I would do it if I could; but it's so new here, and so strange, and so fine,—and melancholy—." I stopped, fearing I might say too much, or had already said it, and we took another look at each other.

Before she spoke again, she turned her eyes from me, and looked at the dress she wore, and at the dressing-table, and finally at herself in the looking-glass.

"So new to him," she muttered, "so old to me; so strange to him, so familiar to me; so melancholy to both of us! Call Estella."

As she was still looking at the reflection of herself, I thought she was still talking to herself, and kept quiet.

"Call Estella," she repeated, flashing a look at me. "You can do that. Call Estella. At the door."

To stand in the dark in a mysterious passage of an unknown house, bawling Estella to a scornful young lady neither visible nor responsive, and feeling it a dreadful liberty so to roar out her name, was almost as bad as playing to order. But she answered at last, and her light came along the dark passage like a star.

Miss Havisham beckoned her to come close, and took up a jewel from the table, and tried its effect upon her fair young bosom and against her pretty brown hair. "Your own, one day, my dear, and you will use it well. Let me see you play cards with this boy."

"With this boy? Why, he is a common laboring boy!"

I thought I overheard Miss Havisham answer,—only it seemed so unlikely,—"Well? You can break his heart."

"What do you play, boy?" asked Estella of myself, with the greatest disdain.

"Nothing but beggar my neighbor, miss."

"Beggar him," said Miss Havisham to Estella. So we sat down to cards.

It was then I began to understand that everything in the room had stopped, like the watch and the clock, a long time ago. I noticed that Miss Havisham put down the jewel exactly on the spot from which she had taken it up. As Estella dealt the cards, I glanced at the dressing-table again, and saw that the shoe upon it, once white, now yellow, had never been worn. I glanced down at the foot from which the shoe was absent, and saw that the silk stocking on it, once white, now yellow, had been trodden ragged. Without this arrest of everything, this standing still of all the pale decayed objects, not even the withered bridal dress on the collapsed form could have looked so like grave-clothes, or the long veil so like a shroud.

So she sat, corpse-like, as we played at cards; the frillings and trimmings on her bridal dress, looking like earthy paper. I knew nothing then of the discoveries that are occasionally made of bodies buried in ancient times, which fall to powder in the moment of being distinctly seen; but, I have often thought since, that she must have looked as if the admission of the natural light of day would have struck her to dust.

"He calls the knaves Jacks, this boy!" said Estella with disdain, before our first game was out. "And what coarse hands he has! And what thick boots!"

I had never thought of being ashamed of my hands before; but I began to consider them a very indifferent pair. Her contempt for me was so strong, that it became infectious, and I caught it.

She won the game, and I dealt. I misdealt, as was only natural, when I knew she was lying in wait for me to do wrong; and she denounced me for a stupid, clumsy laboring-boy.

"You say nothing of her," remarked Miss Havisham to me, as she looked on. "She says many hard things of you, but you say nothing of her. What do you think of her?"

"I don't like to say," I stammered.

"Tell me in my ear," said Miss Havisham, bending down.

"I think she is very proud," I replied, in a whisper.

"Anything else?"

"I think she is very pretty."

"Anything else?"

"I think she is very insulting." (She was looking at me then with a look of supreme aversion.)

"Anything else?"

"I think I should like to go home."

"And never see her again, though she is so pretty?"

"I am not sure that I shouldn't like to see her again, but I should like to go home now."

"You shall go soon," said Miss Havisham, aloud. "Play the game out."

Saving for the one weird smile at first, I should have felt almost sure that Miss Havisham's face could not smile. It had dropped into a watchful and brooding expression,—most likely when all the things about her had become transfixed,—and it looked as if nothing could ever lift it up again. Her chest had dropped, so that she stooped; and her voice had dropped, so that she spoke low, and with a dead lull upon her; altogether, she had the appearance of having dropped body and soul, within and without, under the weight of a crushing blow.

I played the game to an end with Estella, and she beggared me. She threw the cards down on the table when she had won them all, as if she despised them for having been won of me.

"When shall I have you here again?" said Miss Havisham. "Let me think."

I was beginning to remind her that to-day was Wednesday, when she checked me with her former impatient movement of the fingers of her right hand.

"There, there! I know nothing of days of the week; I know nothing of weeks of the year. Come again after six days. You hear?"

"Yes, ma'am."

"Estella, take him down. Let him have something to eat, and let him roam and look about him while he eats. Go, Pip."

I followed the candle down, as I had followed the candle up, and she stood it in the place where we had found it. Until she opened the side entrance, I had fancied, without thinking about it, that it must necessarily be night-time. The rush of the daylight quite confounded me, and made me feel as if I had been in the candlelight of the strange room many hours.

"You are to wait here, you boy," said Estella; and disappeared and closed the door.

I took the opportunity of being alone in the courtyard to look at my coarse hands and my common boots. My opinion of those accessories was not favorable. They had never troubled me before, but they troubled me now, as vulgar appendages. I determined to ask Joe why he had ever taught me to call those picture-cards Jacks, which ought to be called knaves. I wished Joe had been rather more genteelly brought up, and then I should have been so too.

She came back, with some bread and meat and a little mug of beer. She put the mug down on the stones of the yard, and gave me the bread and meat without looking at me, as insolently as if I were a dog in disgrace. I was so humiliated, hurt, spurned, offended, angry, sorry,—I cannot hit upon the right name for the smart—God knows what its name was,—that tears started to my eyes. The moment they sprang there, the girl looked at me with a quick delight in having been the cause of them. This gave me power to keep them back and to look at her: so, she gave a contemptuous toss—but with a sense, I thought, of having made too sure that I was so wounded—and left me.

But when she was gone, I looked about me for a place to hide my face in, and got behind one of the gates in the brewery-lane, and leaned my sleeve against the wall there, and leaned my forehead on it and cried. As I cried, I kicked the wall, and took a hard twist at my hair; so bitter were my feelings, and so sharp was the smart without a name, that needed counteraction.

My sister's bringing up had made me sensitive. In the little world in which children have their existence whosoever brings them up, there is nothing so finely perceived and so finely felt as injustice. It may be only small injustice that the child can be exposed to; but the child is small, and its world is small, and its rocking-horse stands as many hands high, according to scale, as a big-boned Irish hunter. Within myself, I had sustained, from my babyhood, a perpetual conflict with injustice. I had known, from the time when I could speak, that my sister, in her capricious and violent coercion, was unjust to me. I had cherished a profound conviction that her bringing me up by hand gave her no right to bring me up by jerks. Through all my punishments, disgraces, fasts, and vigils, and other penitential performances, I had nursed this assurance; and to my communing so much with it, in a solitary and unprotected way, I in great part refer the fact that I was morally timid and very sensitive.

I got rid of my injured feelings for the time by kicking them into the brewery wall, and twisting them out of my hair, and then I smoothed my face with my sleeve, and came from behind the gate. The bread and meat were acceptable, and the beer was warming and tingling, and I was soon in spirits to look about me.

To be sure, it was a deserted place, down to the pigeon-house in the brewery-yard, which had been blown crooked on its pole by some high wind, and would have made the pigeons think themselves at sea, if there had been any pigeons there to be rocked by it. But there were no pigeons in the dove-cot, no horses in the stable, no pigs in the sty, no malt in the storehouse, no smells of grains and beer in the copper or the vat. All the uses and scents of the brewery might have evaporated with its last reek of smoke. In a by-yard, there was a wilderness of empty casks, which had a certain sour remembrance of better days lingering about them; but it was too sour to be accepted as a sample of the beer that was gone,—and in this respect I remember those recluses as being like most others.

Behind the furthest end of the brewery, was a rank garden with an old wall; not so high but that I could struggle up and hold on long enough to look over it, and see that the rank garden was the garden of the house, and that it was overgrown with tangled weeds, but that there was a track upon the green and yellow paths, as if some one sometimes walked there, and that Estella was walking away from me even then. But she seemed to be everywhere. For when I yielded to the temptation presented by the casks, and began to walk on them, I saw her walking on them at the end of the yard of casks. She had her back towards me, and held her pretty brown hair spread out in her two hands, and never looked round, and passed out of my view directly.

So, in the brewery itself,—by which I mean the large paved lofty place in which they used to make the beer, and where the brewing utensils still were. When I first went into it, and, rather oppressed by its gloom, stood near the door looking about me, I saw her pass among the extinguished fires, and ascend some light iron stairs, and go out by a gallery high overhead, as if she were going out into the sky.

It was in this place, and at this moment, that a strange thing happened to my fancy. I thought it a strange thing then, and I thought it a stranger thing long afterwards. I turned my eyes—a little dimmed by looking up at the frosty light—towards a great wooden beam in a low nook of the building near me on my right hand, and I saw a figure hanging there by the neck. A figure all in yellow white, with but one shoe to the feet; and it hung so, that I could see that the faded trimmings of the dress were like earthy paper, and that the face was Miss Havisham's, with a movement going over the whole countenance as if she were trying to call to me. In the terror of seeing the figure, and in the terror of being certain that it had not been there a moment before, I at first ran from it, and then ran towards it. And my terror was greatest of all when I found no figure there.

Nothing less than the frosty light of the cheerful sky, the sight of people passing beyond the bars of the court-yard gate, and the reviving influence of the rest of the bread and meat and beer, would have brought me round. Even with those aids, I might not have come to myself as soon as I did, but that I saw Estella approaching with the keys, to let me out. She would have some fair reason for looking down upon me, I thought, if she saw me frightened; and she would have no fair reason.

She gave me a triumphant glance in passing me, as if she rejoiced that my hands were so coarse and my boots were so thick, and she opened the gate, and stood holding it. I was passing out without looking at her, when she touched me with a taunting hand.

"Why don't you cry?"

"Because I don't want to."

"You do," said she. "You have been crying till you are half blind, and you are near crying again now."

She laughed contemptuously, pushed me out, and locked the gate upon me. I went straight to Mr Pumblechook's, and was immensely relieved to find him not at home. So, leaving word with the shopman on what day I was wanted at Miss Havisham's again, I set off on the four-mile walk to our forge; pondering, as I went along, on all I had seen, and deeply revolving that I was a common laboring-boy; that my hands were coarse; that my boots were thick; that I had fallen into a despicable habit of calling knaves Jacks; that I was much more ignorant than I had considered myself last night, and generally that I was in a low-lived bad way.

~

Charles Dickens (1812–1870) was one of the most popular Victorian writers. His books were originally published in installments, with suspenseful endings to each chapter leaving readers desperate for more. His best-known works include *A Tale of Two Cities*, *Great Expectations* **and the novella** *A Christmas Carol.*

The Tell-Tale Heart

Edgar Allan Poe

TRUE!—nervous—very, very dreadfully nervous I had been and am; but why will you say that I am mad? The disease had sharpened my senses—not destroyed—not dulled them. Above all was the sense of hearing acute. I heard all things in the heaven and in the earth. I heard many things in hell. How, then, am I mad? Hearken! and observe how healthily—how calmly I can tell you the whole story.

It is impossible to say how first the idea entered my brain; but once conceived, it haunted me day and night. Object there was none. Passion there was none. I loved the old man. He had never wronged me. He had never given me insult. For his gold I had no desire. I think it was his eye! yes, it was this! He had the eye of a vulture—a pale blue eye, with a film over it. Whenever it fell upon me, my blood ran cold; and so by degrees—very gradually—I made up my mind to take the life of the old man, and thus rid myself of the eye forever.

Now this is the point. You fancy me mad. Madmen know nothing. But you should have seen me. You should have seen how wisely I proceeded—with what caution—with what foresight—with what dissimulation I went to work! I was never kinder to the old man than during the whole week before I killed him. And every night, about midnight, I turned the latch of his door and opened it—oh so gently! And then, when I had made an opening sufficient for my head, I put in a dark lantern, all closed, closed, that no light shone out, and then I thrust in my head. Oh, you would have laughed to see how cunningly I thrust it in! I moved it slowly—very, very slowly, so that I might not disturb the old man's sleep. It took me an hour to place my whole head within the opening so far that I could see him as he lay upon his bed. Ha! would a madman have been so wise as this? And then, when my head was well in the room, I undid the lantern cautiously—oh, so cautiously—cautiously (for the hinges creaked)—I undid it just so much that a single thin ray fell upon the vulture eye. And this I did for seven long nights—every night just at midnight—but I found the eye always closed; and so it was impossible to do the work; for it was not the old man who vexed me, but his Evil Eye. And every morning, when the day broke, I went boldly into the chamber, and spoke courageously to him, calling him by name in a hearty tone, and inquiring how he has passed the night. So you see he would have been a very profound old man, indeed, to suspect that every night, just at twelve, I looked in upon him while he slept.

Upon the eighth night I was more than usually cautious in opening the door. A watch's minute hand moves more quickly than did mine. Never before that night had I felt the extent of my own powers—of my sagacity. I could scarcely contain my feelings of triumph. To think that there I was, opening the door, little by little, and he not even to dream of my secret deeds or thoughts. I fairly chuckled at the idea; and perhaps he heard me; for he moved on the bed suddenly, as if startled. Now you may think that I drew back—but no. His room was as black as pitch with the thick darkness, (for the shutters were close fastened, through fear of robbers,) and so I knew that he could not see the opening of the door, and I kept pushing it on steadily, steadily.

I had my head in, and was about to open the lantern, when my thumb slipped upon the tin fastening, and the old man sprang up in bed, crying out—"Who's there?"

I kept quite still and said nothing. For a whole hour I did not move a muscle, and in the meantime I did not hear him lie down. He was still sitting up in the bed listening;—just as I have done, night after night, hearkening to the death watches in the wall.

Presently I heard a slight groan, and I knew it was the groan of mortal terror. It was not a groan of pain or of grief—oh, no!—it was the low stifled sound that arises from the bottom of the soul when overcharged with awe. I knew the sound well. Many a night, just at midnight, when all the world slept, it has welled up from my own bosom, deepening, with its dreadful echo, the terrors that distracted me. I say I knew it well. I knew what the old man felt, and pitied him, although I chuckled at heart. I knew that he had been lying awake ever since the first slight noise, when he had turned in the bed. His fears had been ever since growing upon him. He had been trying to fancy them causeless, but could not. He had been saying to himself—"It is nothing but the wind in the chimney—it is only a mouse crossing the floor," or "It is merely a cricket which has made a single chirp." Yes, he had been trying to comfort himself with these suppositions: but he had found all in vain. All in vain; because Death, in approaching him had stalked with his black shadow before him, and enveloped the victim. And it was the mournful influence of the unperceived shadow that caused him to feel—although he neither saw nor heard—to feel the presence of my head within the room.

When I had waited a long time, very patiently, without hearing him lie down, I resolved to open a little—a very, very little crevice in the lantern. So I opened it—you cannot imagine how stealthily, stealthily—until, at length a simple dim ray, like the thread of the spider, shot from out the crevice and fell full upon the vulture eye.

It was open—wide, wide open—and I grew furious as I gazed upon it. I saw it with perfect distinctness—all a dull blue, with a hideous veil over it that chilled the very marrow in my bones; but I could see nothing else of the old man's face or person: for I had directed the ray as if by instinct, precisely upon the damned spot.

And have I not told you that what you mistake for madness is but over-acuteness of the sense?—now, I say, there came to my ears a low, dull, quick sound, such as a watch makes when enveloped in cotton. I knew that sound well, too. It was the beating of the old man's heart. It increased my fury, as the beating of a drum stimulates the soldier into courage.

But even yet I refrained and kept still. I scarcely breathed. I held the lantern motionless. I tried how steadily I could maintain the ray upon the eve. Meantime the hellish tattoo of the heart increased. It grew quicker and quicker, and louder and louder every instant. The old man's terror must have been extreme! It grew louder, I say, louder every moment!—do you mark me well I have told you that I am nervous: so I am. And now at the dead hour of the night, amid the dreadful silence of that old house, so strange a noise as this excited me to uncontrollable terror. Yet, for some minutes longer I refrained and stood still.

But the beating grew louder, louder! I thought the heart must burst. And now a new anxiety seized me—the sound would be heard by a neighbour! The old man's hour had come! With a loud yell, I threw open the lantern and leaped into the room. He shrieked once—once only. In an instant I dragged him to the floor, and pulled the heavy bed over him. I then smiled gaily, to find the deed so far done. But, for many minutes, the heart beat on with a muffled sound. This, however, did not vex me; it would not be heard through the wall. At length it ceased. The old man was dead. I removed the bed and examined the corpse. Yes, he was stone, stone dead. I placed my hand upon the heart and held it there many minutes. There was no pulsation. He was stone dead. His eye would trouble me no more.

If still you think me mad, you will think so no longer when I describe the wise precautions I took for the concealment of the body. The night waned, and I worked hastily, but in silence. First of all I dismembered the corpse. I cut off the head and the arms and the legs.

I then took up three planks from the flooring of the chamber, and deposited all between the scantlings. I then replaced the boards so cleverly, so cunningly, that no human eye—not even his—could have detected any thing wrong. There was nothing to wash out—no stain of any kind—no blood-spot whatever. I had been too wary for that. A tub had caught all—ha! ha!

When I had made an end of these labors, it was four o'clock—still dark as midnight. As the bell sounded the hour, there came a knocking at the street door. I went down to open it with a light heart,—for what had I now to fear? There entered three men, who introduced themselves, with perfect suavity, as officers of the police. A shriek had been heard by a neighbour during the night; suspicion of foul play had been aroused; information had been lodged at the police office, and they (the officers) had been deputed to search the premises.

I smiled,—for what had I to fear? I bade the gentlemen welcome. The shriek, I said, was my own in a dream. The old man, I mentioned, was absent in the country. I took my visitors all over the house. I bade them search—search well. I led them, at length, to his chamber. I showed them his treasures, secure, undisturbed. In the enthusiasm of my confidence, I brought chairs into the room, and desired them here to rest from their fatigues, while I myself, in the wild audacity of my perfect triumph, placed my own seat upon the very spot beneath which reposed the corpse of the victim.

The officers were satisfied. My manner had convinced them. I was singularly at ease. They sat, and while I answered cheerily, they chatted of familiar things. But, ere long, I felt myself getting pale and wished them gone. My head ached, and I fancied a ringing in my ears: but still they sat and still chatted. The ringing became more distinct:—It continued and became more distinct: I talked more freely to get rid of the feeling: but it continued and gained definiteness—until, at length, I found that the noise was not within my ears.

No doubt I now grew very pale;—but I talked more fluently, and with a heightened voice. Yet the sound increased—and what could I do? It was a low, dull, quick sound—much such a sound as a watch makes when enveloped in cotton. I gasped for breath—and yet the officers heard it not. I talked more quickly—more vehemently; but the noise steadily increased. I arose and argued about trifles, in a high key and with violent gesticulations; but the noise steadily increased. Why would they not be gone? I paced the floor to and fro with heavy strides, as if excited to fury by the observations of the men—but the noise steadily increased. Oh

God! what could I do? I foamed—I raved—I swore! I swung the chair upon which I had been sitting, and grated it upon the boards, but the noise arose over all and continually increased. It grew louder—louder—louder! And still the men chatted pleasantly, and smiled. Was it possible they heard not? Almighty God!—no, no! They heard!—they suspected!—they knew!—they were making a mockery of my horror!—this I thought, and this I think. But anything was better than this agony! Anything was more tolerable than this derision! I could bear those hypocritical smiles no longer! I felt that I must scream or die! and now—again!—hark! louder! louder! louder! louder!

"Villains!" I shrieked, "dissemble no more! I admit the deed!—tear up the planks! here, here!—It is the beating of his hideous heart!"

~

Edgar Allan Poe (1809–1849) was an American writer, poet, editor and literary critic from Boston who had a profound impact on American literature. His best-known stories and poems include "The Fall of the House of Usher", "The Tell-Tale Heart", "The Murders in the Rue Morgue" and "The Raven".

From Wuthering Heights

Emily Brontë

What vain weathercocks we are! I, who had determined to hold myself independent of all social intercourse, and thanked my stars that, at length, I had lighted on a spot where it was next to impracticable—I, weak wretch, after maintaining till dusk a struggle with low spirits and solitude, was finally compelled to strike my colours; and under pretence of gaining information concerning the necessities of my establishment, I desired Mrs Dean, when she brought in supper, to sit down while I ate it; hoping sincerely she would prove a regular gossip, and either rouse me to animation or lull me to sleep by her talk.

"You have lived here a considerable time," I commenced; "did you not say sixteen years?"

"Eighteen, sir: I came when the mistress was married, to wait on her; after she died, the master retained me for his housekeeper."

"Indeed."

There ensued a pause. She was not a gossip, I feared; unless about her own affairs, and those could hardly interest me. However, having studied for an interval, with a fist on either knee, and a cloud of meditation over her ruddy countenance, she ejaculated—"Ah, times are greatly changed since then!"

"Yes," I remarked, "you've seen a good many alterations, I suppose?"

"I have: and troubles too," she said.

"Oh, I'll turn the talk on my landlord's family!" I thought to myself. "A good subject to start! And that pretty girl-widow, I should like to know her history: whether she be a native of the country, or, as is more probable, an exotic that the surly indigenae will not recognise for kin." With this intention I asked Mrs Dean why Heathcliff let Thrushcross Grange, and preferred living in a situation and residence so much inferior. "Is he not rich enough to keep the estate in good order?" I inquired.

"Rich, sir!" she returned. "He has nobody knows what money, and every year it increases. Yes, yes, he's rich enough to live in a finer house than this: but he's very near—close-handed; and, if he had meant to flit to Thrushcross Grange, as soon as he heard of a good tenant he could not have borne to miss the chance of getting a few hundreds more. It is strange people should be so greedy, when they are alone in the world!"

"He had a son, it seems?"

"Yes, he had one—he is dead."

"And that young lady, Mrs Heathcliff, is his widow?"

"Yes."

"Where did she come from originally?"

"Why, sir, she is my late master's daughter: Catherine Linton was her maiden name. I nursed her, poor thing! I did wish Mr

Heathcliff would remove here, and then we might have been together again."

"What! Catherine Linton?" I exclaimed, astonished. But a minute's reflection convinced me it was not my ghostly Catherine. "Then," I continued, "my predecessor's name was Linton?"

"It was."

"And who is that Earnshaw: Hareton Earnshaw, who lives with Mr Heathcliff? Are they relations?"

"No; he is the late Mrs Linton's nephew."

"The young lady's cousin, then?"

"Yes; and her husband was her cousin also: one on the mother's, the other on the father's side: Heathcliff married Mr Linton's sister."

"I see the house at Wuthering Heights has 'Earnshaw' carved over the front door. Are they an old family?"

"Very old, sir; and Hareton is the last of them, as our Miss Cathy is of us—I mean, of the Lintons. Have you been to Wuthering Heights? I beg pardon for asking; but I should like to hear how she is!"

"Mrs Heathcliff? She looked very well, and very handsome; yet, I think, not very happy."

"Oh dear, I don't wonder! And how did you like the master?"

"A rough fellow, rather, Mrs Dean. Is not that his character?

"Rough as a saw-edge, and hard as whinstone! The less you meddle with him the better."

"He must have had some ups and downs in life to make him such a churl. Do you know anything of his history?"

"It's a cuckoo's, sir—I know all about it: except where he was born, and who were his parents, and how he got his money at first. And Hareton has been cast out like an unfledged dunnock! The unfortunate lad is the only one in all this parish that does not guess how he has been cheated."

"Well, Mrs Dean, it will be a charitable deed to tell me something of my neighbours: I feel I shall not rest if I go to bed; so be good enough to sit and chat an hour."

"Oh, certainly, sir! I'll just fetch a little sewing, and then I'll sit as long as you please. But you've caught cold: I saw you shivering, and you must have some gruel to drive it out."

The worthy woman bustled off, and I crouched nearer the fire; my head felt hot, and the rest of me chill: moreover, I was excited, almost to a pitch of foolishness, through my nerves and brain. This caused me to feel, not uncomfortable, but rather fearful (as I am still) of serious effects from the incidents of to-day and yesterday. She returned presently, bringing a smoking basin and a basket of work; and, having placed the former on the hob, drew in her seat, evidently pleased to find me so companionable.

Before I came to live here, she commenced—waiting no farther invitation to her story—I was almost always at Wuthering Heights; because my mother had nursed Mr Hindley Earnshaw, that was Hareton's father, and I got used to playing with the children: I ran errands too, and helped to make hay, and hung about the farm ready for anything that anybody would set me to. One fine summer morning—it was the beginning of harvest, I remember—Mr Earnshaw, the old master, came down-stairs, dressed for a journey; and, after he had told Joseph what was to be done during the day, he turned to Hindley, and Cathy, and me—for I sat eating my porridge with them—and he said, speaking to his son, "Now, my bonny man, I'm going to Liverpool to-day, what shall I bring you? You may choose what you like: only let it be little, for I shall walk there and back: sixty miles each way, that is a long spell!" Hindley named a fiddle, and then he asked Miss Cathy; she was hardly six years old, but she could ride any horse in the stable, and she chose a whip. He did not forget me; for he had a kind heart, though he was rather severe sometimes. He promised to bring me a pocketful of apples and pears, and then he kissed his children, said good-bye, and set off.

It seemed a long while to us all—the three days of his absence—and often did little Cathy ask when he would be home. Mrs Earnshaw expected him by supper-time on the third evening, and she put the meal off hour after hour; there were no signs of his coming, however, and at last the children got tired of running down to the gate to look. Then it grew dark; she would have had them to bed, but they begged sadly to be allowed to stay up; and, just about eleven o'clock, the door-latch was raised quietly, and in stepped the master. He threw himself into a chair, laughing and groaning, and bid them all stand off, for he was nearly killed—he would not have such another walk for the three kingdoms.

"And at the end of it to be flighted to death!" he said, opening his great-coat, which he held bundled up in his arms. "See here, wife! I was never so beaten with anything in my life: but you must e'en take it as a gift of God; though it's as dark almost as if it came from the devil."

We crowded round, and over Miss Cathy's head I had a peep at a dirty, ragged, black-haired child; big enough both to walk and talk: indeed, its face looked older than Catherine's; yet when it was set on its feet, it only stared round, and repeated over and over again some gibberish that nobody could understand. I was frightened, and Mrs Earnshaw was ready to fling it out of doors: she did fly up, asking how he could fashion to bring that gipsy brat into the house, when they had their own bairns to feed and fend for? What he meant to do with it, and whether he were mad? The master tried to explain the matter; but he was really half dead with fatigue, and all that I could make out, amongst her scolding, was a tale of his seeing it starving, and houseless, and as good as dumb, in the streets of Liverpool, where he picked it up and inquired for its owner. Not a soul knew to whom it belonged, he said; and his money and time being both limited, he thought it better to take it home with him at once, than run into vain expenses there: because he was determined he would not leave it as he found it. Well, the conclusion was, that my mistress grumbled herself calm; and Mr Earnshaw told me to wash it, and give it clean things, and let it sleep with the children.

Hindley and Cathy contented themselves with looking and listening till peace was restored: then, both began searching their father's pockets for the presents he had promised them. The former was a boy of fourteen, but when he drew out what had been a fiddle, crushed to morsels in the great-coat, he blubbered aloud; and Cathy, when she learned the master had lost her whip in attending on the stranger, showed her humour by grinning and spitting at the stupid little thing; earning for her pains a sound blow from her father, to teach her cleaner manners. They entirely refused to have it in bed with them, or even in their room; and I had no more sense, so I put it on the landing of the stairs, hoping it might be gone on the morrow. By chance, or else attracted by hearing his voice, it crept to Mr Earnshaw's door, and there he found it on quitting his chamber. Inquiries were made as to how it got there; I was obliged to confess, and in recompense for my cowardice and inhumanity was sent out of the house.

This was Heathcliff's first introduction to the family. On coming back a few days afterwards (for I did not consider my banishment perpetual), I found they had christened him "Heathcliff": it was the name of a son who died in childhood, and it has served him ever since, both for Christian and surname. Miss Cathy and he were now very thick; but Hindley hated him: and to say the truth I did the same; and we plagued and went on with him shamefully: for I wasn't reasonable enough to feel my injustice, and the mistress never put in a word on his behalf when she saw him wronged.

He seemed a sullen, patient child; hardened, perhaps, to ill-treatment: he would stand Hindley's blows without winking or shedding a tear, and my pinches moved him only to draw in a breath and open his eyes, as if he had hurt himself by accident, and nobody was to blame. This endurance made old Earnshaw furious, when he discovered his son persecuting the poor fatherless child, as he called him. He took to Heathcliff strangely, believing all he said (for that matter, he said precious little, and generally the truth), and petting him up far above Cathy, who was too mischievous and wayward for a favourite.

So, from the very beginning, he bred bad feeling in the house; and at Mrs Earnshaw's death, which happened in less than two years after, the young master had learned to regard his father as an oppressor rather than a friend, and Heathcliff as a usurper of his parent's affections and his privileges; and he grew bitter with brooding over these injuries. I sympathised a while; but when the children fell ill of the measles, and I had to tend them, and take on me the cares of a woman at once, I changed my idea. Heathcliff was dangerously sick; and while he lay at the worst he would have me constantly by his pillow: I suppose he felt I did a good deal for him, and he hadn't wit to guess that I was compelled to do it. However, I will say this, he was the quietest child that ever nurse watched over. The difference between him and the others forced me to be less partial. Cathy and her brother harassed me terribly: he was as uncomplaining as a lamb; though hardness, not gentleness, made him give little trouble.

He got through, and the doctor affirmed it was in a great measure owing to me, and praised me for my care. I was vain of his commendations, and softened towards the being by whose means I earned them, and thus Hindley lost his last ally: still

I couldn't dote on Heathcliff, and I wondered often what my master saw to admire so much in the sullen boy; who never, to my recollection, repaid his indulgence by any sign of gratitude. He was not insolent to his benefactor, he was simply insensible; though knowing perfectly the hold he had on his heart, and conscious he had only to speak and all the house would be obliged to bend to his wishes. As an instance, I remember Mr Earnshaw once bought a couple of colts at the parish fair, and gave the lads each one. Heathcliff took the handsomest, but it soon fell lame, and when he discovered it, he said to Hindley—

"You must exchange horses with me: I don't like mine; and if you won't I shall tell your father of the three thrashings you've given me this week, and show him my arm, which is black to the shoulder." Hindley put out his tongue, and cuffed him over the ears. "You'd better do it at once," he persisted, escaping to the porch (they were in the stable): "you will have to: and if I speak of these blows, you'll get them again with interest." "Off, dog!" cried Hindley, threatening him with an iron weight used for weighing potatoes and hay. "Throw it," he replied, standing still, "and then I'll tell how you boasted that you would turn me out of doors as soon as he died, and see whether he will not turn you out directly." Hindley threw it, hitting him on the breast, and down he fell, but staggered up immediately, breathless and white; and, had not I prevented it, he would have gone just so to the master, and got full revenge by letting his condition plead for him, intimating who had caused it. "Take my colt, Gipsy, then!" said young Earnshaw. "And I pray that he may break your neck: take him, and be damned, you beggarly interloper! and wheedle my father out of all he has: only afterwards show him what you are, imp of Satan.—And take that, I hope he'll kick out your brains!"

Heathcliff had gone to loose the beast, and shift it to his own stall; he was passing behind it, when Hindley finished his speech by knocking him under its feet, and without stopping to examine whether his hopes were fulfilled, ran away as fast as he could. I was surprised to witness how coolly the child gathered himself up, and went on with his intention; exchanging saddles and all, and then sitting down on a bundle of hay to overcome the qualm which the violent blow occasioned, before he entered the house. I persuaded him easily to let me lay the blame of his bruises on the horse: he minded little what tale was told since he had what he wanted. He complained so seldom, indeed, of such stirs as these, that I really thought him not vindictive: I was deceived completely, as you will hear.

~

Emily Brontë (1818–1848), sister of novelists Charlotte Brontë and Anne Brontë, is best known for her only novel, ***Wuthering Heights*****, and a collection of poems. She is often lauded as one of the most intensely original and passionate voices in English literature.**

In A Library

Emily Dickinson

A precious, mouldering pleasure 't is
To meet an antique book,
In just the dress his century wore;
A privilege, I think,

His venerable hand to take,
And warming in our own,
A passage back, or two, to make
To times when he was young.

His quaint opinions to inspect,
His knowledge to unfold
On what concerns our mutual mind,
The literature of old;

What interested scholars most,
What competitions ran
When Plato was a certainty.
And Sophocles a man;

When Sappho was a living girl,
And Beatrice wore
The gown that Dante deified.
Facts, centuries before,

He traverses familiar,
As one should come to town
And tell you all your dreams were true;
He lived where dreams were sown.

His presence is enchantment,
You beg him not to go;
Old volumes shake their vellum heads
And tantalize, just so.

~

Emily Dickinson (1830–1886) was one of the most important poets in the American canon. Her most popular works include "I'm Nobody! Who Are You?", "'Hope'" Is the Thing with Feathers", "A Bird, Came Down the Walk" and "My Life Had Stood—A Loaded Gun".

From The Great Gatsby

F. Scott Fitzgerald

There was music from my neighbor's house through the summer nights. In his blue gardens men and girls came and went like moths among the whisperings and the champagne and the stars. At high tide in the afternoon I watched his guests diving from the tower of his raft or taking the sun on the hot sand of his beach while his two motor-boats slit the waters of the Sound, drawing aquaplanes over cataracts of foam. On week-ends his Rolls-Royce became an omnibus, bearing parties to and from the city, between nine in the morning and long past midnight, while his station wagon scampered like a brisk yellow bug to meet all trains. And on Mondays eight servants including an extra gardener toiled all day with mops and scrubbing-brushes and hammers and garden-shears, repairing the ravages of the night before.

Every Friday five crates of oranges and lemons arrived from a fruiterer in New York—every Monday these same oranges and lemons left his back door in a pyramid of pulpless halves. There was a machine in the kitchen which could extract the juice of two hundred oranges in half an hour, if a little button was pressed two hundred times by a butler's thumb.

At least once a fortnight a corps of caterers came down with several hundred feet of canvas and enough colored lights to make a Christmas tree of Gatsby's enormous garden. On buffet tables, garnished with glistening hors-d'oeuvre, spiced baked hams crowded against salads of harlequin designs and pastry pigs and turkeys bewitched to a dark gold. In the main hall a bar with a real brass rail was set up, and stocked with gins and liquors and with cordials so long forgotten that most of his female guests were too young to know one from another.

By seven o'clock the orchestra has arrived—no thin five-piece affair but a whole pitful of oboes and trombones and saxophones and viols and cornets and piccolos and low and high drums. The last swimmers have come in from the beach now and are dressing upstairs; the cars from New York are parked five deep in the drive, and already the halls and salons and verandas are gaudy with primary colors and hair shorn in strange new ways and shawls beyond the dreams of Castile. The bar is in full swing and floating rounds of cocktails permeate the garden outside until the air is alive with chatter and laughter and casual innuendo and introductions forgotten on the spot and enthusiastic meetings between women who never knew each other's names.

The lights grow brighter as the earth lurches away from the sun and now the orchestra is playing yellow cocktail music and the opera of voices pitches a key higher. Laughter is easier, minute by minute, spilled with prodigality, tipped out at a cheerful word. The groups change more swiftly, swell with new arrivals, dissolve and form in the same breath—already there are wanderers, confident girls who weave here and there among the stouter and more stable, become for a sharp, joyous moment the center of a group and then excited with triumph glide on through the sea-change of faces and voices and color under the constantly changing light.

Suddenly one of these gypsies in trembling opal, seizes a cocktail out of the air, dumps it down for courage and moving her hands like Frisco dances out alone on the canvas platform. A momentary hush; the orchestra leader varies his rhythm obligingly for her and there is a burst of chatter as the erroneous news goes around that she is Gilda Gray's understudy from the "Follies." The party has begun.

I believe that on the first night I went to Gatsby's house I was one of the few guests who had actually been invited. People were not invited—they went there. They got into automobiles which bore them out to Long Island and somehow they ended up at Gatsby's door. Once there they were introduced by somebody who knew Gatsby and after that they conducted themselves according to the rules of behavior associated with amusement parks. Sometimes they came and went without having met Gatsby at all, came for the party with a simplicity of heart that was its own ticket of admission.

I had been actually invited. A chauffeur in a uniform of robin's egg blue crossed my lawn early that Saturday morning with a surprisingly formal note from his employer—the honor would be entirely Gatsby's, it said, if I would attend his "little party" that night. He had seen me several times and had intended to call on me long before but a peculiar combination of circumstances had prevented it—signed Jay Gatsby in a majestic hand.

Dressed up in white flannels I went over to his lawn a little after seven and wandered around rather ill-at-ease among swirls and eddies of people I didn't know—though here and there was a face I had noticed on the commuting train. I was immediately struck by the number of young Englishmen dotted about; all well dressed, all looking a little hungry and all talking in low earnest voices to solid and prosperous Americans. I was sure that they were selling something: bonds or insurance or automobiles. They were, at least, agonizingly aware of the easy money in the vicinity and convinced that it was theirs for a few words in the right key.

As soon as I arrived I made an attempt to find my host but the two or three people of whom I asked his whereabouts stared at me in such an amazed way and denied so vehemently any knowledge of his movements that I slunk off in the direction of the cocktail table—the only place in the garden where a single man could linger without looking purposeless and alone.

I was on my way to get roaring drunk from sheer embarrassment when Jordan Baker came out of the house and stood at the head of the marble steps, leaning a little backward and looking with contemptuous interest down into the garden.

Welcome or not, I found it necessary to attach myself to someone before I should begin to address cordial remarks to the passers-by.

"Hello!" I roared, advancing toward her. My voice seemed unnaturally loud across the garden.

"I thought you might be here," she responded absently as I came up.

"I remembered you lived next door to—"

She held my hand impersonally, as a promise that she'd take care of me in a minute, and gave ear to two girls in twin yellow dresses who stopped at the foot of the steps.

"Hello!" they cried together. "Sorry you didn't win."

That was for the golf tournament. She had lost in the finals the week before.

"You don't know who we are," said one of the girls in yellow, "but we met you here about a month ago."

"You've dyed your hair since then," remarked Jordan, and I started but the girls had moved casually on and her remark was addressed to the premature moon, produced like the supper, no doubt, out of a caterer's basket. With Jordan's slender golden arm resting in mine we descended the steps and sauntered about the garden. A tray of cocktails floated at us through the twilight and we sat down at a table with the two girls in yellow and three men, each one introduced to us as Mr Mumble.

"Do you come to these parties often?" inquired Jordan of the girl beside her.

"The last one was the one I met you at," answered the girl, in an alert, confident voice. She turned to her companion: "Wasn't it for you, Lucille?"

It was for Lucille, too.

"I like to come," Lucille said. "I never care what I do, so I always have a good time. When I was here last I tore my gown on a chair, and he asked me my name and address—inside of a week I got a package from Croirier's with a new evening gown in it."

"Did you keep it?" asked Jordan.

"Sure I did. I was going to wear it tonight, but it was too big in the bust and had to be altered. It was gas blue with lavender beads. Two hundred and sixty-five dollars."

"There's something funny about a fellow that'll do a thing like that," said the other girl eagerly. "He doesn't want any trouble with ANYbody."

"Who doesn't?" I inquired.

"Gatsby. Somebody told me—"

The two girls and Jordan leaned together confidentially.

"Somebody told me they thought he killed a man once."

A thrill passed over all of us. The three Mr Mumbles bent forward and listened eagerly.

"I don't think it's so much THAT," argued Lucille skeptically; "it's more that he was a German spy during the war."

One of the men nodded in confirmation.

"I heard that from a man who knew all about him, grew up with him in Germany," he assured us positively.

"Oh, no," said the first girl, "it couldn't be that, because he was in the American army during the war." As our credulity switched back to her she leaned forward with enthusiasm. "You look at him sometimes when he thinks nobody's looking at him. I'll bet he killed a man."

She narrowed her eyes and shivered. Lucille shivered. We all turned and looked around for Gatsby. It was testimony to the romantic speculation he inspired that there were whispers about him from those who found little that it was necessary to whisper about in this world.

The first supper—there would be another one after midnight—was now being served, and Jordan invited me to join her own party who were spread around a table on the other side of the garden. There were three married couples and Jordan's escort, a persistent undergraduate given to violent innuendo and obviously under the impression that sooner or later Jordan was going to yield him up her person to a greater or lesser degree. Instead of rambling this party had preserved a dignified homogeneity, and assumed to itself the function of representing the staid nobility of the countryside—East Egg condescending to West Egg, and carefully on guard against its spectroscopic gayety.

"Let's get out," whispered Jordan, after a somehow wasteful and inappropriate half hour. "This is much too polite for me."

We got up, and she explained that we were going to find the host—I had never met him, she said, and it was making me uneasy. The undergraduate nodded in a cynical, melancholy way.

The bar, where we glanced first, was crowded but Gatsby was not there. She couldn't find him from the top of the steps, and he wasn't on the veranda. On a chance we tried an important-looking door, and walked into a high Gothic library, panelled with carved English oak, and probably transported complete from some ruin overseas.

A stout, middle-aged man with enormous owl-eyed spectacles was sitting somewhat drunk on the edge of a great table, staring with unsteady concentration at the shelves of books. As we entered he wheeled excitedly around and examined Jordan from head to foot.

"What do you think?" he demanded impetuously.

"About what?"

He waved his hand toward the book-shelves.

"About that. As a matter of fact you needn't bother to ascertain. I ascertained. They're real."

"The books?"

He nodded.

"Absolutely real—have pages and everything. I thought they'd be a nice durable cardboard. Matter of fact, they're absolutely real. Pages and—Here! Lemme show you."

Taking our skepticism for granted, he rushed to the bookcases and returned with Volume One of the "Stoddard Lectures."

"See!" he cried triumphantly. "It's a bona fide piece of printed matter. It fooled me. This fella's a regular Belasco. It's a triumph. What thoroughness! What realism! Knew when to stop too—didn't cut the pages. But what do you want? What do you expect?"

He snatched the book from me and replaced it hastily on its shelf muttering that if one brick was removed the whole library was liable to collapse.

"Who brought you?" he demanded. "Or did you just come? I was brought. Most people were brought."

Jordan looked at him alertly, cheerfully without answering.

"I was brought by a woman named Roosevelt," he continued. "Mrs Claud Roosevelt. Do you know her? I met her somewhere last night. I've been drunk for about a week now, and I thought it might sober me up to sit in a library."

"Has it?"

"A little bit, I think. I can't tell yet. I've only been here an hour. Did I tell you about the books? They're real. They're—"

"You told us."

We shook hands with him gravely and went back outdoors.

There was dancing now on the canvas in the garden, old men pushing young girls backward in eternal graceless circles, superior couples holding each other tortuously, fashionably and keeping in the corners—and a great number of single girls dancing individualistically or relieving the orchestra for a moment of the burden of the banjo or the traps. By midnight the hilarity had increased. A celebrated tenor had sung in Italian and a notorious contralto had sung in jazz and between the numbers people were doing "stunts" all over the garden, while happy vacuous bursts of laughter rose toward the summer sky. A pair of stage "twins"—who turned out to be the girls in yellow—did a baby act in costume and champagne was served in glasses bigger than finger bowls. The moon had risen higher, and floating in the Sound was a triangle of silver scales, trembling a little to the stiff, tinny drip of the banjoes on the lawn.

I was still with Jordan Baker. We were sitting at a table with a man of about my age and a rowdy little girl who gave way upon the slightest provocation to uncontrollable laughter. I was enjoying myself now. I had taken two finger bowls of champagne and the scene had changed before my eyes into something significant, elemental and profound.

At a lull in the entertainment the man looked at me and smiled.

"Your face is familiar," he said, politely. "Weren't you in the Third Division during the war?"

"Why, yes. I was in the Ninth Machine-Gun Battalion."

"I was in the Seventh Infantry until June nineteen-eighteen. I knew I'd seen you somewhere before."

We talked for a moment about some wet, grey little villages in France. Evidently he lived in this vicinity for he told me that he had just bought a hydroplane and was going to try it out in the morning.

"Want to go with me, old sport? Just near the shore along the Sound."

"What time?"

"Any time that suits you best."

It was on the tip of my tongue to ask his name when Jordan looked around and smiled.

"Having a gay time now?" she inquired.

"Much better." I turned again to my new acquaintance. "This is an unusual party for me. I haven't even seen the host. I live over there—" I waved my hand at the invisible hedge in the distance, "and this man Gatsby sent over his chauffeur with an invitation."

For a moment he looked at me as if he failed to understand.

"I'm Gatsby," he said suddenly.

"What!" I exclaimed. "Oh, I beg your pardon."

"I thought you knew, old sport. I'm afraid I'm not a very good host."

He smiled understandingly—much more than understandingly. It was one of those rare smiles with a quality of eternal reassurance in it, that you may come across four or five times in life. It faced—or seemed to face—the whole external world for an instant, and then concentrated on YOU with an irresistible prejudice in your favor. It understood you just so far as you wanted to be understood, believed in you as you would like to believe in yourself and assured you that it had precisely the impression of you that, at your best, you hoped to convey. Precisely at that point it vanished—and I was looking at an elegant young rough-neck, a year or two over thirty, whose elaborate formality of speech just missed being absurd. Some time before he introduced himself I'd got a strong impression that he was picking his words with care.

Almost at the moment when Mr Gatsby identified himself a butler hurried toward him with the information that Chicago was calling him on the wire. He excused himself with a small bow that included each of us in turn.

"If you want anything just ask for it, old sport," he urged me. "Excuse me. I will rejoin you later."

When he was gone I turned immediately to Jordan—constrained to assure her of my surprise. I had expected that Mr Gatsby would be a florid and corpulent person in his middle years.

"Who is he?" I demanded. "Do you know?"

"He's just a man named Gatsby."

"Where is he from, I mean? And what does he do?"

"Now YOU're started on the subject," she answered with a wan smile. "Well, he told me once he was an Oxford man."

A dim background started to take shape behind him but at her next remark it faded away.

"However, I don't believe it."

"Why not?"

"I don't know," she insisted, "I just don't think he went there."

Something in her tone reminded me of the other girl's "I think he killed a man," and had the effect of stimulating my curiosity. I would have accepted without question the information that Gatsby sprang from the swamps of Louisiana or from the lower East Side of New York.

That was comprehensible. But young men didn't—at least in my provincial inexperience I believed they didn't—drift coolly out of nowhere and buy a palace on Long Island Sound.

"Anyhow he gives large parties," said Jordan, changing the subject with an urbane distaste for the concrete. "And I like large parties. They're so intimate. At small parties there isn't any privacy."

There was the boom of a bass drum, and the voice of the orchestra leader rang out suddenly above the echolalia of the garden.

"Ladies and gentlemen," he cried. "At the request of Mr Gatsby we are going to play for you Mr Vladmir Tostoff's latest work, which attracted so much attention at Carnegie Hall last May. If you read the papers you know there was a big sensation." He smiled with jovial condescension, and added: "Some sensation!" Whereupon everybody laughed.

"The piece is known," he concluded lustily, "as 'Vladmir Tostoff's Jazz History of the World!'"

The nature of Mr Tostoff's composition eluded me, because just as it began my eyes fell on Gatsby, standing alone on the marble steps and looking from one group to another with approving eyes. His tanned skin was drawn attractively tight on his face and his short hair looked as though it were trimmed every day. I could see nothing sinister about him. I wondered if the fact that he was not drinking helped to set him off from his guests, for it seemed to me that he grew more correct as the fraternal hilarity increased. When the "Jazz History of the World" was over, girls were putting their heads on men's shoulders in a puppyish, convivial way, girls were swooning backward playfully into men's arms, even into groups, knowing that someone would arrest their falls—but no one swooned backward on Gatsby, and no French bob touched Gatsby's shoulder, and no singing quartets were formed with Gatsby's head for one link.

"I beg your pardon."

Gatsby's butler was suddenly standing beside us.

"Miss Baker?" he inquired. "I beg your pardon, but Mr Gatsby would like to speak to you alone."

"With me?" she exclaimed in surprise.

"Yes, madame."

She got up slowly, raising her eyebrows at me in astonishment, and followed the butler toward the house. I noticed that she wore her evening-dress, all her dresses, like sports clothes—there was a jauntiness about her movements as if she had first learned to walk upon golf courses on clean, crisp mornings.

I was alone and it was almost two. For some time confused and intriguing sounds had issued from a long, many-windowed room which overhung the terrace. Eluding Jordan's undergraduate, who was now engaged in an obstetrical conversation with two chorus girls, and who implored me to join him, I went inside.

The large room was full of people. One of the girls in yellow was playing the piano, and beside her stood a tall, red-haired young lady from a famous chorus, engaged in song. She had drunk a quantity of champagne, and during the course of her song she had decided, ineptly, that everything was very, very sad—she was not only singing, she was weeping too. Whenever there was a pause in the song she filled it with gasping, broken sobs, and then took up the lyric again in a quavering soprano. The tears coursed down her cheeks—not freely, however, for when they came into contact with her heavily beaded eyelashes they assumed an inky colour, and pursued the rest of their way in slow black rivulets. A humorous suggestion was made that she sing the notes on her face, whereupon she threw up her hands, sank into a chair, and went off into a deep vinous sleep.

"She had a fight with a man who says he's her husband," explained a girl at my elbow.

I looked around. Most of the remaining women were now having fights with men said to be their husbands. Even Jordan's party, the quartet from East Egg, were rent asunder by dissension. One of the men was talking with curious intensity to a young actress, and his wife, after attempting to laugh at the situation in a dignified and indifferent way, broke down entirely and resorted to flank attacks—at intervals she appeared suddenly at his side like an angry diamond, and hissed: "You promised!" into his ear.

The reluctance to go home was not confined to wayward men. The hall was at present occupied by two deplorably sober men and their highly indignant wives. The wives were sympathizing with each other in slightly raised voices.

"Whenever he sees I'm having a good time he wants to go home."

"Never heard anything so selfish in my life."

"We're always the first ones to leave."

"So are we."

"Well, we're almost the last tonight," said one of the men sheepishly. "The orchestra left half an hour ago."

In spite of the wives' agreement that such malevolence was beyond credibility, the dispute ended in a short struggle, and both wives were lifted, kicking, into the night.

As I waited for my hat in the hall the door of the library opened and Jordan Baker and Gatsby came out together. He was saying some last word to her, but the eagerness in his manner tightened abruptly into formality as several people approached him to say goodbye.

Jordan's party were calling impatiently to her from the porch, but she lingered for a moment to shake hands.

"I've just heard the most amazing thing," she whispered. "How long were we in there?"

"Why, about an hour."

"It was… simply amazing," she repeated abstractedly. "But I swore I wouldn't tell it and here I am tantalizing you." She yawned gracefully in my face. "Please come and see me… Phone book… Under the name of Mrs Sigourney Howard… My aunt…" She was hurrying off as she talked—her brown hand waved a jaunty salute as she melted into her party at the door.

Rather ashamed that on my first appearance I had stayed so late, I joined the last of Gatsby's guests, who were clustered around him. I wanted to explain that I'd hunted for him early in the evening and to apologize for not having known him in the garden.

"Don't mention it," he enjoined me eagerly. "Don't give it another thought, old sport." The familiar expression held no more familiarity than the hand which reassuringly brushed my shoulder. "And don't forget we're going up in the hydroplane tomorrow morning, at nine o'clock."

Then the butler, behind his shoulder:

"Philadelphia wants you on the phone, sir."

"All right, in a minute. Tell them I'll be right there… Good night."

"Good night."

"Good night." He smiled—and suddenly there seemed to be a pleasant significance in having been among the last to go, as if he had desired it all the time. "Good night, old sport… Good night."

But as I walked down the steps I saw that the evening was not quite over. Fifty feet from the door a dozen headlights illuminated a bizarre and tumultuous scene. In the ditch beside the road, right side up, but violently shorn of one wheel, rested a new coupé which had left Gatsby's drive not two minutes before. The sharp jut of a wall accounted for the detachment of the wheel, which was now getting considerable attention from half a dozen curious chauffeurs. However, as they had left their cars blocking the road, a harsh, discordant din from those in the rear had been audible for some time, and added to the already violent confusion of the scene.

A man in a long duster had dismounted from the wreck and now stood in the middle of the road, looking from the car to the tyre and from the tyre to the observers in a pleasant, puzzled way.

"See!" he explained. "It went in the ditch."

The fact was infinitely astonishing to him, and I recognized first the unusual quality of wonder, and then the man—it was the late patron of Gatsby's library.

"How'd it happen?"

He shrugged his shoulders.

"I know nothing whatever about mechanics," he said decisively.

"But how did it happen? Did you run into the wall?"

"Don't ask me," said Owl Eyes, washing his hands of the whole matter. "I know very little about driving—next to nothing. It happened, and that's all I know."

"Well, if you're a poor driver you oughtn't to try driving at night."

"But I wasn't even trying," he explained indignantly, "I wasn't even trying."

An awed hush fell upon the bystanders.

"Do you want to commit suicide?"

"You're lucky it was just a wheel! A bad driver and not even *try*ing!"

"You don't understand," explained the criminal. "I wasn't driving. There's another man in the car."

The shock that followed this declaration found voice in a sustained "Ah-h-h!" as the door of the coupé swung slowly open. The crowd—it was now a crowd—stepped back involuntarily, and when the door had opened wide there was a ghostly pause. Then, very gradually, part by part, a pale, dangling individual stepped out of the wreck, pawing tentatively at the ground with a large uncertain dancing shoe.

Blinded by the glare of the headlights and confused by the incessant groaning of the horns, the apparition stood swaying for a moment before he perceived the man in the duster.

"Wha's matter?" he inquired calmly. "Did we run outa gas?"

"Look!"

Half a dozen fingers pointed at the amputated wheel—he stared at it for a moment, and then looked upward as though he suspected that it had dropped from the sky.

"It came off," someone explained.

He nodded.

"At first I din' notice we'd stopped."

A pause. Then, taking a long breath and straightening his shoulders, he remarked in a determined voice:

"Wonder'ff tell me where there's a gas'line station?"

At least a dozen men, some of them a little better off than he was, explained to him that wheel and car were no longer joined by any physical bond.

"Back out," he suggested after a moment. "Put her in reverse."

"But the *wheel*'s off!"

He hesitated.

"No harm in trying," he said.

The caterwauling horns had reached a crescendo and I turned away and cut across the lawn toward home. I glanced back once. A wafer of a moon was shining over Gatsby's house, making the night fine as before, and surviving the laughter and the sound of his still glowing garden. A sudden emptiness seemed to flow now from the windows and the great doors, endowing with complete isolation the figure of the host, who stood on the porch, his hand up in a formal gesture of farewell.

Reading over what I have written so far, I see I have given the impression that the events of three nights several weeks apart were all that absorbed me. On the contrary, they were merely casual events in a crowded summer, and, until much later, they absorbed me infinitely less than my personal affairs.

Most of the time I worked. In the early morning the sun threw my shadow westward as I hurried down the white chasms of lower New York to the Probity Trust. I knew the other clerks and young bond-salesmen by their first names, and lunched with them in dark, crowded restaurants on little pig sausages and mashed potatoes and coffee. I even had a short affair with a girl who lived in Jersey City and worked in the accounting department, but her brother began throwing mean looks in my direction, so when she went on her vacation in July I let it blow quietly away.

I took dinner usually at the Yale Club—for some reason it was the gloomiest event of my day—and then I went upstairs to the library and studied investments and securities for a conscientious hour. There were generally a few rioters around, but they never came into the library, so it was a good place to work. After that, if the night was mellow, I strolled down Madison Avenue past the old Murray Hill Hotel, and over 33rd Street to the Pennsylvania Station.

I began to like New York, the racy, adventurous feel of it at night, and the satisfaction that the constant flicker of men and women and machines gives to the restless eye. I liked to walk up Fifth Avenue and pick out romantic women from the crowd and imagine that in a few minutes I was going to enter into their lives, and no one would ever know or disapprove.

Sometimes, in my mind, I followed them to their apartments on the corners of hidden streets, and they turned and smiled back at me before they faded through a door into warm darkness. At the enchanted metropolitan twilight I felt a haunting loneliness sometimes, and felt it in others—poor young clerks who loitered in front of windows waiting until it was time for a solitary restaurant dinner—young clerks in the dusk, wasting the most poignant moments of night and life.

Again at eight o'clock, when the dark lanes of the Forties were lined five deep with throbbing taxicabs, bound for the theatre district, I felt a sinking in my heart. Forms leaned together in the taxis as they waited, and voices sang, and there was laughter from unheard jokes, and lighted cigarettes made unintelligible circles inside. Imagining that I, too, was hurrying towards gaiety and sharing their intimate excitement, I wished them well.

For a while I lost sight of Jordan Baker, and then in midsummer I found her again. At first I was flattered to go places with her, because she was a golf champion, and everyone knew her name. Then it was something more. I wasn't actually in love, but I felt a sort of tender curiosity. The bored haughty face that she turned to the world concealed something—most affectations conceal something eventually, even though they don't in the beginning—and one day I found what it was. When we were on a house-party together up in Warwick, she left a borrowed car out in the rain with the top down, and then lied about it—and suddenly I remembered the story about her that had eluded me that night at Daisy's. At her first big golf tournament there was a row that nearly reached the newspapers—a suggestion that she had moved her ball from a bad lie in the semifinal round. The thing approached the proportions of a scandal—then died away. A caddy retracted his statement, and the only other witness admitted that he might have been mistaken. The incident and the name had remained together in my mind.

Jordan Baker instinctively avoided clever, shrewd men, and now I saw that this was because she felt safer on a plane where any divergence from a code would be thought impossible. She was incurably dishonest. She wasn't able to endure being at a disadvantage and, given this unwillingness, I suppose she had begun dealing in subterfuges when she was very young in order to keep that cool, insolent smile turned to the world and yet satisfy the demands of her hard, jaunty body.

It made no difference to me. Dishonesty in a woman is a thing you never blame deeply—I was casually sorry, and then I forgot. It was on that same house-party that we had a curious conversation about driving a car. It started because she passed so close to some workmen that our fender flicked a button on one man's coat.

"You're a rotten driver," I protested. "Either you ought to be more careful, or you oughtn't to drive at all."

"I am careful."

"No, you're not."

"Well, other people are," she said lightly.

"What's that got to do with it?"

"They'll keep out of my way," she insisted. "It takes two to make an accident."

"Suppose you met somebody just as careless as yourself."

"I hope I never will," she answered. "I hate careless people. That's why I like you."

Her grey, sun-strained eyes stared straight ahead, but she had deliberately shifted our relations, and for a moment I thought I loved her. But I am slow-thinking and full of interior rules that act as brakes on my desires, and I knew that first I had to get myself definitely out of that tangle back home. I'd been writing letters once a week and signing them: "Love, Nick," and all I could think of was how, when that certain girl played tennis, a faint moustache of perspiration appeared on her upper lip. Nevertheless there was a vague understanding that had to be tactfully broken off before I was free.

Everyone suspects himself of at least one of the cardinal virtues, and this is mine: I am one of the few honest people that I have ever known.

~

Francis Scott Fitzgerald (1896–1940) was an American writer of novels and short stories, whose works have been seen as evocative of the Jazz Age. He has written dozens of short stories that treat themes of youth, despair and age, including "The Curious Case of Benjamin Button", and novels such as ***Tender is the Night*** **and** ***The Great Gatsby*****.**

From A Little Princess

Frances Hodgson Burnett

A French Lesson

When Sara entered the schoolroom the next morning everybody looked at her with wide, interested eyes. By that time every pupil—from Lavinia Herbert, who was nearly thirteen and felt quite grown up, to Lottie Legh, who was only just four and the baby of the school—had heard a great deal about her. They knew very certainly that she was Miss Minchin's show pupil and was considered a credit to the establishment. One or two of them had even caught a glimpse of her French maid, Mariette, who had arrived the evening before. Lavinia had managed to pass Sara's room when the door was open, and had seen Mariette opening a box which had arrived late from some shop.

"It was full of petticoats with lace frills on them—frills and frills," she whispered to her friend Jessie as she bent over her geography. "I saw her shaking them out. I heard Miss Minchin say to Miss Amelia that her clothes were so grand that they were ridiculous for a child. My mamma says that children should be dressed simply. She has got one of those petticoats on now. I saw it when she sat down."

"She has silk stockings on!" whispered Jessie, bending over her geography also. "And what little feet! I never saw such little feet."

"Oh," sniffed Lavinia, spitefully, "that is the way her slippers are made. My mamma says that even big feet can be made to look small if you have a clever shoemaker. I don't think she is pretty at all. Her eyes are such a queer color."

"She isn't pretty as other pretty people are," said Jessie, stealing a glance across the room; "but she makes you want to look at her again. She has tremendously long eyelashes, but her eyes are almost green."

Sara was sitting quietly in her seat, waiting to be told what to do. She had been placed near Miss Minchin's desk. She was not abashed at all by the many pairs of eyes watching her. She was interested and looked back quietly at the children who looked at her. She wondered what they were thinking of, and if they liked Miss Minchin, and if they cared for their lessons, and if any of them had a papa at all like her own. She had had a long talk with Emily about her papa that morning.

"He is on the sea now, Emily," she had said. "We must be very great friends to each other and tell each other things. Emily, look at me. You have the nicest eyes I ever saw—but I wish you could speak."

She was a child full of imaginings and whimsical thoughts, and one of her fancies was that there would be a great deal of comfort in even pretending that Emily was alive and really heard and understood. After Mariette had dressed her in her dark-blue schoolroom frock and tied her hair with a dark-blue ribbon, she went to Emily, who sat in a chair of her own, and gave her a book.

"You can read that while I am downstairs," she said; and, seeing Mariette looking at her curiously, she spoke to her with a serious little face.

"What I believe about dolls," she said, "is that they can do things they will not let us know about. Perhaps, really, Emily can read and talk and walk, but she will only do it when people are out of the room. That is her secret. You see, if people knew that dolls could do things, they would make them work. So, perhaps, they have promised each other to keep it a secret. If you stay in the room, Emily will just sit there and stare; but if you go out, she will begin to read, perhaps, or go and look out of the window. Then if she heard either of us coming, she would just run back and jump into her chair and pretend she had been there all the time."

"Comme elle est drole!" Mariette said to herself, and when she went downstairs she told the head housemaid about it. But she had already begun to like this odd little girl who had such an intelligent small face and such perfect manners. She had taken care of children before who were not so polite. Sara was a very fine little person, and had a gentle, appreciative way of saying, "If you please, Mariette," "Thank you, Mariette," which was very charming. Mariette told the head housemaid that she thanked her as if she was thanking a lady.

"Elle a l'air d'une princesse, cette petite," she said. Indeed, she was very much pleased with her new little mistress and liked her place greatly.

After Sara had sat in her seat in the schoolroom for a few minutes, being looked at by the pupils, Miss Minchin rapped in a dignified manner upon her desk.

"Young ladies," she said, "I wish to introduce you to your new companion." All the little girls rose in their places, and Sara rose also. "I shall expect you all to be very agreeable to Miss Crewe; she has just come to us from a great distance—in fact, from India. As soon as lessons are over you must make each other's acquaintance."

The pupils bowed ceremoniously, and Sara made a little curtsy, and then they sat down and looked at each other again.

"Sara," said Miss Minchin in her schoolroom manner, "come here to me."

She had taken a book from the desk and was turning over its leaves. Sara went to her politely.

"As your papa has engaged a French maid for you," she began, "I conclude that he wishes you to make a special study of the French language."

Sara felt a little awkward.

"I think he engaged her," she said, "because he—he thought I would like her, Miss Minchin."

"I am afraid," said Miss Minchin, with a slightly sour smile, "that you have been a very spoiled little girl and always imagine that things are done because you like them. My impression is that your papa wished you to learn French."

If Sara had been older or less punctilious about being quite polite to people, she could have explained herself in a very few words. But, as it was, she felt a flush rising on her cheeks. Miss Minchin was a very severe and imposing person, and she seemed so absolutely sure that Sara knew nothing whatever of French that she felt as if it would be almost rude to correct her. The truth was that Sara could not remember the time when she had not seemed to know French. Her father had often spoken it to her when she had been a baby. Her mother had been a

French woman, and Captain Crewe had loved her language, so it happened that Sara had always heard and been familiar with it.

"I—I have never really learned French, but—but—" she began, trying shyly to make herself clear.

One of Miss Minchin's chief secret annoyances was that she did not speak French herself, and was desirous of concealing the irritating fact. She, therefore, had no intention of discussing the matter and laying herself open to innocent questioning by a new little pupil.

"That is enough," she said with polite tartness. "If you have not learned, you must begin at once. The French master, Monsieur Dufarge, will be here in a few minutes. Take this book and look at it until he arrives."

Sara's cheeks felt warm. She went back to her seat and opened the book. She looked at the first page with a grave face. She knew it would be rude to smile, and she was very determined not to be rude. But it was very odd to find herself expected to study a page which told her that "le pere" meant "the father," and "la mere" meant "the mother."

Miss Minchin glanced toward her scrutinizingly.

"You look rather cross, Sara," she said. "I am sorry you do not like the idea of learning French."

"I am very fond of it," answered Sara, thinking she would try again; "but—"

"You must not say 'but' when you are told to do things," said Miss Minchin. "Look at your book again."

And Sara did so, and did not smile, even when she found that "le fils" meant "the son," and "le frere" meant "the brother."

"When Monsieur Dufarge comes," she thought, "I can make him understand."

Monsieur Dufarge arrived very shortly afterward. He was a very nice, intelligent, middle-aged Frenchman, and he looked interested when his eyes fell upon Sara trying politely to seem absorbed in her little book of phrases.

"Is this a new pupil for me, madame?" he said to Miss Minchin. "I hope that is my good fortune."

"Her papa—Captain Crewe—is very anxious that she should begin the language. But I am afraid she has a childish prejudice against it. She does not seem to wish to learn," said Miss Minchin.

"I am sorry of that, mademoiselle," he said kindly to Sara. "Perhaps, when we begin to study together, I may show you that it is a charming tongue."

Little Sara rose in her seat. She was beginning to feel rather desperate, as if she were almost in disgrace. She looked up into Monsieur Dufarge's face with her big, green-gray eyes, and they were quite innocently appealing. She knew that he would understand as soon as she spoke. She began to explain quite simply in pretty and fluent French. Madame had not understood. She had not learned French exactly—not out of books—but her papa and other people had always spoken it to her, and she had read it and written it as she had read and written English. Her papa loved it, and she loved it because he did. Her dear mamma, who had died when she was born, had been French. She would be glad to learn anything monsieur would teach her, but what she had tried to explain to madame was that she already knew the words in this book—and she held out the little book of phrases.

When she began to speak Miss Minchin started quite violently and sat staring at her over her eyeglasses, almost indignantly, until she had finished. Monsieur Dufarge began to smile, and his smile was one of great pleasure. To hear this pretty childish voice speaking his own language so simply and charmingly made him feel almost as if he were in his native land—which in dark, foggy days in London sometimes seemed worlds away. When she had finished, he took the phrase book from her, with a look almost affectionate. But he spoke to Miss Minchin.

"Ah, madame," he said, "there is not much I can teach her. She has not LEARNED French; she is French. Her accent is exquisite."

"You ought to have told me," exclaimed Miss Minchin, much mortified, turning to Sara.

"I—I tried," said Sara. "I—I suppose I did not begin right."

Miss Minchin knew she had tried, and that it had not been her fault that she was not allowed to explain. And when she saw that the pupils had been listening and that Lavinia and Jessie were giggling behind their French grammars, she felt infuriated.

"Silence, young ladies!" she said severely, rapping upon the desk. "Silence at once!"

And she began from that minute to feel rather a grudge against her show pupil.

~

Frances Hodgson Burnett (1849–1924) was born in England and raised in the United States. Popular children's books by Burnett include *A Little Princess, The Secret Garden* **and** *Little Lord Fauntleroy*, **which she also developed into a play. There have been several film and television adaptations of her works.**

The Lady, or The Tiger?

Frank R. Stockton

In the very olden time there lived a semi-barbaric king, whose ideas, though somewhat polished and sharpened by the progressiveness of distant Latin neighbors, were still large, florid, and untrammeled, as became the half of him which was barbaric. He was a man of exuberant fancy, and, withal, of an authority so irresistible that, at his will, he turned his varied fancies into facts. He was greatly given to self-communing, and, when he and himself agreed upon anything, the thing was done. When every member of his domestic and political systems moved smoothly in its appointed course, his nature was bland and genial; but, whenever there was a little hitch, and some of his orbs got out of their orbits, he was blander and more genial still, for nothing pleased him so much as to make the crooked straight and crush down uneven places.

Among the borrowed notions by which his barbarism had become semified was that of the public arena, in which, by exhibitions of manly and beastly valor, the minds of his subjects were refined and cultured.

But even here the exuberant and barbaric fancy asserted itself. The arena of the king was built, not to give the people an opportunity of hearing the rhapsodies of dying gladiators, nor to enable them to view the inevitable conclusion of a conflict between religious opinions and hungry jaws, but for purposes far better adapted to widen and develop the mental energies of the people. This vast amphitheater, with its encircling galleries, its mysterious vaults, and its unseen passages, was an agent of poetic justice, in which crime was punished, or virtue rewarded, by the decrees of an impartial and incorruptible chance.

When a subject was accused of a crime of sufficient importance to interest the king, public notice was given that on an appointed day the fate of the accused person would be decided in the king's arena, a structure which well deserved its name, for, although its form and plan were borrowed from afar, its purpose emanated solely from the brain of this man, who, every barleycorn a king, knew no tradition to which he owed more allegiance than pleased his fancy, and who ingrafted on every adopted form of human thought and action the rich growth of his barbaric idealism.

When all the people had assembled in the galleries, and the king, surrounded by his court, sat high up on his throne of royal state on one side of the arena, he gave a signal, a door beneath him opened, and the accused subject stepped out into the amphitheater. Directly opposite him, on the other side of the inclosed space, were two doors, exactly alike and side by side. It was the duty and the privilege of the person on trial to walk directly to these doors and open one of them.

He could open either door he pleased; he was subject to no guidance or influence but that of the aforementioned impartial and incorruptible chance. If he opened the one, there came out of it a hungry tiger, the fiercest and most cruel that could be procured, which immediately sprang upon him and tore him to pieces as a punishment for his guilt. The moment that the case of the criminal was thus decided, doleful iron bells were clanged, great wails went up from the hired mourners posted on the outer rim of the arena, and the vast audience, with bowed heads and downcast hearts, wended slowly their homeward way, mourning greatly that one so young and fair, or so old and respected, should have merited so dire a fate.

But, if the accused person opened the other door, there came forth from it a lady, the most suitable to his years and station that his majesty could select among his fair subjects, and to this lady he was immediately married, as a reward of his innocence. It mattered not that he might already possess a wife and family, or that his affections might be engaged upon an object of his own selection; the king allowed no such subordinate arrangements to interfere with his great scheme of retribution and reward. The exercises, as in the other instance, took place immediately, and in the arena. Another door opened beneath the king, and a priest, followed by a band of choristers, and dancing maidens blowing joyous airs on golden horns and treading an epithalamic measure, advanced to where the pair stood, side by side, and the wedding was promptly and cheerily solemnized. Then the gay brass bells rang forth their merry peals, the people shouted glad hurrahs, and the innocent man, preceded by children strewing flowers on his path, led his bride to his home.

This was the king's semi-barbaric method of administering justice. Its perfect fairness is obvious. The criminal could not know out of which door would come the lady; he opened either he pleased, without having the slightest idea whether, in the next instant, he was to be devoured or married. On some occasions the tiger came out of one door, and on some out of the other. The decisions of this tribunal were not only fair, they were positively determinate: the accused person was instantly punished if he found himself guilty, and, if innocent, he was rewarded on the spot, whether he liked it or not. There was no escape from the judgments of the king's arena.

The institution was a very popular one. When the people gathered together on one of the great trial days, they never knew whether they were to witness a bloody slaughter or a hilarious wedding. This element of uncertainty lent an interest to the occasion which it could not otherwise have attained. Thus, the masses were entertained and pleased, and the thinking part of the community could bring no charge of unfairness against this plan, for did not the accused person have the whole matter in his own hands?

This semi-barbaric king had a daughter as blooming as his most florid fancies, and with a soul as fervent and imperious as his own. As is usual in such cases, she was the apple of his eye, and was loved by him above all humanity. Among his courtiers was a young man of that fineness of blood and lowness of station common to the conventional heroes of romance who love royal maidens. This royal maiden was well satisfied with her lover, for he was handsome and brave to a degree unsurpassed in all this kingdom, and she loved him with an ardor that had enough of barbarism in it to make it exceedingly warm and strong. This love affair moved on happily for many months, until one day the king happened to discover its existence. He did not hesitate nor waver in regard to his duty in the premises. The youth was immediately cast into prison, and a day was appointed for his trial in the king's arena. This, of course, was an especially important occasion, and his majesty, as well as all the people, was greatly interested in the workings and development of this trial. Never before had such a case occurred; never before had a subject dared to love the daughter of the king. In after years such things became commonplace enough, but then they were in no slight degree novel and startling.

The tiger-cages of the kingdom were searched for the most savage and relentless beasts, from which the fiercest monster might be selected for the arena; and the ranks of maiden youth and beauty throughout the land were carefully surveyed by competent judges in order that the young man might have a fitting bride in case fate did not determine for him a different destiny. Of course, everybody knew that the deed with which the accused was charged had been done. He had loved the princess, and neither he, she, nor any one else, thought of denying the fact; but the king would not think of allowing any fact of this kind to interfere with the workings of the tribunal, in which he took such great delight and satisfaction. No matter how the affair turned out, the youth would be disposed of, and the king would take an aesthetic pleasure in watching the course of events, which would determine whether or not the young man had done wrong in allowing himself to love the princess.

The appointed day arrived. From far and near the people gathered, and thronged the great galleries of the arena, and crowds, unable to gain admittance, massed themselves against its outside walls. The king and his court were in their places, opposite the twin doors, those fateful portals, so terrible in their similarity.

All was ready. The signal was given. A door beneath the royal party opened, and the lover of the princess walked into the arena. Tall, beautiful, fair, his appearance was greeted with a low hum of admiration and anxiety. Half the audience had not known so grand a youth had lived among them. No wonder the princess loved him! What a terrible thing for him to be there!

As the youth advanced into the arena he turned, as the custom was, to bow to the king, but he did not think at all of that royal personage. His eyes were fixed upon the princess, who sat to the right of her father. Had it not been for the moiety of barbarism in her nature it is probable that lady would not have been there, but her intense and fervid soul would not allow her to be absent on an occasion in which she was so terribly interested. From the moment that the decree had gone forth that her lover should decide his fate in the king's arena, she had thought of nothing, night or day, but this great event and the various subjects connected with it. Possessed of more power, influence, and force of character than any one who had ever before been interested in such a case, she had done what no other person had done,—she had possessed herself of the secret of the doors. She knew in which of the two rooms, that lay behind those doors, stood the cage of the tiger, with its open front, and in which waited the lady. Through these thick doors, heavily curtained with skins on the inside, it was impossible that any noise or suggestion should come from within to the person who should approach to raise the latch of one of them. But gold, and the power of a woman's will, had brought the secret to the princess.

And not only did she know in which room stood the lady ready to emerge, all blushing and radiant, should her door be opened, but she knew who the lady was. It was one of the fairest and loveliest of the damsels of the court who had been selected as the reward of the accused youth, should he be proved innocent of the crime of aspiring to one so far above him; and the princess hated her. Often had she seen, or imagined that she had seen, this fair creature throwing glances of admiration upon the person of her lover, and sometimes she thought these glances were perceived, and even returned. Now and then she had seen them talking together; it was but for a moment or two, but much can be said in a brief space; it may have been on most unimportant topics, but how could she know that? The girl was lovely, but she had dared to raise her eyes to the loved one of the princess; and, with all the intensity of the savage blood transmitted to her through long lines of wholly barbaric ancestors, she hated the woman who blushed and trembled behind that silent door.

When her lover turned and looked at her, and his eye met hers as she sat there, paler and whiter than any one in the vast ocean of anxious faces about her, he saw, by that power of quick perception which is given to those whose souls are one, that she knew behind which door crouched the tiger, and behind which stood the lady. He had expected her to know it. He understood her nature, and his soul was assured that she would never rest until she had made plain to herself this thing, hidden to all other lookers-on, even to the king. The only hope for the youth in which there was any element of certainty was based upon the success of the princess in discovering this mystery; and the moment he looked upon her, he saw she had succeeded, as in his soul he knew she would succeed.

Then it was that his quick and anxious glance asked the question: "Which?" It was as plain to her as if he shouted it from where he stood. There was not an instant to be lost. The question was asked in a flash; it must be answered in another.

Her right arm lay on the cushioned parapet before her. She raised her hand, and made a slight, quick movement toward the right. No one but her lover saw her. Every eye but his was fixed on the man in the arena.

He turned, and with a firm and rapid step he walked across the empty space. Every heart stopped beating, every breath was held, every eye was fixed immovably upon that man. Without the slightest hesitation, he went to the door on the right, and opened it.

Now, the point of the story is this: Did the tiger come out of that door, or did the lady?

The more we reflect upon this question, the harder it is to answer. It involves a study of the human heart which leads us through devious mazes of passion, out of which it is difficult to find our way. Think of it, fair reader, not as if the decision of the question depended upon yourself, but upon that hot-blooded, semi-barbaric princess, her soul at a white heat beneath the combined fires of despair and jealousy. She had lost him, but who should have him?

How often, in her waking hours and in her dreams, had she started in wild horror, and covered her face with her hands as she thought of her lover opening the door on the other side of which waited the cruel fangs of the tiger!

But how much oftener had she seen him at the other door! How in her grievous reveries had she gnashed her teeth, and torn her hair, when she saw his start of rapturous delight as he opened the door of the lady! How her soul had burned in agony when she had seen him rush to meet that woman, with her flushing cheek and sparkling eye of triumph; when she had seen him lead her forth, his whole frame kindled with the joy of recovered life; when she had heard the glad shouts from the multitude, and the wild ringing of the happy bells; when she had seen the priest, with his joyous followers, advance to the couple, and make them man and wife before her very eyes; and when she had seen them walk away together upon their path of flowers, followed by the tremendous shouts of the hilarious multitude, in which her one despairing shriek was lost and drowned!

Would it not be better for him to die at once, and go to wait for her in the blessed regions of semi-barbaric futurity?

And yet, that awful tiger, those shrieks, that blood!

Her decision had been indicated in an instant, but it had been made after days and nights of anguished deliberation. She had known she would be asked, she had decided what she would answer, and, without the slightest hesitation, she had moved her hand to the right.

The question of her decision is one not to be lightly considered, and it is not for me to presume to set myself up as the one person able to answer it. And so I leave it with all of you: Which came out of the opened door,—the lady, or the tiger?

~

Frank Richard Stockton (1834–1902) was an American popular novelist and short-story writer of mainly humorous fiction, best known for his allegorical fairy tales for all ages. His popular works include *The Floating Prince, and Other Fairy Tales; The Casting Away of Mrs Lecks and Mrs Aleshine* and *The House of Martha*.

The Diamond Necklace

Guy de Maupassant

The girl was one of those pretty and charming young creatures who sometimes are born, as if by a slip of fate, into a family of clerks. She had no dowry, no expectations, no way of being known, understood, loved, married by any rich and distinguished man; so she let herself be married to a little clerk of the Ministry of Public Instruction.

She dressed plainly because she could not dress well, but she was unhappy as if she had really fallen from a higher station; since with women there is neither caste nor rank, for beauty, grace and charm take the place of family and birth. Natural ingenuity, instinct for what is elegant, a supple mind are their sole hierarchy, and often make of women of the people the equals of the very greatest ladies.

Mathilde suffered ceaselessly, feeling herself born to enjoy all delicacies and all luxuries. She was distressed at the poverty of her dwelling, at the bareness of the walls, at the shabby chairs, the ugliness of the curtains. All those things, of which another woman of her rank would never even have been conscious, tortured her and made her angry. The sight of the little Breton peasant who did her humble housework aroused in her despairing regrets and bewildering dreams. She thought of silent antechambers hung with Oriental tapestry, illumined by tall bronze candelabra, and of two great footmen in knee breeches who sleep in the big armchairs, made drowsy by the oppressive heat of the stove. She thought of long reception halls hung with ancient silk, of the dainty cabinets containing priceless curiosities and of the little coquettish perfumed reception rooms made for chatting at five o'clock with intimate friends, with men famous and sought after, whom all women envy and whose attention they all desire.

When she sat down to dinner, before the round table covered with a tablecloth in use three days, opposite her husband, who uncovered the soup tureen and declared with a delighted air, "Ah, the good soup! I don't know anything better than that," she thought of dainty dinners, of shining silverware, of tapestry that peopled the walls with ancient personages and with strange birds flying in the midst of a fairy forest; and she thought of delicious dishes served on marvellous plates and of the whispered gallantries to which you listen with a sphinxlike smile while you are eating the pink meat of a trout or the wings of a quail.

She had no gowns, no jewels, nothing. And she loved nothing but that. She felt made for that. She would have liked so much to please, to be envied, to be charming, to be sought after.

She had a friend, a former schoolmate at the convent, who was rich, and whom she did not like to go to see any more because she felt so sad when she came home.

But one evening her husband reached home with a triumphant air and holding a large envelope in his hand.

"There," said he, "there is something for you."

She tore the paper quickly and drew out a printed card which bore these words:

> *The Minister of Public Instruction and Madame Georges Ramponneau request the honor of M. and Madame Loisel's company at the palace of the Ministry on Monday evening, January 18th.*

Instead of being delighted, as her husband had hoped, she threw the invitation on the table crossly, muttering:

"What do you wish me to do with that?"

"Why, my dear, I thought you would be glad. You never go out, and this is such a fine opportunity. I had great trouble to get it. Every one wants to go; it is very select, and they are not giving many invitations to clerks. The whole official world will be there."

She looked at him with an irritated glance and said impatiently:

"And what do you wish me to put on my back?"

He had not thought of that. He stammered:

"Why, the gown you go to the theatre in. It looks very well to me."

He stopped, distracted, seeing that his wife was weeping. Two great tears ran slowly from the corners of her eyes toward the corners of her mouth.

"What's the matter? What's the matter?" he answered.

By a violent effort she conquered her grief and replied in a calm voice, while she wiped her wet cheeks:

"Nothing. Only I have no gown, and, therefore, I can't go to this ball. Give your card to some colleague whose wife is better equipped than I am."

He was in despair. He resumed:

"Come, let us see, Mathilde. How much would it cost, a suitable gown, which you could use on other occasions—something very simple?"

She reflected several seconds, making her calculations and wondering also what sum she could ask without drawing on herself an immediate refusal and a frightened exclamation from the economical clerk.

Finally she replied hesitating:

"I don't know exactly, but I think I could manage it with four hundred francs."

He grew a little pale, because he was laying aside just that amount to buy a gun and treat himself to a little shooting next summer on the plain of Nanterre, with several friends who went to shoot larks there of a Sunday.

But he said:

"Very well. I will give you four hundred francs. And try to have a pretty gown."

The day of the ball drew near and Madame Loisel seemed sad, uneasy, anxious. Her frock was ready, however. Her husband said to her one evening:

"What is the matter? Come, you have seemed very queer these last three days."

And she answered:

"It annoys me not to have a single piece of jewelry, not a single ornament, nothing to put on. I shall look poverty-stricken. I would almost rather not go at all."

"You might wear natural flowers," said her husband. "They're very stylish at this time of year. For ten francs you can get two or three magnificent roses."

She was not convinced.

"No; there's nothing more humiliating than to look poor among other women who are rich."

"How stupid you are!" her husband cried. "Go look up your friend, Madame Forestier, and ask her to lend you some jewels. You're intimate enough with her to do that."

She uttered a cry of joy:

"True! I never thought of it."

The next day she went to her friend and told her of her distress.

Madame Forestier went to a wardrobe with a mirror, took out a large jewel box, brought it back, opened it and said to Madame Loisel:

"Choose, my dear."

She saw first some bracelets, then a pearl necklace, then a Venetian gold cross set with precious stones, of admirable workmanship. She tried on the ornaments before the mirror, hesitated and could not make up her mind to part with them, to give them back. She kept asking:

"Haven't you any more?"

"Why, yes. Look further; I don't know what you like."

Suddenly she discovered, in a black satin box, a superb diamond necklace, and her heart throbbed with an immoderate desire. Her hands trembled as she took it. She fastened it round her throat, outside her high-necked waist, and was lost in ecstasy at her reflection in the mirror.

Then she asked, hesitating, filled with anxious doubt:

"Will you lend me this, only this?"

"Why, yes, certainly."

She threw her arms round her friend's neck, kissed her passionately, then fled with her treasure.

The night of the ball arrived. Madame Loisel was a great success. She was prettier than any other woman present, elegant, graceful, smiling and wild with joy. All the men looked at her, asked her name, sought to be introduced. All the attaches of the Cabinet wished to waltz with her. She was remarked by the minister himself.

She danced with rapture, with passion, intoxicated by pleasure, forgetting all in the triumph of her beauty, in the glory of her success, in a sort of cloud of happiness comprised of all this homage, admiration, these awakened desires and of that sense of triumph which is so sweet to woman's heart.

She left the ball about four o'clock in the morning. Her husband had been sleeping since midnight in a little deserted anteroom with three other gentlemen whose wives were enjoying the ball.

He threw over her shoulders the wraps he had brought, the modest wraps of common life, the poverty of which contrasted with the elegance of the ball dress. She felt this and wished to escape so as not to be remarked by the other women, who were enveloping themselves in costly furs.

Loisel held her back, saying: "Wait a bit. You will catch cold outside. I will call a cab."

But she did not listen to him and rapidly descended the stairs. When they reached the street they could not find a carriage and began to look for one, shouting after the cabmen passing at a distance.

They went toward the Seine in despair, shivering with cold. At last they found on the quay one of those ancient night cabs which, as though they were ashamed to show their shabbiness during the day, are never seen round Paris until after dark.

It took them to their dwelling in the Rue des Martyrs, and sadly they mounted the stairs to their flat. All was ended for her. As to him, he reflected that he must be at the ministry at ten o'clock that morning.

She removed her wraps before the glass so as to see herself once more in all her glory. But suddenly she uttered a cry. She no longer had the necklace around her neck!

"What is the matter with you?" demanded her husband, already half undressed.

She turned distractedly toward him.

"I have—I have—I've lost Madame Forestier's necklace," she cried.

He stood up, bewildered.

"What!—how? Impossible!"

They looked among the folds of her skirt, of her cloak, in her pockets, everywhere, but did not find it.

"You're sure you had it on when you left the ball?" he asked.

"Yes, I felt it in the vestibule of the minister's house."

"But if you had lost it in the street we should have heard it fall. It must be in the cab."

"Yes, probably. Did you take his number?"

"No. And you—didn't you notice it?"

"No."

They looked, thunderstruck, at each other. At last Loisel put on his clothes.

"I shall go back on foot," said he, "over the whole route, to see whether I can find it."

He went out. She sat waiting on a chair in her ball dress, without strength to go to bed, overwhelmed, without any fire, without a thought.

Her husband returned about seven o'clock. He had found nothing.

He went to police headquarters, to the newspaper offices to offer a reward; he went to the cab companies—everywhere, in fact, whither he was urged by the least spark of hope.

She waited all day, in the same condition of mad fear before this terrible calamity.

Loisel returned at night with a hollow, pale face. He had discovered nothing.

"You must write to your friend," said he, "that you have broken the clasp of her necklace and that you are having it mended. That will give us time to turn round."

She wrote at his dictation.

At the end of a week they had lost all hope. Loisel, who had aged five years, declared:

"We must consider how to replace that ornament."

The next day they took the box that had contained it and went to the jeweler whose name was found within. He consulted his books.

"It was not I, madame, who sold that necklace; I must simply have furnished the case."

Then they went from jeweler to jeweler, searching for a necklace like the other, trying to recall it, both sick with chagrin and grief.

They found, in a shop at the Palais Royal, a string of diamonds that seemed to them exactly like the one they had lost. It was worth forty thousand francs. They could have it for thirty-six.

So they begged the jeweler not to sell it for three days yet. And they made a bargain that he should buy it back for thirty-four thousand francs, in case they should find the lost necklace before the end of February.

Loisel possessed eighteen thousand francs which his father had left him. He would borrow the rest.

He did borrow, asking a thousand francs of one, five hundred of another, five louis here, three louis there. He gave notes, took up ruinous obligations, dealt with usurers and all the race of lenders. He compromised all the rest of his life, risked signing a note without even knowing whether he could meet it; and, frightened by the trouble yet to come, by the black misery that was about to fall upon him, by the prospect of all the physical privations and moral tortures that he was to suffer, he went to get the new necklace, laying upon the jeweler's counter thirty-six thousand francs.

When Madame Loisel took back the necklace Madame Forestier said to her with a chilly manner:

"You should have returned it sooner; I might have needed it."

She did not open the case, as her friend had so much feared. If she had detected the substitution, what would she have thought, what would she have said? Would she not have taken Madame Loisel for a thief?

Thereafter Madame Loisel knew the horrible existence of the needy. She bore her part, however, with sudden heroism. That dreadful debt must be paid. She would pay it. They dismissed their servant; they changed their lodgings; they rented a garret under the roof.

She came to know what heavy housework meant and the odious cares of the kitchen. She washed the dishes, using her dainty fingers and rosy nails on greasy pots and pans. She washed the soiled linen, the shirts and the dishcloths, which she dried upon a line; she carried the slops down to the street every morning and carried up the water, stopping for breath at every landing. And dressed like a woman of the people, she went to the fruiterer, the grocer, the butcher, a basket on her arm, bargaining, meeting with impertinence, defending her miserable money, sou by sou.

Every month they had to meet some notes, renew others, obtain more time.

Her husband worked evenings, making up a tradesman's accounts, and late at night he often copied manuscript for five sous a page.

This life lasted ten years.

At the end of ten years they had paid everything, everything, with the rates of usury and the accumulations of the compound interest.

Madame Loisel looked old now. She had become the woman of impoverished households—strong and hard and rough. With frowsy hair, skirts askew and red hands, she talked loud while washing the floor with great swishes of water. But sometimes, when her husband was at the office, she sat down near the window and she thought of that gay evening of long ago, of that ball where she had been so beautiful and so admired.

What would have happened if she had not lost that necklace? Who knows? who knows? How strange and changeful is life! How small a thing is needed to make or ruin us!

But one Sunday, having gone to take a walk in the Champs Elysees to refresh herself after the labors of the week, she suddenly perceived a woman who was leading a child. It was Madame Forestier, still young, still beautiful, still charming.

Madame Loisel felt moved. Should she speak to her? Yes, certainly. And now that she had paid, she would tell her all about it. Why not?

She went up.

"Good-day, Jeanne."

The other, astonished to be familiarly addressed by this plain good-wife, did not recognize her at all and stammered:

"But—madame!—I do not know—You must have mistaken."

"No. I am Mathilde Loisel."

Her friend uttered a cry.

"Oh, my poor Mathilde! How you are changed!"

"Yes, I have had a pretty hard life, since I last saw you, and great poverty—and that because of you!"

"Of me! How so?"

"Do you remember that diamond necklace you lent me to wear at the ministerial ball?"

"Yes. Well?"

"Well, I lost it."

"What do you mean? You brought it back."

"I brought you back another exactly like it. And it has taken us ten years to pay for it. You can understand that it was not easy for us, for us who had nothing. At last it is ended, and I am very glad."

Madame Forestier had stopped.

"You say that you bought a necklace of diamonds to replace mine?"

"Yes. You never noticed it, then! They were very similar."

And she smiled with a joy that was at once proud and ingenuous.

Madame Forestier, deeply moved, took her hands.

"Oh, my poor Mathilde! Why, my necklace was paste! It was worth at most only five hundred francs!"

~

Henri Ren Albert Guy de Maupassant (1850–1893) was a popular French author who wrote under the pen name Guy de Maupassant. He is considered one of the fathers of the modern short story. His works include "The Necklace", "A Piece of String", "Mademoiselle Fifi" and "The Hand".

Clay

James Joyce

The matron had given her leave to go out as soon as the women's tea was over and Maria looked forward to her evening out. The kitchen was spick and span: the cook said you could see yourself in the big copper boilers. The fire was nice and bright and on one of the side-tables were four very big barmbracks. These barmbracks seemed uncut; but if you went closer you would see that they had been cut into long thick even slices and were ready to be handed round at tea. Maria had cut them herself.

Maria was a very, very small person indeed but she had a very long nose and a very long chin. She talked a little through her nose, always soothingly: *"Yes, my dear,"* and *"No, my dear."* She was always sent for when the women quarrelled over their tubs and always succeeded in making peace. One day the matron had said to her:

"Maria, you are a veritable peace-maker!"

And the sub-matron and two of the Board ladies had heard the compliment. And Ginger Mooney was always saying what she wouldn't do to the dummy who had charge of the irons if it wasn't for Maria. Everyone was so fond of Maria.

The women would have their tea at six o'clock and she would be able to get away before seven. From Ballsbridge to the Pillar, twenty minutes; from the Pillar to Drumcondra, twenty minutes; and twenty minutes to buy the things. She would be there before eight. She took out her purse with the silver clasps and read again the words *A Present from Belfast*. She was very fond of that purse because Joe had brought it to her five years before when he and Alphy had gone to Belfast on a Whit-Monday trip. In the purse were two half-crowns and some coppers. She would have five shillings clear after paying tram fare. What a nice evening they would have, all the children singing! Only she hoped that Joe wouldn't come in drunk. He was so different when he took any drink.

Often he had wanted her to go and live with them; but she would have felt herself in the way (though Joe's wife was ever so nice with her) and she had become accustomed to the life of the laundry. Joe was a good fellow. She had nursed him and Alphy too; and Joe used often say:

"Mamma is mamma but Maria is my proper mother."

After the break-up at home the boys had got her that position in the *Dublin by Lamplight* laundry, and she liked it. She used to have such a bad opinion of Protestants but now she thought they were very nice people, a little quiet and serious, but still very nice people to live with. Then she had her plants in the conservatory and she liked looking after them. She had lovely ferns and wax-plants and, whenever anyone came to visit her, she always gave the visitor one or two slips from her conservatory. There was one thing she didn't like and that was the tracts on the walks; but the matron was such a nice person to deal with, so genteel.

When the cook told her everything was ready she went into the women's room and began to pull the big bell. In a few minutes the women began to come in by twos and threes, wiping their steaming hands in their petticoats and pulling down the sleeves of their blouses over their red steaming arms. They settled down before their huge mugs which the cook and the dummy filled up with hot tea, already mixed with milk and sugar in huge tin cans. Maria superintended the distribution of the barmbrack and saw that every woman got her four slices. There was a great deal of laughing and joking during the meal. Lizzie Fleming said Maria was sure to get the ring and, though Fleming had said that for so many Hallow Eves, Maria had to laugh and say she didn't want any ring or man either; and when she laughed her grey-green eyes sparkled with disappointed shyness and the tip of her nose nearly met the tip of her chin. Then Ginger Mooney lifted up her mug of tea and proposed Maria's health while all the other women clattered with their mugs on the table, and said she was sorry she hadn't a sup of porter to drink it in. And Maria laughed again till the tip of her nose nearly met the tip of her chin and till her minute body nearly shook itself asunder because she knew that Mooney meant well though, of course, she had the notions of a common woman.

But wasn't Maria glad when the women had finished their tea and the cook and the dummy had begun to clear away the tea-things! She went into her little bedroom and, remembering that the next morning was a mass morning, changed the hand of the alarm from seven to six. Then she took off her working skirt and her house-boots and laid her best skirt out on the bed and her tiny dress-boots beside the foot of the bed. She changed her blouse too and, as she stood before the mirror, she thought of how she used to dress for mass on Sunday morning when she was a young girl; and she looked with quaint affection at the diminutive body which she had so often adorned. In spite of its years she found it a nice tidy little body.

When she got outside the streets were shining with rain and she was glad of her old brown waterproof. The tram was full and she had to sit on the little stool at the end of the car, facing all the people, with her toes barely touching the floor. She arranged in her mind all she was going to do and thought how much better it was to be independent and to have your own money in your pocket. She hoped they would have a nice evening. She was sure they would but she could not help thinking what a pity it was Alphy and Joe were not speaking. They were always falling out now but when they were boys together they used to be the best of friends: but such was life.

She got out of her tram at the Pillar and ferreted her way quickly among the crowds. She went into Downes's cake-shop but the shop was so full of people that it was a long time before she could get herself attended to. She bought a dozen of mixed penny cakes, and at last came out of the shop laden with a big bag. Then she thought what else would she buy: she wanted to buy something really nice. They would be sure to have plenty of apples and nuts. It was hard to know what to buy and all she could think of was cake. She decided to buy some plumcake but Downes's plumcake had not enough almond icing on top of it so she went over to a shop in Henry Street. Here she was a long time in suiting herself and the stylish young lady behind the counter, who was evidently a little annoyed by her, asked her was it wedding-cake she wanted to buy. That made Maria blush and smile at the young lady; but the young lady took it all very seriously and finally cut a thick slice of plumcake, parcelled it up and said:

"Two-and-four, please."

She thought she would have to stand in the Drumcondra tram because none of the young men seemed to notice her but an elderly gentleman made room for her. He was a stout gentleman and he wore a brown hard hat; he had a square red face and a greyish moustache. Maria thought he was a colonel-looking gentleman and she reflected how much more polite he was than the young men who simply stared straight before them. The gentleman began to chat with her about Hallow Eve and the rainy weather. He supposed the bag was full of good things for the little ones and said it was only right that the youngsters should enjoy themselves while they were young. Maria agreed with him and favoured him with demure nods and hems. He was very nice with her, and when she was getting out at the Canal Bridge she thanked him and bowed, and he bowed to her and raised his hat and smiled agreeably, and while she was going up along the terrace, bending her tiny head under the rain, she thought how easy it was to know a gentleman even when he has a drop taken.

Everybody said: *"O, here's Maria!"* when she came to Joe's house. Joe was there, having come home from business, and all the children had their Sunday dresses on. There were two big girls in from next door and games were going on. Maria gave the bag of cakes to the eldest boy, Alphy, to divide and Mrs Donnelly said it was too good of her to bring such a big bag of cakes and made all the children say:

"Thanks, Maria."

But Maria said she had brought something special for papa and mamma, something they would be sure to like, and she began to look for her plumcake. She tried in Downes's bag and then in the pockets of her waterproof and then on the hallstand but nowhere could she find it. Then she asked all the children had any of them eaten it—by mistake, of course—but the children all said no and looked as if they did not like to eat cakes if they were to be accused of stealing. Everybody had a solution for the mystery and Mrs Donnelly said it was plain that Maria had left it behind her in the tram. Maria, remembering how confused the gentleman with the greyish moustache had made her, coloured with shame and vexation and disappointment. At the thought of the failure of her little surprise and of the two and fourpence she had thrown away for nothing she nearly cried outright.

But Joe said it didn't matter and made her sit down by the fire. He was very nice with her. He told her all that went on in his office, repeating for her a smart answer which he had made to the manager. Maria did not understand why Joe laughed so much over the answer he had made but she said that the manager must have been a very overbearing person to deal with. Joe said he wasn't so bad when you knew how to take him, that he was a decent sort so long as you didn't rub him the wrong way. Mrs Donnelly played the piano for the children and they danced and sang. Then the two next-door girls handed round the nuts. Nobody could find the nutcrackers and Joe was nearly getting cross over it and asked how did they expect Maria to crack nuts without a nutcracker. But Maria said she didn't like nuts and that they weren't to bother about her. Then Joe asked would she take a bottle of stout and Mrs Donnelly said there was port wine too in the house if she would prefer that. Maria said she would rather they didn't ask her to take anything: but Joe insisted.

So Maria let him have his way and they sat by the fire talking over old times and Maria thought she would put in a good word for Alphy. But Joe cried that God might strike him stone dead if ever he spoke a word to his brother again and Maria said she was sorry she had mentioned the matter. Mrs Donnelly told her husband it was a great shame for him to speak that way of his own flesh and blood but Joe said that Alphy was no brother of his and there was nearly being a row on the head of it. But Joe said he would not lose his temper on account of the night it was and asked his wife to open some more stout. The two next-door girls had arranged some Hallow Eve games and soon everything was merry again. Maria was delighted to see the children so merry and Joe and his wife in such good spirits. The next-door girls put some saucers on the table and then led the children up to the table, blindfold. One got the prayer-book and the other three got the water; and when one of the next-door girls got the ring Mrs Donnelly shook her finger at the blushing girl as much as to say: *O, I know all about it!* They insisted then on blindfolding Maria and leading her up to the table to see what she would get; and, while they were putting on the bandage, Maria laughed and laughed again till the tip of her nose nearly met the tip of her chin.

They led her up to the table amid laughing and joking and she put her hand out in the air as she was told to do. She moved her hand about here and there in the air and descended on one of the saucers. She felt a soft wet substance with her fingers and was surprised that nobody spoke or took off her bandage. There was a pause for a few seconds; and then a great deal of scuffling and whispering. Somebody said something about the garden, and at last Mrs Donnelly said something very cross to one of the next-door girls and told her to throw it out at once: that was no play. Maria understood that it was wrong that time and so she had to do it over again: and this time she got the prayer-book.

After that Mrs Donnelly played Miss McCloud's Reel for the children and Joe made Maria take a glass of wine. Soon they were all quite merry again and Mrs Donnelly said Maria would enter a convent before the year was out because she had got the prayer-book. Maria had never seen Joe so nice to her as he was that night, so full of pleasant talk and reminiscences. She said they were all very good to her.

At last the children grew tired and sleepy and Joe asked Maria would she not sing some little song before she went, one of the old songs. Mrs Donnelly said *"Do, please, Maria!"* and so Maria had to get up and stand beside the piano. Mrs Donnelly bade the children be quiet and listen to Maria's song. Then she played the prelude and said *"Now, Maria!"* and Maria, blushing very much began to sing in a tiny quavering voice. She sang *I Dreamt that I Dwelt*, and when she came to the second verse she sang again:

I dreamt that I dwelt in marble halls
With vassals and serfs at my side
And of all who assembled within those walls
That I was the hope and the pride.
I had riches too great to count, could boast
Of a high ancestral name,
But I also dreamt, which pleased me most,
That you loved me still the same.

But no one tried to show her her mistake; and when she had ended her song Joe was very much moved. He said that there was no time like the long ago and no music for him like poor old Balfe, whatever other people might say; and his eyes filled up so much with tears that he could not find what he was looking for and in the end he had to ask his wife to tell him where the corkscrew was.

~

James Joyce (1882–1941) was an Irish writer, poet and literary critic. He is best known for his landmark novel ***Ulysses*** **and its successor** ***Finnegans Wake*****, as well as the short story collection** ***Dubliners*** **and the semi-autobiographical novel** ***A Portrait of the Artist as a Young Man*****.**

From Pride And Prejudice

Jane Austen

Chapter I

It is a truth universally acknowledged, that a single man in possession of a good fortune must be in want of a wife.

However little known the feelings or views of such a man may be on his first entering a neighbourhood, this truth is so well fixed in the minds of the surrounding families, that he is considered as the rightful property of some one or other of their daughters.

"My dear Mr Bennet," said his lady to him one day, "have you heard that Netherfield Park is let at last?"

Mr Bennet replied that he had not.

"But it is," returned she; "for Mrs Long has just been here, and she told me all about it."

Mr Bennet made no answer.

"Do not you want to know who has taken it?" cried his wife, impatiently.

"*You* want to tell me, and I have no objection to hearing it."

This was invitation enough.

"Why, my dear, you must know, Mrs Long says that Netherfield is taken by a young man of large fortune from the north of England; that he came down on Monday in a chaise and four to see the place, and was so much delighted with it that he agreed with Mr Morris immediately; that he is to take possession before Michaelmas, and some of his servants are to be in the house by the end of next week."

"What is his name?"

"Bingley."

"Is he married or single?"

"Oh, single, my dear, to be sure! A single man of large fortune; four or five thousand a year. What a fine thing for our girls!"

"How so? how can it affect them?"

"My dear Mr Bennet," replied his wife, "how can you be so tiresome? You must know that I am thinking of his marrying one of them."

"Is that his design in settling here?"

"Design? Nonsense, how can you talk so! But it is very likely that he *may* fall in love with one of them, and therefore you must visit him as soon as he comes."

"I see no occasion for that. You and the girls may go—or you may send them by themselves, which perhaps will be still better; for as you are as handsome as any of them, Mr Bingley might like you the best of the party."

"My dear, you flatter me. I certainly *have* had my share of beauty, but I do not pretend to be anything extraordinary now. When a woman has five grown-up daughters, she ought to give over thinking of her own beauty."

"In such cases, a woman has not often much beauty to think of."

"But, my dear, you must indeed go and see Mr Bingley when he comes into the neighbourhood."

"It is more than I engage for, I assure you."

"But consider your daughters. Only think what an establishment it would be for one of them. Sir William and Lady Lucas are determined to go, merely on that account; for in general, you know, they visit no new comers. Indeed you must go, for it will be impossible for *us* to visit him, if you do not."

"You are over scrupulous, surely. I dare say Mr Bingley will be very glad to see you; and I will send a few lines by you to assure him of my hearty consent to his marrying whichever he chooses of the girls—though I must throw in a good word for my little Lizzy."

"I desire you will do no such thing. Lizzy is not a bit better than the others: and I am sure she is not half so handsome as Jane, nor half so good-humoured as Lydia. But you are always giving *her* the preference."

"They have none of them much to recommend them," replied he: "they are all silly and ignorant like other girls; but Lizzy has something more of quickness than her sisters."

"Mr Bennet, how can you abuse your own children in such a way? You take delight in vexing me. You have no compassion on my poor nerves."

"You mistake me, my dear. I have a high respect for your nerves. They are my old friends. I have heard you mention them with consideration these twenty years at least."

"Ah, you do not know what I suffer."

"But I hope you will get over it, and live to see many young men of four thousand a year come into the neighbourhood."

"It will be no use to us, if twenty such should come, since you will not visit them."

"Depend upon it, my dear, that when there are twenty, I will visit them all."

Mr Bennet was so odd a mixture of quick parts, sarcastic humour, reserve, and caprice, that the experience of three-and-twenty years had been insufficient to make his wife understand his character. *Her* mind was less difficult to develope. She was a woman of mean understanding, little information, and uncertain temper. When she was discontented, she fancied herself nervous. The business of her life was to get her daughters married: its solace was visiting and news.

Chapter II

Mr Bennet was among the earliest of those who waited on Mr Bingley. He had always intended to visit him, though to the last always assuring his wife that he should not go; and till the evening after the visit was paid she had no knowledge of it. It was then disclosed in the following manner. Observing his second daughter employed in trimming a hat, he suddenly addressed her with,—

"I hope Mr Bingley will like it, Lizzy."

"We are not in a way to know *what* Mr Bingley likes," said her mother, resentfully, "since we are not to visit."

"But you forget, mamma," said Elizabeth, "that we shall meet him at the assemblies, and that Mrs Long has promised to introduce him."

"I do not believe Mrs Long will do any such thing. She has two nieces of her own. She is a selfish, hypocritical woman, and I have no opinion of her."

"No more have I," said Mr Bennet; "and I am glad to find that you do not depend on her serving you."

Mrs Bennet deigned not to make any reply; but, unable to contain herself, began scolding one of her daughters.

"Don't keep coughing so, Kitty, for heaven's sake! Have a little compassion on my nerves. You tear them to pieces."

"Kitty has no discretion in her coughs," said her father; "she times them ill."

"I do not cough for my own amusement," replied Kitty, fretfully. "When is your next ball to be, Lizzy?"

"To-morrow fortnight."

"Ay, so it is," cried her mother, "and Mrs Long does not come back till the day before; so, it will be impossible for her to introduce him, for she will not know him herself."

"Then, my dear, you may have the advantage of your friend, and introduce Mr Bingley to *her*."

"Impossible, Mr Bennet, impossible, when I am not acquainted with him myself; how can you be so teasing?"

"I honour your circumspection. A fortnight's acquaintance is certainly very little. One cannot know what a man really is by the end of a fortnight. But if *we* do not venture, somebody else will; and after all, Mrs Long and her nieces must stand their chance; and, therefore, as she will think it an act of kindness, if you decline the office, I will take it on myself."

The girls stared at their father. Mrs Bennet said only, "Nonsense, nonsense!"

"What can be the meaning of that emphatic exclamation?" cried he. "Do you consider the forms of introduction, and the stress that is laid on them, as nonsense? I cannot quite agree with you *there*. What say you, Mary? For you are a young lady of deep reflection, I know, and read great books, and make extracts."

Mary wished to say something very sensible, but knew not how.

"While Mary is adjusting her ideas," he continued, "let us return to Mr Bingley."

"I am sick of Mr Bingley," cried his wife.

"I am sorry to hear *that*; but why did you not tell me so before? If I had known as much this morning, I certainly would not have called on him. It is very unlucky; but as I have actually paid the visit, we cannot escape the acquaintance now."

The astonishment of the ladies was just what he wished—that of Mrs Bennet perhaps surpassing the rest; though when the first tumult of joy was over, she began to declare that it was what she had expected all the while.

"How good it was in you, my dear Mr Bennet! But I knew I should persuade you at last. I was sure you loved your girls too well to neglect such an acquaintance. Well, how pleased I am! And it is such a good joke, too, that you should have gone this morning, and never said a word about it till now."

"Now, Kitty, you may cough as much as you choose," said Mr Bennet; and, as he spoke, he left the room, fatigued with the raptures of his wife.

"What an excellent father you have, girls," said she, when the door was shut. "I do not know how you will ever make him amends for his kindness; or me either, for that matter. At our time of life, it is not so pleasant, I can tell you, to be making new acquaintances every day; but for your sakes we would do anything. Lydia, my love, though you *are* the youngest, I dare say Mr Bingley will dance with you at the next ball."

"Oh," said Lydia, stoutly, "I am not afraid; for though I *am* the youngest, I'm the tallest."

The rest of the evening was spent in conjecturing how soon he would return Mr Bennet's visit, and determining when they should ask him to dinner.

Chapter III

Not all that Mrs Bennet, however, with the assistance of her five daughters, could ask on the subject, was sufficient to draw from her husband any satisfactory description of Mr Bingley. They attacked him in various ways, with barefaced questions, ingenious suppositions, and distant surmises; but he eluded the skill of them all; and they were at last obliged to accept the second-hand intelligence of their neighbour, Lady Lucas. Her report was highly favourable. Sir William had been delighted with him. He was quite young, wonderfully handsome, extremely agreeable, and, to crown the whole, he meant to be at the next assembly with a large party. Nothing could be more delightful! To be fond of dancing was a certain step towards falling in love; and very lively hopes of Mr Bingley's heart were entertained.

"If I can but see one of my daughters happily settled at Netherfield," said Mrs Bennet to her husband, "and all the others equally well married, I shall have nothing to wish for."

In a few days Mr Bingley returned Mr Bennet's visit, and sat about ten minutes with him in his library. He had entertained hopes of being admitted to a sight of the young ladies, of whose beauty he had heard much; but he saw only the father. The ladies were somewhat more fortunate, for they had the advantage of ascertaining, from an upper window, that he wore a blue coat and rode a black horse.

An invitation to dinner was soon afterwards despatched; and already had Mrs Bennet planned the courses that were to do credit to her housekeeping, when an answer arrived which deferred it all. Mr Bingley was obliged to be in town the following day, and consequently unable to accept the honour of their invitation, etc. Mrs Bennet was quite disconcerted. She could not imagine what business he could have in town so soon after his arrival in Hertfordshire; and she began to fear that he might always be flying about from one place to another, and never settled at Netherfield as he ought to be. Lady Lucas quieted her fears a little by starting the idea of his being gone to London only to get a large party for the ball; and a report soon followed that Mr Bingley was to bring twelve ladies and seven gentlemen with him to the assembly. The girls grieved over such a number of ladies; but were comforted the day before the ball by hearing that, instead of twelve, he had brought only six with him from London, his five sisters and a cousin. And when the party entered the assembly-room, it consisted of only five altogether: Mr Bingley, his two sisters, the husband of the eldest, and another young man.

Mr Bingley was good-looking and gentlemanlike: he had a pleasant countenance, and easy, unaffected manners. His sisters were fine women, with an air of decided fashion. His brother-in-law, Mr Hurst, merely looked the gentleman; but his friend Mr Darcy soon drew the attention of the room by his fine, tall person, handsome features, noble mien, and the report, which was in general circulation within five minutes after his entrance, of his having ten thousand a year. The gentlemen pronounced him to be a fine figure of a man, the ladies declared he was much handsomer than Mr Bingley, and he was looked at with great admiration for about half the evening, till his manners gave a disgust which turned the tide of his popularity; for he was discovered to be proud, to be above his company, and above being pleased; and not all his large estate in Derbyshire could save him from having a most forbidding, disagreeable countenance, and being unworthy to be compared with his friend.

Mr Bingley had soon made himself acquainted with all the principal people in the room: he was lively and unreserved, danced every dance, was angry that the ball closed so early, and talked of giving one himself at Netherfield. Such amiable qualities must speak for themselves. What a contrast between him and his friend!

Mr Darcy danced only once with Mrs Hurst and once with Miss Bingley, declined being introduced to any other lady, and spent the rest of the evening in walking about the room, speaking occasionally to one of his own party. His character was decided. He was the proudest, most disagreeable man in the world, and everybody hoped that he would never come there again. Amongst the most violent against him was Mrs Bennet, whose dislike of his general behaviour was sharpened into particular resentment by his having slighted one of her daughters.

Elizabeth Bennet had been obliged, by the scarcity of gentlemen, to sit down for two dances; and during part of that time, Mr Darcy had been standing near enough for her to overhear a conversation between him and Mr Bingley, who came from the dance for a few minutes to press his friend to join it.

"Come, Darcy," said he, "I must have you dance. I hate to see you standing about by yourself in this stupid manner. You had much better dance."

"I certainly shall not. You know how I detest it, unless I am particularly acquainted with my partner. At such an assembly as this, it would be insupportable. Your sisters are engaged, and there is not another woman in the room whom it would not be a punishment to me to stand up with."

"I would not be so fastidious as you are," cried Bingley, "for a kingdom! Upon my honour, I never met with so many pleasant girls in my life as I have this evening; and there are several of them, you see, uncommonly pretty."

"*You* are dancing with the only handsome girl in the room," said Mr Darcy, looking at the eldest Miss Bennet.

"Oh, she is the most beautiful creature I ever beheld! But there is one of her sisters sitting down just behind you, who is very pretty, and I dare say very agreeable. Do let me ask my partner to introduce you."

"Which do you mean?" and turning round, he looked for a moment at Elizabeth, till, catching her eye, he withdrew his own, and coldly said, "She is tolerable: but not handsome enough to tempt *me*; and I am in no humour at present to give consequence to young ladies who are slighted by other men. You had better return to your partner and enjoy her smiles, for you are wasting your time with me."

Mr Bingley followed his advice. Mr Darcy walked off; and Elizabeth remained with no very cordial feelings towards him. She told the story, however, with great spirit among her friends; for she had a lively, playful disposition, which delighted in anything ridiculous.

The evening altogether passed off pleasantly to the whole family. Mrs Bennet had seen her eldest daughter much admired by the Netherfield party. Mr Bingley had danced with her twice, and she had been distinguished by his sisters. Jane was as much gratified by this as her mother could be, though in a quieter way. Elizabeth felt Jane's pleasure. Mary had heard herself mentioned to Miss Bingley as the most accomplished girl in the neighbourhood; and Catherine and Lydia had been fortunate enough to be never without partners, which was all that they had yet learnt to care for at a ball. They returned, therefore, in good spirits to Longbourn, the village where they lived, and of which they were the principal inhabitants. They found Mr Bennet still up. With a book, he was regardless of time; and on the present occasion he had a good deal of curiosity as to the event of an evening which had raised such splendid expectations. He had rather hoped that all his wife's views on the stranger would be disappointed; but he soon found that he had a very different story to hear.

"Oh, my dear Mr Bennet," as she entered the room, "we have had a most delightful evening, a most excellent ball. I wish you had been there. Jane was so admired, nothing could be like it. Everybody said how well she looked; and Mr Bingley thought her quite beautiful, and danced with her twice. Only think of *that*, my dear: he actually danced with her twice; and she was the only creature in the room that he asked a second time. First of all, he asked Miss Lucas. I was so vexed to see him stand up with her; but, however, he did not admire her at all; indeed, nobody can, you know; and he seemed quite struck with Jane as she was going down the dance. So he inquired who she was, and got introduced, and asked her for the two next. Then, the two third he danced with Miss King, and the two fourth with Maria Lucas, and the two fifth with Jane again, and the two sixth with Lizzy, and the *Boulanger*—"

"If he had had any compassion for *me*," cried her husband impatiently, "he would not have danced half so much! For God's sake, say no more of his partners. O that he had sprained his ancle in the first dance!"

"Oh, my dear," continued Mrs Bennet, "I am quite delighted with him. He is so excessively handsome! and his sisters are charming women. I never in my life saw anything more elegant than their dresses. I dare say the lace upon Mrs Hurst's gown—"

Here she was interrupted again. Mr Bennet protested against any description of finery. She was therefore obliged to seek another branch of the subject, and related, with much bitterness of spirit, and some exaggeration, the shocking rudeness of Mr Darcy.

"But I can assure you," she added, "that Lizzy does not lose much by not suiting *his* fancy; for he is a most disagreeable, horrid man, not at all worth pleasing. So high and so conceited, that there was no enduring him! He walked here, and he walked there, fancying himself so very great! Not handsome enough to dance with! I wish you had been there, my dear, to have given him one of your set-downs. I quite detest the man."

~

Jane Austen (1775–1817) was an English novelist and writer, best known for novels such as *Pride and Prejudice, Sense and Sensibility, Mansfield Park, Emma* and *Persuasion*, **among others. Her works provide amusing and informative insights into the life of the British nobility, and are read and studied around the world even today.**

Three Questions

Leo Tolstoy

It once occurred to a certain king, that if he always knew the right time to begin everything; if he knew who were the right people to listen to, and whom to avoid; and, above all, if he always knew what was the most important thing to do, he would never fail in anything he might undertake.

And this thought having occurred to him, he had it proclaimed throughout his kingdom that he would give a great reward to any one who would teach him what was the right time for every action, and who were the most necessary people, and how he might know what was the most important thing to do.

And learned men came to the King, but they all answered his questions differently.

In reply to the first question, some said that to know the right time for every action, one must draw up in advance, a table of days, months and years, and must live strictly according to it. Only thus, said they, could everything be done at its proper time. Others declared that it was impossible to decide beforehand the right time for every action; but that, not letting oneself be absorbed in idle pastimes, one should always attend to all that was going on, and then do what was most needful. Others, again, said that however attentive the King might be to what was going on, it was impossible for one man to decide correctly the right time for every action, but that he should have a Council of wise men, who would help him to fix the proper time for everything.

But then again others said there were some things which could not wait to be laid before a Council, but about which one had at once to decide whether to undertake them or not. But in order to decide that, one must know beforehand what was going to happen. It is only magicians who know that; and, therefore, in order to know the right time for every action, one must consult magicians.

Equally various were the answers to the second question. Some said, the people the King most needed were his councillors; others, the priests; others, the doctors; while some said the warriors were the most necessary.

To the third question, as to what was the most important occupation: some replied that the most important thing in the world was science. Others said it was skill in warfare; and others, again, that it was religious worship.

All the answers being different, the King agreed with none of them, and gave the reward to none. But still wishing to find the right answers to his questions, he decided to consult a hermit, widely renowned for his wisdom.

The hermit lived in a wood which he never quitted, and he received none but common folk. So the King put on simple clothes, and before reaching the hermit's cell dismounted from his horse, and, leaving his body-guard behind, went on alone.

When the King approached, the hermit was digging the ground in front of his hut. Seeing the King, he greeted him and went on digging. The hermit was frail and weak, and each time he stuck his spade into the ground and turned a little earth, he breathed heavily.

The King went up to him and said: "I have come to you, wise hermit, to ask you to answer three questions: How can I learn to do the right thing at the right time? Who are the people I most need, and to whom should I, therefore, pay more attention than to the rest? And, what affairs are the most important, and need my first attention?"

The hermit listened to the King, but answered nothing. He just spat on his hand and recommenced digging.

"You are tired," said the King, "let me take the spade and work awhile for you."

"Thanks!" said the hermit, and, giving the spade to the King, he sat down on the ground.

When he had dug two beds, the King stopped and repeated his questions. The hermit again gave no answer, but rose, stretched out his hand for the spade, and said:

"Now rest awhile-and let me work a bit."

But the King did not give him the spade, and continued to dig. One hour passed, and another. The sun began to sink behind the trees, and the King at last stuck the spade into the ground, and said:

"I came to you, wise man, for an answer to my questions. If you can give me none, tell me so, and I will return home."

"Here comes some one running," said the hermit, "let us see who it is."

The King turned round, and saw a bearded man come running out of the wood. The man held his hands pressed against his stomach, and blood was flowing from under them. When he reached the King, he fell fainting on the ground moaning feebly. The King and the hermit unfastened the man's clothing. There was a large wound in his stomach. The King washed it as best he could, and bandaged it with his handkerchief and with a towel the hermit had. But the blood would not stop flowing, and the King again and again removed the bandage soaked with warm blood, and washed and rebandaged the wound. When at last the blood ceased flowing, the man revived and asked for something to drink. The King brought fresh water and gave it to him. Meanwhile the sun had set, and it had become cool. So the King, with the hermit's help, carried the wounded man into the hut and laid him on the bed. Lying on the bed the man closed his eyes and was quiet; but the King was so tired with his walk and with the work he had done, that he crouched down on the threshold, and also fell asleep—so soundly that he slept all through the short summer night. When he awoke in the morning, it was long before he could remember where he was, or who was the strange bearded man lying on the bed and gazing intently at him with shining eyes.

"Forgive me!" said the bearded man in a weak voice, when he saw that the King was awake and was looking at him.

"I do not know you, and have nothing to forgive you for," said the King.

"You do not know me, but I know you. I am that enemy of yours who swore to revenge himself on you, because you executed his brother and seized his property. I knew you had gone alone to see the hermit, and I resolved to kill you on your way back. But the day passed and you did not return. So I came out from my ambush to find you, and I came upon your bodyguard, and they recognized me, and wounded me. I escaped from them, but should have bled to death had you not dressed my wound. I wished to kill you, and you have saved my life. Now, if I live, and if you wish it, I will serve you as your most faithful slave, and will bid my sons do the same. Forgive me!"

The King was very glad to have made peace with his enemy so easily, and to have gained him for a friend, and he not only forgave him, but said he would send his servants and his own physician to attend him, and promised to restore his property.

Having taken leave of the wounded man, the King went out into the porch and looked around for the hermit. Before going away he wished once more to beg an answer to the questions he had put. The hermit was outside, on his knees, sowing seeds in the beds that had been dug the day before.

The King approached him, and said:

"For the last time, I pray you to answer my questions, wise man."

"You have already been answered!" said the hermit, still crouching on his thin legs, and looking up at the King, who stood before him.

"How answered? What do you mean?" asked the King.

"Do you not see," replied the hermit. "If you had not pitied my weakness yesterday, and had not dug those beds for me, but had gone your way, that man would have attacked you, and you would have repented of not having stayed with me. So the most important time was when you were digging the beds; and I was the most important man; and to do me good was your most important business. Afterwards when that man ran to us, the most important time was when you were attending to him, for if you had not bound up his wounds he would have died without having made peace with you. So he was the most important man, and what you did for him was your most important business. Remember then: there is only one time that is important—Now! It is the most important time because it is the only time when we have any power. The most necessary man is he with whom you are, for no man knows whether he will ever have dealings with any one else: and the most important affair is, to do him good, because for that purpose alone was man sent into this life!"

~

Leo Tolstoy (1828–1910) is best known to the world because of *War and Peace*, his epic in prose, and *Anna Karenina*, one of the most splendid novels in any language. But during his lifetime Tolstoy also wrote enough shorter works to fill many volumes, including "The Cossacks" and "Family Happiness".

From Little Women

Louisa May Alcott

The Laurence Boy

"Jo! Jo! Where are you?" cried Meg at the foot of the garret stairs.

"Here!" answered a husky voice from above, and, running up, Meg found her sister eating apples and crying over the Heir of Redclyffe, wrapped up in a comforter on an old three-legged sofa by the sunny window. This was Jo's favorite refuge, and here she loved to retire with half a dozen russets and a nice book, to enjoy the quiet and the society of a pet rat who lived near by and didn't mind her a particle. As Meg appeared, Scrabble whisked into his hole. Jo shook the tears off her cheeks and waited to hear the news.

"Such fun! Only see! A regular note of invitation from Mrs Gardiner for tomorrow night!" cried Meg, waving the precious paper and then proceeding to read it with girlish delight.

"'Mrs Gardiner would be happy to see Miss March and Miss Josephine at a little dance on New Year's Eve.' Marmee is willing we should go, now what shall we wear?"

"What's the use of asking that, when you know we shall wear our poplins, because we haven't got anything else?" answered Jo with her mouth full.

"If I only had a silk!" sighed Meg. "Mother says I may when I'm eighteen perhaps, but two years is an everlasting time to wait."

"I'm sure our pops look like silk, and they are nice enough for us. Yours is as good as new, but I forgot the burn and the tear in mine. Whatever shall I do? The burn shows badly, and I can't take any out."

"You must sit still all you can and keep your back out of sight. The front is all right. I shall have a new ribbon for my hair, and Marmee will lend me her little pearl pin, and my new slippers are lovely, and my gloves will do, though they aren't as nice as I'd like."

"Mine are spoiled with lemonade, and I can't get any new ones, so I shall have to go without," said Jo, who never troubled herself much about dress.

"You must have gloves, or I won't go," cried Meg decidedly. "Gloves are more important than anything else. You can't dance without them, and if you don't I should be so mortified."

"Then I'll stay still. I don't care much for company dancing. It's no fun to go sailing round. I like to fly about and cut capers."

"You can't ask Mother for new ones, they are so expensive, and you are so careless. She said when you spoiled the others that she shouldn't get you any more this winter. Can't you make them do?"

"I can hold them crumpled up in my hand, so no one will know how stained they are. That's all I can do. No! I'll tell you how we can manage, each wear one good one and carry a bad one. Don't you see?"

"Your hands are bigger than mine, and you will stretch my glove dreadfully," began Meg, whose gloves were a tender point with her.

"Then I'll go without. I don't care what people say!" cried Jo, taking up her book.

"You may have it, you may! Only don't stain it, and do behave nicely. Don't put your hands behind you, or stare, or say 'Christopher Columbus!' will you?"

"Don't worry about me. I'll be as prim as I can and not get into any scrapes, if I can help it. Now go and answer your note, and let me finish this splendid story."

So Meg went away to 'accept with thanks', look over her dress, and sing blithely as she did up her one real lace frill, while Jo finished her story, her four apples, and had a game of romps with Scrabble.

On New Year's Eve the parlor was deserted, for the two younger girls played dressing maids and the two elder were absorbed in the all-important business of 'getting ready for the party'. Simple as the toilets were, there was a great deal of running up and down, laughing and talking, and at one time a strong smell of burned hair pervaded the house. Meg wanted a few curls about her face, and Jo undertook to pinch the papered locks with a pair of hot tongs.

"Ought they to smoke like that?" asked Beth from her perch on the bed.

"It's the dampness drying," replied Jo.

"What a queer smell! It's like burned feathers," observed Amy, smoothing her own pretty curls with a superior air.

"There, now I'll take off the papers and you'll see a cloud of little ringlets," said Jo, putting down the tongs.

She did take off the papers, but no cloud of ringlets appeared, for the hair came with the papers, and the horrified hairdresser laid a row of little scorched bundles on the bureau before her victim.

"Oh, oh, oh! What have you done? I'm spoiled! I can't go! My hair, oh, my hair!" wailed Meg, looking with despair at the uneven frizzle on her forehead.

"Just my luck! You shouldn't have asked me to do it. I always spoil everything. I'm so sorry, but the tongs were too hot, and so I've made a mess," groaned poor Jo, regarding the little black pancakes with tears of regret.

"It isn't spoiled. Just frizzle it, and tie your ribbon so the ends come on your forehead a bit, and it will look like the last fashion. I've seen many girls do it so," said Amy consolingly.

"Serves me right for trying to be fine. I wish I'd let my hair alone," cried Meg petulantly.

"So do I, it was so smooth and pretty. But it will soon grow out again," said Beth, coming to kiss and comfort the shorn sheep.

After various lesser mishaps, Meg was finished at last, and by the united exertions of the entire family Jo's hair was got up and her dress on. They looked very well in their simple suits, Meg's in silvery drab, with a blue velvet snood, lace frills, and the pearl pin. Jo in maroon, with a stiff, gentlemanly linen collar, and a white chrysanthemum or two for her only ornament. Each put on one nice light glove, and carried one soiled one, and all pronounced the effect "quite easy and fine". Meg's high-heeled slippers were very tight and hurt her, though she would not own it, and Jo's nineteen hairpins all seemed stuck straight into her head, which was not exactly comfortable, but, dear me, let us be elegant or die.

"Have a good time, dearies!" said Mrs March, as the sisters went daintily down the walk. "Don't eat much supper, and come away at eleven when I send Hannah for you." As the gate clashed behind them, a voice cried from a window...

"Girls, girls! Have you you both got nice pocket handkerchiefs?"

"Yes, yes, spandy nice, and Meg has cologne on hers," cried Jo, adding with a laugh as they went on, "I do believe Marmee would ask that if we were all running away from an earthquake."

"It is one of her aristocratic tastes, and quite proper, for a real lady is always known by neat boots, gloves, and handkerchief," replied Meg, who had a good many little 'aristocratic tastes' of her own.

"Now don't forget to keep the bad breadth out of sight, Jo. Is my sash right? And does my hair look very bad?" said Meg, as she turned from the glass in Mrs Gardiner's dressing room after a prolonged prink.

"I know I shall forget. If you see me doing anything wrong, just remind me by a wink, will you?" returned Jo, giving her collar a twitch and her head a hasty brush.

"No, winking isn't ladylike. I'll lift my eyebrows if any thing is wrong, and nod if you are all right. Now hold your shoulder straight, and take short steps, and don't shake hands if you are introduced to anyone. It isn't the thing."

"How do you learn all the proper ways? I never can. Isn't that music gay?"

Down they went, feeling a trifle timid, for they seldom went to parties, and informal as this little gathering was, it was an event to them. Mrs Gardiner, a stately old lady, greeted them kindly and handed them over to the eldest of her six daughters. Meg knew Sallie and was at her ease very soon, but Jo, who didn't care much for girls or girlish gossip, stood about, with her back carefully against the wall, and felt as much out of place as a colt in a flower garden. Half a dozen jovial lads were talking about skates in another part of the room, and she longed to go and join them, for skating was one of the joys of her life. She telegraphed her wish to Meg, but the eyebrows went up so alarmingly that she dared not stir. No one came to talk to her, and one by one the group dwindled away till she was left alone. She could not roam about and amuse herself, for the burned breadth would show, so she stared at people rather forlornly till the dancing began. Meg was asked at once, and the tight slippers tripped about so briskly that none would have guessed the pain their wearer suffered smilingly. Jo saw a big red headed youth approaching her corner, and fearing he meant to engage her, she slipped into a curtained recess, intending to peep and enjoy herself in peace. Unfortunately, another bashful person had chosen the same refuge, for, as the curtain fell behind her, she found herself face to face with the 'Laurence boy'.

"Dear me, I didn't know anyone was here!" stammered Jo, preparing to back out as speedily as she had bounced in.

But the boy laughed and said pleasantly, though he looked a little startled, "Don't mind me, stay if you like."

"Shan't I disturb you?"

"Not a bit. I only came here because I don't know many people and felt rather strange at first, you know."

"So did I. Don't go away, please, unless you'd rather."

The boy sat down again and looked at his pumps, till Jo said, trying to be polite and easy, "I think I've had the pleasure of seeing you before. You live near us, don't you?"

"Next door." And he looked up and laughed outright, for Jo's prim manner was rather funny when he remembered how they had chatted about cricket when he brought the cat home.

That put Jo at her ease and she laughed too, as she said, in her heartiest way, "We did have such a good time over your nice Christmas present."

"Grandpa sent it."

"But you put it into his head, didn't you, now?"

"How is your cat, Miss March?" asked the boy, trying to look sober while his black eyes shone with fun.

"Nicely, thank you, Mr Laurence. But I am not Miss March, I'm only Jo," returned the young lady.

"I'm not Mr Laurence, I'm only Laurie."

"Laurie Laurence, what an odd name."

"My first name is Theodore, but I don't like it, for the fellows called me Dora, so I made them say Laurie instead."

"I hate my name, too, so sentimental! I wish every one would say Jo instead of Josephine. How did you make the boys stop calling you Dora?"

"I thrashed 'em."

"I can't thrash Aunt March, so I suppose I shall have to bear it." And Jo resigned herself with a sigh.

"Don't you like to dance, Miss Jo?" asked Laurie, looking as if he thought the name suited her.

"I like it well enough if there is plenty of room, and everyone is lively. In a place like this I'm sure to upset something, tread on people's toes, or do something dreadful, so I keep out of mischief and let Meg sail about. Don't you dance?"

"Sometimes. You see I've been abroad a good many years, and haven't been into company enough yet to know how you do things here."

"Abroad!" cried Jo. "Oh, tell me about it! I love dearly to hear people describe their travels."

Laurie didn't seem to know where to begin, but Jo's eager questions soon set him going, and he told her how he had been at school in Vevay, where the boys never wore hats and had a fleet of boats on the lake, and for holiday fun went on walking trips about Switzerland with their teachers.

"Don't I wish I'd been there!" cried Jo. "Did you go to Paris?"

"We spent last winter there."

"Can you talk French?"

"We were not allowed to speak anything else at Vevay."

"Do say some! I can read it, but can't pronounce."

"Quel nom a cette jeune demoiselle en les pantoufles jolis?"

"How nicely you do it! Let me see ... you said, 'Who is the young lady in the pretty slippers', didn't you?"

"Oui, mademoiselle."

"It's my sister Margaret, and you knew it was! Do you think she is pretty?"

"Yes, she makes me think of the German girls, she looks so fresh and quiet, and dances like a lady."

Jo quite glowed with pleasure at this boyish praise of her sister, and stored it up to repeat to Meg. Both peeped and criticized and chatted till they felt like old acquaintances. Laurie's bashfulness soon wore off, for Jo's gentlemanly demeanor amused and set him at his ease, and Jo was her merry self again, because her dress was forgotten and nobody lifted their eyebrows at her. She liked the 'Laurence boy' better than ever and took several good looks at him, so that she might describe him to the girls, for they had no brothers, very few male cousins, and boys were almost unknown creatures to them.

"Curly black hair, brown skin, big black eyes, handsome nose, fine teeth, small hands and feet, taller than I am, very polite, for a boy, and altogether jolly. Wonder how old he is?"

It was on the tip of Jo's tongue to ask, but she checked herself in time and, with unusual tact, tried to find out in a round-about way.

"I suppose you are going to college soon? I see you pegging away at your books, no, I mean studying hard." And Jo blushed at the dreadful 'pegging' which had escaped her.

Laurie smiled but didn't seem shocked, and answered with a shrug. "Not for a year or two. I won't go before seventeen, anyway."

"Aren't you but fifteen?" asked Jo, looking at the tall lad, whom she had imagined seventeen already.

"Sixteen, next month."

"How I wish I was going to college! You don't look as if you liked it."

"I hate it! Nothing but grinding or skylarking. And I don't like the way fellows do either, in this country."

"What do you like?"

"To live in Italy, and to enjoy myself in my own way."

Jo wanted very much to ask what his own way was, but his black brows looked rather threatening as he knit them, so she changed the subject by saying, as her foot kept time, "That's a splendid polka! Why don't you go and try it?"

"If you will come too," he answered, with a gallant little bow.

"I can't, for I told Meg I wouldn't, because..." There Jo stopped, and looked undecided whether to tell or to laugh.

"Because, what?"

"You won't tell?"

"Never!"

"Well, I have a bad trick of standing before the fire, and so I burn my frocks, and I scorched this one, and though it's nicely mended, it shows, and Meg told me to keep still so no one would see it. You may laugh, if you want to. It is funny, I know."

But Laurie didn't laugh. He only looked down a minute, and the expression of his face puzzled Jo when he said very gently, "Never mind that. I'll tell you how we can manage. There's a long hall out there, and we can dance grandly, and no one will see us. Please come."

Jo thanked him and gladly went, wishing she had two neat gloves when she saw the nice, pearl-colored ones her partner wore. The hall was empty, and they had a grand polka, for Laurie danced well, and taught her the German step, which delighted Jo, being full of swing and spring. When the music stopped, they sat down on the stairs to get their breath, and Laurie was in the midst of an account of a students' festival at Heidelberg when Meg appeared in search of her sister. She beckoned, and Jo reluctantly followed her into a side room, where she found her on a sofa, holding her foot, and looking pale.

"I've sprained my ankle. That stupid high heel turned and gave me a sad wrench. It aches so, I can hardly stand, and I don't know how I'm ever going to get home," she said, rocking to and fro in pain.

"I knew you'd hurt your feet with those silly shoes. I'm sorry. But I don't see what you can do, except get a carriage, or stay here all night," answered Jo, softly rubbing the poor ankle as she spoke.

"I can't have a carriage without its costing ever so much. I dare say I can't get one at all, for most people come in their own, and it's a long way to the stable, and no one to send."

"I'll go."

"No, indeed! It's past nine, and dark as Egypt. I can't stop here, for the house is full. Sallie has some girls staying with her. I'll rest till Hannah comes, and then do the best I can."

"I'll ask Laurie. He will go," said Jo, looking relieved as the idea occurred to her.

"Mercy, no! Don't ask or tell anyone. Get me my rubbers, and put these slippers with our things. I can't dance anymore, but as soon as supper is over, watch for Hannah and tell me the minute she comes."

"They are going out to supper now. I'll stay with you. I'd rather."

"No, dear, run along, and bring me some coffee. I'm so tired I can't stir."

So Meg reclined, with rubbers well hidden, and Jo went blundering away to the dining room, which she found after going into a china closet, and opening the door of a room where old Mr Gardiner was taking a little private refreshment. Making a dart at the table, she secured the coffee, which she immediately spilled, thereby making the front of her dress as bad as the back.

"Oh, dear, what a blunderbuss I am!" exclaimed Jo, finishing Meg's glove by scrubbing her gown with it.

"Can I help you?" said a friendly voice. And there was Laurie, with a full cup in one hand and a plate of ice in the other.

"I was trying to get something for Meg, who is very tired, and someone shook me, and here I am in a nice state," answered Jo, glancing dismally from the stained skirt to the coffee-colored glove.

"Too bad! I was looking for someone to give this to. May I take it to your sister?"

"Oh, thank you! I'll show you where she is. I don't offer to take it myself, for I should only get into another scrape if I did."

Jo led the way, and as if used to waiting on ladies, Laurie drew up a little table, brought a second installment of coffee and ice for Jo, and was so obliging that even particular Meg pronounced him a 'nice boy'. They had a merry time over the bonbons and mottoes, and were in the midst of a quiet game of *Buzz*, with two or three other young people who had strayed in, when Hannah appeared. Meg forgot her foot and rose so quickly that she was forced to catch hold of Jo, with an exclamation of pain.

"Hush! Don't say anything," she whispered, adding aloud, "It's nothing. I turned my foot a little, that's all," and limped upstairs to put her things on.

Hannah scolded, Meg cried, and Jo was at her wits' end, till she decided to take things into her own hands. Slipping out, she ran down and, finding a servant, asked if he could get her a carriage. It happened to be a hired waiter who knew nothing about the neighborhood and Jo was looking round for help when Laurie, who had heard what she said, came up and offered his grandfather's carriage, which had just come for him, he said.

"It's so early! You can't mean to go yet?" began Jo, looking relieved but hesitating to accept the offer.

"I always go early, I do, truly! Please let me take you home. It's all on my way, you know, and it rains, they say."

That settled it, and telling him of Meg's mishap, Jo gratefully accepted and rushed up to bring down the rest of the party. Hannah hated rain as much as a cat does so she made no trouble, and they rolled away in the luxurious close carriage, feeling very festive and elegant. Laurie went on the box so Meg could keep her foot up, and the girls talked over their party in freedom.

"I had a capital time. Did you?" asked Jo, rumpling up her hair, and making herself comfortable.

"Yes, till I hurt myself. Sallie's friend, Annie Moffat, took a fancy to me, and asked me to come and spend a week with her when Sallie does. She is going in the spring when the opera comes, and it will be perfectly splendid, if Mother only lets me go," answered Meg, cheering up at the thought.

"I saw you dancing with the red headed man I ran away from. Was he nice?"

"Oh, very! His hair is auburn, not red, and he was very polite, and I had a delicious redowa with him."

"He looked like a grasshopper in a fit when he did the new step. Laurie and I couldn't help laughing. Did you hear us?"

"No, but it was very rude. What were you about all that time, hidden away there?"

Jo told her adventures, and by the time she had finished they were at home. With many thanks, they said good night and crept in, hoping to disturb no one, but the instant their door creaked, two little nightcaps bobbed up, and two sleepy but eager voices cried out...

"Tell about the party! Tell about the party!"

With what Meg called 'a great want of manners' Jo had saved some bonbons for the little girls, and they soon subsided, after hearing the most thrilling events of the evening.

"I declare, it really seems like being a fine young lady, to come home from the party in a carriage and sit in my dressing gown with a maid to wait on me," said Meg, as Jo bound up her foot with arnica and brushed her hair.

"I don't believe fine young ladies enjoy themselves a bit more than we do, in spite of our burned hair, old gowns, one glove apiece and tight slippers that sprain our ankles when we are silly enough to wear them." And I think Jo was quite right.

~

Louisa May Alcott (1832–1888) was an American writer best known for *Little Women*, often ranked among the best and most popular novels of all time. She wrote two sequels to this book about the March family, *Little Men* and *Jo's Boys*, as well as other books for young readers including *Eight Cousins* and *An Old-Fashioned Girl*. Alcott also wrote thrillers and ghost stories for adults under the pseudonym A.M. Bernard.

From The Adventures of Tom Sawyer

Mark Twain

"TOM!"

No answer.

"TOM!"

No answer.

"What's gone with that boy, I wonder? You TOM!"

No answer.

The old lady pulled her spectacles down and looked over them about the room; then she put them up and looked out under them. She seldom or never looked *through* them for so small a thing as a boy; they were her state pair, the pride of her heart, and were built for "style," not service—she could have seen through a pair of stove-lids just as well. She looked perplexed for a moment, and then said, not fiercely, but still loud enough for the furniture to hear:

"Well, I lay if I get hold of you I'll—"

She did not finish, for by this time she was bending down and punching under the bed with the broom, and so she needed breath to punctuate the punches with. She resurrected nothing but the cat.

"I never did see the beat of that boy!"

She went to the open door and stood in it and looked out among the tomato vines and "jimpson" weeds that constituted the garden. No Tom. So she lifted up her voice at an angle calculated for distance and shouted:

"Y-o-u-u TOM!"

There was a slight noise behind her and she turned just in time to seize a small boy by the slack of his roundabout and arrest his flight.

"There! I might 'a' thought of that closet. What you been doing in there?"

"Nothing."

"Nothing! Look at your hands. And look at your mouth. What *is* that truck?"

"I don't know, aunt."

"Well, I know. It's jam—that's what it is. Forty times I've said if you didn't let that jam alone I'd skin you. Hand me that switch."

The switch hovered in the air—the peril was desperate—

"My! Look behind you, aunt!"

The old lady whirled round, and snatched her skirts out of danger. The lad fled on the instant, scrambled up the high board-fence, and disappeared over it.

His aunt Polly stood surprised a moment, and then broke into a gentle laugh.

"Hang the boy, can't I never learn anything? Ain't he played me tricks enough like that for me to be looking out for him by this time? But old fools is the biggest fools there is. Can't learn an old dog new tricks, as the saying is. But my goodness, he never plays them alike, two days, and how is a body to know what's coming? He 'pears to know just how long he can torment me before I get my dander up, and he knows if he can make out to put me off for a minute or make me laugh, it's all down again and I can't hit him a lick. I ain't doing my duty by that boy, and that's the Lord's truth, goodness knows. Spare the rod and spile the child, as the Good Book says. I'm a laying up sin and suffering for us both, I know. He's full of the Old Scratch, but laws-a-me! he's my own dead sister's boy, poor thing, and I ain't got the heart to lash him, somehow. Every time I let him off, my conscience does hurt me so, and every time I hit him my old heart most breaks. Well-a-well, man that is born of woman is of few days and full of trouble, as the Scripture says, and I reckon it's so. He'll play hookey this evening, * and [* Southwestern for "afternoon"] I'll just be obleeged to make him work, tomorrow, to punish him. It's mighty hard to make him work Saturdays, when all the boys is having holiday, but he hates work more than he hates anything else, and I've *got* to do some of my duty by him, or I'll be the ruination of the child."

Tom did play hookey, and he had a very good time. He got back home barely in season to help Jim, the small colored boy, saw next-day's wood and split the kindlings before supper—at least he was there in time to tell his adventures to Jim while Jim did three-fourths of the work. Tom's younger brother (or rather half-brother) Sid was already through with his part of the work (picking up chips), for he was a quiet boy, and had no adventurous, trouble-some ways.

While Tom was eating his supper, and stealing sugar as opportunity offered, Aunt Polly asked him questions that were full of guile, and very deep—for she wanted to trap him into damaging revealments. Like many other simple-hearted souls, it was her pet vanity to believe she was endowed with a talent for dark and mysterious diplomacy, and she loved to contemplate her most transparent devices as marvels of low cunning. Said she:

"Tom, it was middling warm in school, warn't it?"

"Yes'm."

"Powerful warm, warn't it?"

"Yes'm."

"Didn't you want to go in a-swimming, Tom?"

A bit of a scare shot through Tom—a touch of uncomfortable suspicion. He searched Aunt Polly's face, but it told him nothing. So he said:

"No'm—well, not very much."

The old lady reached out her hand and felt Tom's shirt, and said:

"But you ain't too warm now, though." And it flattered her to reflect that she had discovered that the shirt was dry without anybody knowing that that was what she had in her mind. But in spite of her, Tom knew where the wind lay, now. So he forestalled what might be the next move:

"Some of us pumped on our heads—mine's damp yet. See?"

Aunt Polly was vexed to think she had overlooked that bit of circumstantial evidence, and missed a trick. Then she had a new inspiration:

"Tom, you didn't have to undo your shirt collar where I sewed it, to pump on your head, did you? Unbutton your jacket!"

The trouble vanished out of Tom's face. He opened his jacket. His shirt collar was securely sewed.

"Bother! Well, go 'long with you. I'd made sure you'd played hookey and been a-swimming. But I forgive ye, Tom. I reckon you're a kind of a singed cat, as the saying is—better'n you look. *This* time."

She was half sorry her sagacity had miscarried, and half glad that Tom had stumbled into obedient conduct for once.

But Sidney said:

"Well, now, if I didn't think you sewed his collar with white thread, but it's black."

"Why, I did sew it with white! Tom!"

But Tom did not wait for the rest. As he went out at the door he said:

"Siddy, I'll lick you for that."

In a safe place Tom examined two large needles which were thrust into the lapels of his jacket, and had thread bound about them—one needle carried white thread and the other black. He said:

"She'd never noticed if it hadn't been for Sid. Confound it! sometimes she sews it with white, and sometimes she sews it with black. I wish to gee-miny she'd stick to one or t'other—I can't keep the run of 'em. But I bet you I'll lam Sid for that. I'll learn him!"

He was not the Model Boy of the village. He knew the model boy very well though—and loathed him.

Within two minutes, or even less, he had forgotten all his troubles. Not because his troubles were one whit less heavy and bitter to him than a man's are to a man, but because a new and powerful interest bore them down and drove them out of his mind for the time—just as men's misfortunes are forgotten in the excitement of new enterprises. This new interest was a valued novelty in whistling, which he had just acquired from a negro, and he was suffering to practise it un-disturbed. It consisted in a peculiar bird-like turn, a sort of liquid warble, produced by touching the tongue to the roof of the mouth at short intervals in the midst of the music—the reader probably remembers how to do it, if he has ever been a boy. Diligence and attention soon gave him the knack of it, and he strode down the street with his mouth full of harmony and his soul full of gratitude. He felt much as an astronomer feels who has discovered a new planet—no doubt, as far as strong, deep, unalloyed pleasure is concerned, the advantage was with the boy, not the astronomer.

The summer evenings were long. It was not dark, yet. Presently Tom checked his whistle. A stranger was before him—a boy a shade larger than himself. A new-comer of any age or either sex was an im-pressive curiosity in the poor little shabby village of St. Petersburg. This boy was well dressed, too—well dressed on a week-day. This was simply astounding. His cap was a dainty thing, his close-buttoned blue cloth roundabout was new and natty, and so were his pantaloons. He had shoes on—and it was only Friday. He even wore a necktie, a bright bit of ribbon. He had a citified air about him that ate into Tom's vitals. The more Tom stared at the splendid marvel, the higher he turned up his nose at his finery and the shabbier and shabbier his own outfit seemed to him to grow. Neither boy spoke. If one moved, the other moved—but only sidewise, in a circle; they kept face to face and eye to eye all the time. Finally Tom said:

"I can lick you!"

"I'd like to see you try it."

"Well, I can do it."

"No you can't, either."

"Yes I can."

"No you can't."

"I can."

"You can't."

"Can!"

"Can't!"

An uncomfortable pause. Then Tom said:

"What's your name?"

"Tisn't any of your business, maybe."

"Well I 'low I'll *make* it my business."

"Well why don't you?"

"If you say much, I will."

"Much—much—*much*. There now."

"Oh, you think you're mighty smart, *don't* you? I could lick you with one hand tied behind me, if I wanted to."

"Well why don't you *do* it? You *say* you can do it."

"Well I *will*, if you fool with me."

"Oh yes—I've seen whole families in the same fix."

"Smarty! You think you're *some*, now, *don't* you? Oh, what a hat!"

"You can lump that hat if you don't like it. I dare you to knock it off—and anybody that'll take a dare will suck eggs."

"You're a liar!"

"You're another."

"You're a fighting liar and dasn't take it up."

"Aw—take a walk!"

"Say—if you give me much more of your sass I'll take and bounce a rock off'n your head."

"Oh, of *course* you will."

"Well I *will*."

"Well why don't you *do* it then? What do you keep *saying* you will for? Why don't you *do* it? It's because you're afraid."

"I *ain't* afraid."

"You are."

"I ain't."

"You are."

Another pause, and more eying and sidling around each other. Presently they were shoulder to shoulder. Tom said:

"Get away from here!"

"Go away yourself!"

"I won't."

"I won't either."

So they stood, each with a foot placed at an angle as a brace, and both shoving with might and main, and glowering at each other with hate. But neither could get an advantage. After struggling till both were hot and flushed, each relaxed his strain with watchful caution, and Tom said:

"You're a coward and a pup. I'll tell my big brother on you, and he can thrash you with his little finger, and I'll make him do it, too."

"What do I care for your big brother? I've got a brother that's bigger than he is—and what's more, he can throw him over that fence, too." [Both brothers were imaginary.]

"That's a lie."

"*Your* saying so don't make it so."

Tom drew a line in the dust with his big toe, and said:

"I dare you to step over that, and I'll lick you till you can't stand up. Anybody that'll take a dare will steal sheep."

The new boy stepped over promptly, and said:

"Now you said you'd do it, now let's see you do it."

"Don't you crowd me now; you better look out."

"Well, you *said* you'd do it—why don't you do it?"

"By jingo! for two cents I *will* do it."

The new boy took two broad coppers out of his pocket and held them out with derision. Tom struck them to the ground. In an instant both boys were rolling and tumbling in the dirt, gripped together like cats; and for the space of a minute they tugged and tore at each other's hair and clothes, punched and scratched each other's nose, and covered themselves with dust and glory. Presently the confusion took form, and through the fog of battle Tom appeared, seated astride the new boy, and pounding him with his fists. "Holler 'nuff!" said he.

The boy only struggled to free himself. He was crying—mainly from rage.

"Holler 'nuff!"—and the pounding went on.

At last the stranger got out a smothered "'Nuff!" and Tom let him up and said:

"Now that'll learn you. Better look out who you're fooling with next time."

The new boy went off brushing the dust from his clothes, sobbing, snuffling, and occasionally looking back and shaking his head and threatening what he would do to Tom the "next time he caught him out." To which Tom responded with jeers, and started off in high feather, and as soon as his back was turned the new boy snatched up a stone, threw it and hit him between the shoulders and then turned tail and ran like an antelope. Tom chased the traitor home, and thus found out where he lived. He then held a position at the gate for some time, daring the enemy to come outside, but the enemy only made faces at him through the window and declined. At last the enemy's mother appeared, and called Tom a bad, vicious, vulgar child, and ordered him away. So he went away; but he said he "lowed" to "lay" for that boy.

He got home pretty late that night, and when he climbed cautiously in at the window, he uncovered an ambuscade, in the person of his aunt; and when she saw the state his clothes were in her resolution to turn his Saturday holiday into captivity at hard labor became adamantine in its firmness.

~

Samuel Langhorne Clemens (1835–1910), known by his pen name Mark Twain, was an American journalist, humourist, lecturer and novelist popular for his works of fiction *Adventures of Huckleberry Finn*, *The Adventures of Tom Sawyer*, *The Prince and the Pauper* **and non-fiction** *Life on the Mississippi* and *Is Shakespeare Dead?*

THE LAST LEAF

O. HENRY

In a little district west of Washington Square the streets have run crazy and broken themselves into small strips called "places". These "places" make strange angles and curves. One street crosses itself a time or two. An artist once discovered a valuable possibility in this street. Suppose a collector with a bill for paints, paper and canvas should, in traversing this route, suddenly meet himself coming back, without a cent having been paid on account!

So, to quaint old Greenwich Village the art people soon came prowling, hunting for north windows and eighteenth-century gables and Dutch attics and low rents. Then they imported some pewter mugs and a chafing dish or two from Sixth avenue, and became a "colony".

At the top of a squatty, three-story brick Sue and Johnsy had their studio. "Johnsy" was familiar for Joanna. One was from Maine; the other from California. They had met at the *table d'hote* of an Eighth street "Delmonico's", and found their tastes in art, chicory salad and bishop sleeves so congenial that the joint studio resulted.

That was in May. In November a cold, unseen stranger, whom the doctors called Pneumonia, stalked about the colony, touching one here and there with his icy fingers. Over on the east side this ravager strode boldly, smiting his victims by scores, but his feet trod slowly through the maze of the narrow and moss-grown "places".

Mr Pneumonia was not what you would call a chivalric old gentleman. A mite of a little woman with blood thinned by California zephyrs was hardly fair game for the red-fisted, short-breathed old duffer. But Johnsy he smote; and she lay, scarcely moving, on her painted iron bedstead, looking through the small Dutch windowpanes at the blank side of the next brick house.

One morning the busy doctor invited Sue into the hallway with a shaggy, gray eyebrow.

"She has one chance in—let us say, ten," he said, as he shook down the mercury in his clinical thermometer. "And that chance is for her to want to live. This way people have of lining-up on the side of the undertaker makes the entire pharmacopeia look silly. Your little lady has made up her mind that she's not going to get well. Has she anything on her mind?"

"She—she wanted to paint the Bay of Naples some day," said Sue.

"Paint?—bosh! Has she anything on her mind worth thinking about twice—a man, for instance?"

"A man?" said Sue, with a jew's-harp twang in her voice. "Is a man worth—but, no, doctor; there is nothing of the kind."

"Well, it is the weakness, then," said the doctor. "I will do all that science, so far as it may filter through my efforts, can accomplish. But whenever my patient begins to count the carriages in her funeral procession I subtract 50 per cent. from the curative power of medicines. If you will get her to ask one question about the new winter styles in cloak sleeves I will promise you a one-in-five chance for her, instead of one in ten."

After the doctor had gone Sue went into the workroom and cried a Japanese napkin to a pulp. Then she swaggered into Johnsy's room with her drawing board, whistling ragtime.

Johnsy lay, scarcely making a ripple under the bedclothes, with her face toward the window. Sue stopped whistling, thinking she was asleep.

She arranged her board and began a pen-and-ink drawing to illustrate a magazine story. Young artists must pave their way to Art by drawing pictures for magazine stories that young authors write to pave their way to Literature.

As Sue was sketching a pair of elegant horseshow riding trousers and a monocle on the figure of the hero, an Idaho cowboy, she heard a low sound, several times repeated. She went quickly to the bedside.

Johnsy's eyes were open wide. She was looking out the window and counting—counting backward.

"Twelve," she said, and a little later "eleven," and then "ten," and "nine," and then "eight" and "seven," almost together.

Sue looked solicitously out the window. What was there to count? There was only a bare, dreary yard to be seen, and the blank side of the brick house twenty feet away. An old, old ivy vine, gnarled and decayed at the roots, climbed halfway up the brick wall. The cold breath of autumn had stricken its leaves from the vine until its skeleton branches clung, almost bare, to the crumbling bricks.

"What is it, dear?" asked Sue.

"Six," said Johnsy, in almost a whisper. "They're falling faster now. Three days ago there were almost a hundred. It made my head ache to count them. But now it's easy. There goes another one. There are only five left now."

"Five what, dear. Tell your Sudie."

"Leaves. On the ivy vine. When the last one falls I must go, too. I've known that for three days. Didn't the doctor tell you?"

"Oh, I never heard of such nonsense," complained Sue, with magnificent scorn. "What have old ivy leaves to do with your getting well? And you used to love that vine so, you naughty girl. Don't be a goosey. Why, the doctor told me this morning that your chances for getting well real soon were—let's see exactly what he said—he said the chances were ten to one! Why, that's almost as good a chance as we have in New York when we ride on the street cars or walk past a new building. Try to take some broth now, and let Sudie go back to her drawing, so she can sell the editor man with it, and buy port wine for her sick child, and pork chops for her greedy self."

"You needn't get any more wine," said Johnsy, keeping her eyes fixed out the window. "There goes another. No, I don't want any broth. That leaves just four. I want to see the last one fall before it gets dark. Then I'll go, too."

"Johnsy, dear," said Sue, bending over her, "will you promise me to keep your eyes closed, and not look out the window until I am done working? I must hand those drawings in by to-morrow. I need the light, or I would draw the shade down."

"Couldn't you draw in the other room?" asked Johnsy, coldly.

"I'd rather be here by you," said Sue. "Besides I don't want you to keep looking at those silly ivy leaves."

"Tell me as soon as you have finished," said Johnsy, closing her eyes, and lying white and still as a fallen statue, "because I want to see the last one fall. I'm tired of waiting. I'm tired of thinking. I want to turn loose my hold on everything, and go sailing down, down, just like one of those poor, tired leaves."

"Try to sleep," said Sue. "I must call Behrman up to be my model for the old hermit miner. I'll not be gone a minute. Don't try to move 'till I come back."

Old Behrman was a painter who lived on the ground floor beneath them. He was past sixty and had a Michael Angelo's Moses beard curling down from the head of a satyr along the body of an imp. Behrman was a failure in art. Forty years he had wielded the brush without getting near enough to touch the hem of his Mistress's robe. He had been always about to paint a masterpiece, but had never yet begun it. For several years he had painted nothing except now and then a daub in the line of commerce or advertising. He earned a little by serving as a model to those young artists in the colony who could not pay the price of a professional. He drank gin to excess, and still talked of his coming masterpiece. For the rest he was a fierce little old man, who scoffed terribly at softness in any one, and who regarded himself as especial mastiff-in-waiting to protect the two young artists in the studio above.

Sue found Behrman smelling strongly of juniper berries in his dimly lighted den below. In one corner was a blank canvas on an easel that had been waiting there for twenty-five years to receive the first line of the masterpiece. She told him of Johnsy's fancy, and how she feared she would, indeed, light and fragile as a leaf herself, float away when her slight hold upon the world grew weaker.

Old Behrman, with his red eyes, plainly streaming, shouted his contempt and derision for such idiotic imaginings.

"Vass!" he cried. "Is dere people in de world mit der foolishness to die because leafs dey drop off from a confounded vine? I haf not heard of such a thing. No, I will not bose as a model for your fool hermit-dunderhead. Vy do you allow dot silly pusiness to come in der prain of her? Ach, dot poor lettle Miss Johnsy."

"She is very ill and weak," said Sue, "and the fever has left her mind morbid and full of strange fancies. Very well, Mr Behrman, if you do not care to pose for me, you needn't. But I think you are a horrid old—old flibbertigibbet."

"You are just like a woman!" yelled Behrman. "Who said I will not bose? Go on. I come mit you. For half an hour I haf peen trying to say dot I am ready to bose. Gott! dis is not any blace in which one so goot as Miss Yohnsy shall lie sick. Some day I vill baint a masterpiece, and ve shall all go away. Gott! yes."

Johnsy was sleeping when they went upstairs. Sue pulled the shade down to the window-sill, and motioned Behrman into the other room. In there they peered out the window fearfully at the ivy vine. Then they looked at each other for a moment without speaking. A persistent, cold rain was falling, mingled with snow. Behrman, in his old blue shirt, took his seat as the hermit-miner on an upturned kettle for a rock.

When Sue awoke from an hour's sleep the next morning she found Johnsy with dull, wide-open eyes staring at the drawn green shade.

"Pull it up; I want to see," she ordered, in a whisper.

Wearily Sue obeyed.

But, lo! after the beating rain and fierce gusts of wind that had endured through the livelong night, there yet stood out against the brick wall one ivy leaf. It was the last on the vine. Still dark green near its stem, but with its serrated edges tinted with the yellow of dissolution and decay, it hung bravely from a branch some twenty feet above the ground.

"It is the last one," said Johnsy. "I thought it would surely fall during the night. I heard the wind. It will fall to-day, and I shall die at the same time."

"Dear, dear!" said Sue, leaning her worn face down to the pillow, "think of me, if you won't think of yourself. What would I do?"

But Johnsy did not answer. The lonesomest thing in all the world is a soul when it is making ready to go on its mysterious, far journey. The fancy seemed to possess her more strongly as one by one the ties that bound her to friendship and to earth were loosed.

The day wore away, and even through the twilight they could see the lone ivy leaf clinging to its stem against the wall. And then, with the coming of the night the north wind was again loosed, while the rain still beat against the windows and pattered down from the low Dutch eaves.

When it was light enough Johnsy, the merciless, commanded that the shade be raised.

The ivy leaf was still there.

Johnsy lay for a long time looking at it. And then she called to Sue, who was stirring her chicken broth over the gas stove.

"I've been a bad girl, Sudie," said Johnsy. "Something has made that last leaf stay there to show me how wicked I was. It is a sin to want to die. You may bring me a little broth now, and some milk with a little port in it, and—no; bring me a hand-mirror first, and then pack some pillows about me, and I will sit up and watch you cook."

An hour later she said.

"Sudie, some day I hope to paint the Bay of Naples."

The doctor came in the afternoon, and Sue had an excuse to go into the hallway as he left.

"Even chances," said the doctor, taking Sue's thin, shaking hand in his. "With good nursing you'll win. And now I must see another case I have downstairs. Behrman, his name is—some kind of an artist, I believe. Pneumonia, too. He is an old, weak man, and the attack is acute. There is no hope for him; but he goes to the hospital to-day to be made more comfortable."

The next day the doctor said to Sue: "She's out of danger. You've won. Nutrition and care now—that's all."

And that afternoon Sue came to the bed where Johnsy lay, contentedly knitting a very blue and very useless woolen shoulder scarf, and put one arm around her, pillows and all.

"I have something to tell you, white mouse," she said. "Mr Behrman died of pneumonia to-day in the hospital. He was ill only two days. The janitor found him on the morning of the first day in his room downstairs helpless with pain. His shoes and clothing were wet through and icy cold. They couldn't imagine where he had been on such a dreadful night. And then they found a lantern, still lighted, and a ladder that had been dragged from its place, and some scattered brushes, and a palette with green and yellow colors mixed on it, and—look out the window, dear, at the last ivy leaf on the wall. Didn't you wonder why it never fluttered or moved when the wind blew? Ah, darling, it's Behrman's masterpiece—he painted it there the night that the last leaf fell."

~

O. Henry (1862–1910) was an American writer famous for his short stories. His real name was William Sydney Porter. His best-known works include "The Gift of the Magi" and "The Ransom of Red Chief". His stories are known for their surprising, often humorous endings. The O. Henry Prize, named in his honour, is an annual prize given to short story writers to this day.

The Postmaster

Rabindranath Tagore

The postmaster first took up his duties in the village of Ulapur. Though the village was a small one, there was an indigo factory near by, and the proprietor, an Englishman, had managed to get a post office established.

Our postmaster belonged to Calcutta. He felt like a fish out of water in this remote village. His office and living-room were in a dark thatched shed, not far from a green, slimy pond, surrounded on all sides by a dense growth.

The men employed in the indigo factory had no leisure; moreover, they were hardly desirable companions for decent folk. Nor is a Calcutta boy an adept in the art of associating with others. Among strangers he appears either proud or ill at ease. At any rate, the postmaster had but little company; nor had he much to do.

At times he tried his hand at writing a verse or two. That the movement of the leaves and the clouds of the sky were enough to fill life with joy—such were the sentiments to which he sought to give expression. But God knows that the poor fellow would have felt it as the gift of a new life, if some genie of the Arabian Nights had in one night swept away the trees, leaves and all, and replaced them with a macadamised road, hiding the clouds from view with rows of tall houses.

The postmaster's salary was small. He had to cook his own meals, which he used to share with Ratan, an orphan girl of the village, who did odd jobs for him.

When in the evening the smoke began to curl up from the village cowsheds, and the cicalas chirped in every bush; when the mendicants of the Baül sect sang their shrill songs in their daily meeting-place, when any poet, who had attempted to watch the movement of the leaves in the dense bamboo thickets, would have felt a ghostly shiver run down his back, the postmaster would light his little lamp, and call out "Ratan."

Ratan would sit outside waiting for this call, and, instead of coming in at once, would reply, "Did you call me, sir?"

"What are you doing?" the postmaster would ask.

"I must be going to light the kitchen fire," would be the answer.

And the postmaster would say: "Oh, let the kitchen fire be for awhile; light me my pipe first."

At last Ratan would enter, with puffed-out cheeks, vigorously blowing into a flame a live coal to light the tobacco. This would give the postmaster an opportunity of conversing. "Well, Ratan," perhaps he would begin, "do you remember anything of your mother?" That was a fertile subject. Ratan partly remembered, and partly didn't. Her father had been fonder of her than her mother; him she recollected more vividly. He used to come home in the evening after his work, and one or two evenings stood out more clearly than others, like pictures in her memory. Ratan would sit on the floor near the postmaster's feet, as memories crowded in upon her. She called to mind a little brother that she had—and how on some bygone cloudy day she had played at fishing with him on the edge of the pond, with a twig for a make-believe fishing-rod. Such little incidents would drive out greater events from her mind. Thus, as they talked, it would often get very late, and the postmaster would feel too lazy to do any cooking at all. Ratan would then hastily light the fire, and toast some unleavened bread, which, with the cold remnants of the morning meal, was enough for their supper.

On some evenings, seated at his desk in the corner of the big empty shed, the postmaster too would call up memories of his own home, of his mother and his sister, of those for whom in his exile his heart was sad,—memories which were always haunting him, but which he could not talk about with the men of the factory, though he found himself naturally recalling them aloud in the presence of the simple little girl. And so it came about that the girl would allude to his people as mother, brother, and sister, as if she had known them all her life. In fact, she had a complete picture of each one of them painted in her little heart.

One noon, during a break in the rains, there was a cool soft breeze blowing; the smell of the damp grass and leaves in the hot sun felt like the warm breathing of the tired earth on one's body. A persistent bird went on all the afternoon repeating the burden of its one complaint in Nature's audience chamber.

The postmaster had nothing to do. The shimmer of the freshly washed leaves, and the banked-up remnants of the retreating rain-clouds were sights to see; and the postmaster was watching them and thinking to himself: "Oh, if only some kindred soul were near—just one loving human being whom I could hold near my heart!" This was exactly, he went on to think, what that bird was trying to say, and it was the same feeling which the murmuring leaves were striving to express. But no one knows, or would believe, that such an idea might also take possession of an ill-paid village postmaster in the deep, silent mid-day interval of his work.

The postmaster sighed, and called out "Ratan." Ratan was then sprawling beneath the guava-tree, busily engaged in eating unripe guavas. At the voice of her master, she ran up breathlessly, saying: "Were you calling me, Dada?" "I was thinking," said the postmaster, "of teaching you to read." And then for the rest of the afternoon he taught her the alphabet.

Thus, in a very short time, Ratan had got as far as the double consonants.

It seemed as though the showers of the season would never end. Canals, ditches, and hollows were all overflowing with water. Day and night the patter of rain was heard, and the croaking of frogs. The village roads became impassable, and marketing had to be done in punts.

One heavily clouded morning, the postmaster's little pupil had been long waiting outside the door for her call, but, not hearing it as usual, she took up her dog-eared book, and slowly entered the room. She found her master stretched out on his bed, and, thinking that he was resting, she was about to retire on tip-toe, when she suddenly heard her name—"Ratan!" She turned at once and asked: "Were you sleeping, Dada?" The postmaster in a plaintive voice said: "I am not well. Feel my head; is it very hot?"

In the loneliness of his exile, and in the gloom of the rains, his ailing body needed a little tender nursing. He longed to remember the touch on the forehead of soft hands with tinkling bracelets, to imagine the presence of loving womanhood, the nearness of mother and sister. And the exile was not disappointed. Ratan ceased to be a little girl. She at once stepped into the post of mother, called in the village doctor, gave the patient his pills at the proper intervals, sat up all night by his pillow, cooked his gruel for him, and every now and then asked: "Are you feeling a little better, Dada?"

It was some time before the postmaster, with weakened body, was able to leave his sick-bed. "No more of this," said he with decision. "I must get a transfer." He at once wrote off to Calcutta an application for a transfer, on the ground of the unhealthiness of the place.

Relieved from her duties as nurse, Ratan again took up her old place outside the door. But she no longer heard the same old call. She would sometimes peep inside furtively to find the postmaster sitting on his chair, or stretched on his bed, and staring absent-mindedly into the air. While Ratan was awaiting her call, the postmaster was awaiting a reply to his application. The girl read her old lessons over and over again,—her great fear was lest, when the call came, she might be found wanting in the double consonants. At last, after a week, the call did come one evening. With an overflowing heart Ratan rushed into the room with her—"Were you calling me, Dada?"

The postmaster said: "I am going away to-morrow, Ratan."

"Where are you going, Dada?"

"I am going home."

"When will you come back?"

"I am not coming back."

Ratan asked no other question. The postmaster, of his own accord, went on to tell her that his application for a transfer had been rejected, so he had resigned his post and was going home.

For a long time neither of them spoke another word. The lamp went on dimly burning, and from a leak in one corner of the thatch water dripped steadily into an earthen vessel on the floor beneath it.

After a while Ratan rose, and went off to the kitchen to prepare the meal; but she was not so quick about it as on other days. Many new things to think of had entered her little brain. When the postmaster had finished his supper, the girl suddenly asked him: "Dada, will you take me to your home?"

The postmaster laughed. "What an idea!" said he; but he did not think it necessary to explain to the girl wherein lay the absurdity.

That whole night, in her waking and in her dreams, the postmaster's laughing reply haunted her—"What an idea!"

On getting up in the morning, the postmaster found his bath ready. He had stuck to his Calcutta habit of bathing in water drawn and kept in pitchers, instead of taking a plunge in the river as was the custom of the village. For some reason or other, the girl could not ask him about the time of his departure, so she had fetched the water from the river long before sunrise, that it should be ready as early as he might want it. After the bath came a call for Ratan. She entered noiselessly, and looked silently into her master's face for orders. The master said: "You need not be anxious about my going away, Ratan; I shall tell my successor to look after you." These words were kindly meant, no doubt: but inscrutable are the ways of a woman's heart!

Ratan had borne many a scolding from her master without complaint, but these kind words she could not bear. She burst out weeping, and said: "No, no, you need not tell anybody anything at all about me; I don't want to stay on here."

The postmaster was dumbfounded. He had never seen Ratan like this before.

The new incumbent duly arrived, and the postmaster, having given over charge, prepared to depart. Just before starting he called Ratan and said: "Here is something for you; I hope it will keep you for some little time." He brought out from his pocket the whole of his month's salary, retaining only a trifle for his travelling expenses. Then Ratan fell at his feet and cried: "Oh, Dada, I pray you, don't give me anything, don't in any way trouble about me," and then she ran away out of sight.

The postmaster heaved a sigh, took up his carpet bag, put his umbrella over his shoulder, and, accompanied by a man carrying his many-coloured tin trunk, he slowly made for the boat.

When he got in and the boat was under way, and the rain-swollen river, like a stream of tears welling up from the earth, swirled and sobbed at her bows, then he felt a pain at heart; the grief-stricken face of a village girl seemed to represent for him the great unspoken pervading grief of Mother Earth herself. At one time he had an impulse to go back, and bring away along with him that lonesome waif, forsaken of the world. But the wind had just filled the sails, the boat had got well into the middle of the turbulent current, and already the village was left behind, and its outlying burning-ground came in sight.

So the traveller, borne on the breast of the swift-flowing river, consoled himself with philosophical reflections on the numberless meetings and partings going on in the world—on death, the great parting, from which none returns.

But Ratan had no philosophy. She was wandering about the post office in a flood of tears. It may be that she had still a lurking hope in some corner of her heart that her Dada would return, and that is why she could not tear herself away. Alas for our foolish human nature! Its fond mistakes are persistent. The dictates of reason take a long time to assert their own sway. The surest proofs meanwhile are disbelieved. False hope is clung to with all one's might and main, till a day comes when it has sucked the heart dry and it forcibly breaks through its bonds and departs. After that comes the misery of awakening, and then once again the longing to get back into the maze of the same mistakes.

~

Rabindranath Tagore (1861–1941) was the first non-European to win the Nobel Prize in Literature. A poet, writer and preeminent thinker, he composed the Indian national anthem. Some of his best-known works are short stories like "The Runaway" and *Gitanjali*, his award-winning poetry collection. There are museums across India that celebrate his life and work, and universities have been named in his honour.

From Treasure Island

Robert Louis Stevenson

I Go to Bristol

It was longer than the squire imagined ere we were ready for the sea, and none of our first plans—not even Dr Livesey's, of keeping me beside him—could be carried out as we intended. The doctor had to go to London for a physician to take charge of his practice; the squire was hard at work at Bristol; and I lived on at the hall under the charge of old Redruth, the gamekeeper, almost a prisoner, but full of sea-dreams and the most charming anticipations of strange islands and adventures. I brooded by the hour together over the map, all the details of which I well remembered. Sitting by the fire in the housekeeper's room, I approached that island in my fancy from every possible direction; I explored every acre of its surface; I climbed a thousand times to that tall hill they call the Spy-glass, and from the top enjoyed the most wonderful and changing prospects. Sometimes the isle was thick with savages, with whom we fought, sometimes full of dangerous animals that hunted us, but in all my fancies nothing occurred to me so strange and tragic as our actual adventures.

So the weeks passed on, till one fine day there came a letter addressed to Dr Livesey, with this addition, "To be opened, in the case of his absence, by Tom Redruth or young Hawkins." Obeying this order, we found, or rather I found—for the gamekeeper was a poor hand at reading anything but print—the following important news:

Old Anchor Inn, Bristol, March 1, 17—

Dear Livesey—As I do not know whether you are at the hall or still in London, I send this in double to both places.

The ship is bought and fitted. She lies at anchor, ready for sea. You never imagined a sweeter schooner—a child might sail her—two hundred tons; name, *Hispaniola.*

I got her through my old friend, Blandly, who has proved himself throughout the most surprising trump. The admirable fellow literally slaved in my interest, and so, I may say, did everyone in Bristol, as soon as they got wind of the port we sailed for—treasure, I mean.

"Redruth," said I, interrupting the letter, "Dr Livesey will not like that. The squire has been talking, after all."

"Well, who's a better right?" growled the gamekeeper. "A pretty rum go if squire ain't to talk for Dr Livesey, I should think."

At that I gave up all attempts at commentary and read straight on:

Blandly himself found the *Hispaniola*, and by the most admirable management got her for the merest trifle. There is a class of men in Bristol monstrously prejudiced against Blandly. They go the length of declaring that this honest creature would do anything for money, that the *Hispaniola* belonged to him, and that he sold it me absurdly high—the most transparent calumnies. None of them dare, however, to deny the merits of the ship.

So far there was not a hitch. The workpeople, to be sure—riggers and what not—were most annoyingly slow; but time cured that. It was the crew that troubled me.

I wished a round score of men—in case of natives, buccaneers, or the odious French—and I had the worry of the deuce itself to find so much as half a dozen, till the most remarkable stroke of fortune brought me the very man that I required.

I was standing on the dock, when, by the merest accident, I fell in talk with him. I found he was an old sailor, kept a public-house, knew all the seafaring men in Bristol, had lost his health ashore, and wanted a good berth as cook to get to sea again. He had hobbled down there that morning, he said, to get a smell of the salt.

I was monstrously touched—so would you have been—and, out of pure pity, I engaged him on the spot to be ship's cook. Long John Silver, he is called, and has lost a leg; but that I regarded as a recommendation, since he lost it in his country's service, under the immortal Hawke. He has no pension, Livesey. Imagine the abominable age we live in!

Well, sir, I thought I had only found a cook, but it was a crew I had discovered. Between Silver and myself we got together in a few days a company of the toughest old salts imaginable—not pretty to look at, but fellows, by their faces, of the most indomitable spirit. I declare we could fight a frigate.

Long John even got rid of two out of the six or seven I had already engaged. He showed me in a moment that they were just the sort of fresh-water swabs we had to fear in an adventure of importance.

I am in the most magnificent health and spirits, eating like a bull, sleeping like a tree, yet I shall not enjoy a moment till

I hear my old tarpaulins tramping round the capstan. Seaward, ho! Hang the treasure! It's the glory of the sea that has turned my head. So now, Livesey, come post; do not lose an hour, if you respect me.

Let young Hawkins go at once to see his mother, with Redruth for a guard; and then both come full speed to Bristol.

John Trelawney

Postscript—I did not tell you that Blandly, who, by the way, is to send a consort after us if we don't turn up by the end of August, had found an admirable fellow for sailing master—a stiff man, which I regret, but in all other respects a treasure. Long John Silver unearthed a very competent man for a mate, a man named Arrow. I have a boatswain who pipes, Livesey; so things shall go man-o'-war fashion on board the good ship *Hispaniola.*

I forgot to tell you that Silver is a man of substance; I know of my own knowledge that he has a banker's account, which has never been overdrawn. He leaves his wife to manage the inn; and as she is a woman of colour, a pair of old bachelors like you and I may be excused for guessing that it is the wife, quite as much as the health, that sends him back to roving.

J. T.

P.P.S.—Hawkins may stay one night with his mother.

J. T.

You can fancy the excitement into which that letter put me. I was half beside myself with glee; and if ever I despised a man, it was old Tom Redruth, who could do nothing but grumble and lament. Any of the under-gamekeepers would gladly have changed places with him; but such was not the squire's pleasure, and the squire's pleasure was like law among them all. Nobody but old Redruth would have dared so much as even to grumble.

The next morning he and I set out on foot for the Admiral Benbow, and there I found my mother in good health and spirits. The captain, who had so long been a cause of so much discomfort, was gone where the wicked cease from troubling. The squire had had everything repaired, and the public rooms and the sign repainted, and had added some furniture—above all a beautiful armchair for mother in the bar. He had found her a boy as an apprentice also so that she should not want help while I was gone.

It was on seeing that boy that I understood, for the first time, my situation. I had thought up to that moment of the adventures before me, not at all of the home that I was leaving; and now, at sight of this clumsy stranger, who was to stay here in my place beside my mother, I had my first attack of tears. I am afraid I led that boy a dog's life, for as he was new to the work, I had a hundred opportunities of setting him right and putting him down, and I was not slow to profit by them.

The night passed, and the next day, after dinner, Redruth and I were afoot again and on the road. I said good-bye to Mother and the cove where I had lived since I was born, and the dear old Admiral Benbow—since he was repainted, no longer quite so dear. One of my last thoughts was of the captain, who had so often strode along the beach with his cocked hat, his sabre-cut cheek, and his old brass telescope. Next moment we had turned the corner and my home was out of sight.

The mail picked us up about dusk at the Royal George on the heath. I was wedged in between Redruth and a stout old gentleman, and in spite of the swift motion and the cold night air, I must have dozed a great deal from the very first, and then slept like a log up hill and down dale through stage after stage, for when I was awakened at last it was by a punch in the ribs, and I opened my eyes to find that we were standing still before a large building in a city street and that the day had already broken a long time.

"Where are we?" I asked.

"Bristol," said Tom. "Get down."

Mr Trelawney had taken up his residence at an inn far down the docks to superintend the work upon the schooner. Thither we had now to walk, and our way, to my great delight, lay along the quays and beside the great multitude of ships of all sizes and rigs and nations. In one, sailors were singing at their work, in another there were men aloft, high over my head, hanging to threads that seemed no thicker than a spider's. Though I had lived by the shore all my life, I seemed never to have been near the sea till then. The smell of tar and salt was something new. I saw the most wonderful figureheads, that had all been far over the ocean. I saw, besides, many old sailors, with rings in their ears, and whiskers curled in ringlets, and tarry pigtails, and their swaggering, clumsy sea-walk; and if I had seen as many kings or archbishops I could not have been more delighted.

And I was going to sea myself, to sea in a schooner, with a piping boatswain and pig-tailed singing seamen, to sea, bound for an unknown island, and to seek for buried treasure!

While I was still in this delightful dream, we came suddenly in front of a large inn and met Squire Trelawney, all dressed out like a sea-officer, in stout blue cloth, coming out of the door with a smile on his face and a capital imitation of a sailor's walk.

"Here you are," he cried, "and the doctor came last night from London. Bravo! The ship's company complete!"

"Oh, sir," cried I, "when do we sail?"

"Sail!" says he. "We sail tomorrow!"

At the Sign of the Spy-glass

When I had done breakfasting the squire gave me a note addressed to John Silver, at the sign of the Spy-glass, and told me I should easily find the place by following the line of the docks and keeping a bright lookout for a little tavern with a large brass telescope for sign. I set off, overjoyed at this opportunity to see some more of the ships and seamen, and picked my way among a great crowd of people and carts and bales, for the dock was now at its busiest, until I found the tavern in question.

It was a bright enough little place of entertainment. The sign was newly painted; the windows had neat red curtains; the floor was cleanly sanded. There was a street on each side and an open door on both, which made the large, low room pretty clear to see in, in spite of clouds of tobacco smoke.

The customers were mostly seafaring men, and they talked so loudly that I hung at the door, almost afraid to enter.

As I was waiting, a man came out of a side room, and at a glance I was sure he must be Long John. His left leg was cut off close by the hip, and under the left shoulder he carried a crutch, which he managed with wonderful dexterity, hopping about upon it like a bird. He was very tall and strong, with a face as big as a ham—plain and pale, but intelligent and smiling. Indeed, he seemed in the most cheerful spirits, whistling as he moved about among the tables, with a merry word or a slap on the shoulder for the more favoured of his guests.

Now, to tell you the truth, from the very first mention of Long John in Squire Trelawney's letter I had taken a fear in my mind that he might prove to be the very one-legged sailor whom I had watched for so long at the old Benbow. But one look at the man before me was enough. I had seen the captain, and Black Dog, and the blind man, Pew, and I thought I knew what a buccaneer was like—a very different creature, according to me, from this clean and pleasant-tempered landlord.

I plucked up courage at once, crossed the threshold, and walked right up to the man where he stood, propped on his crutch, talking to a customer.

"Mr Silver, sir?" I asked, holding out the note.

"Yes, my lad," said he; "such is my name, to be sure. And who may you be?" And then as he saw the squire's letter, he seemed to me to give something almost like a start.

"Oh!" said he, quite loud, and offering his hand. "I see. You are our new cabin-boy; pleased I am to see you."

And he took my hand in his large firm grasp.

Just then one of the customers at the far side rose suddenly and made for the door. It was close by him, and he was out in the street in a moment. But his hurry had attracted my notice, and I recognized him at glance. It was the tallow-faced man, wanting two fingers, who had come first to the Admiral Benbow.

"Oh," I cried, "stop him! It's Black Dog!"

"I don't care two coppers who he is," cried Silver. "But he hasn't paid his score. Harry, run and catch him."

One of the others who was nearest the door leaped up and started in pursuit.

"If he were Admiral Hawke he shall pay his score," cried Silver; and then, relinquishing my hand, "Who did you say he was?" he asked. "Black what?"

"Dog, sir," said I. "Has Mr Trelawney not told you of the buccaneers? He was one of them."

"So?" cried Silver. "In my house! Ben, run and help Harry. One of those swabs, was he? Was that you drinking with him, Morgan? Step up here."

The man whom he called Morgan—an old, grey-haired, mahogany-faced sailor—came forward pretty sheepishly, rolling his quid.

"Now, Morgan," said Long John very sternly, "you never clapped your eyes on that Black—Black Dog before, did you, now?"

"Not I, sir," said Morgan with a salute.

"You didn't know his name, did you?"

"No, sir."

"By the powers, Tom Morgan, it's as good for you!" exclaimed the landlord. "If you had been mixed up with the like of that, you would never have put another foot in my house, you may lay to that. And what was he saying to you?"

"I don't rightly know, sir," answered Morgan.

"Do you call that a head on your shoulders, or a blessed dead-eye?" cried Long John. "Don't rightly know, don't you! Perhaps you don't happen to rightly know who you was speaking to, perhaps? Come, now, what was he jawing—v'yages, cap'ns, ships? Pipe up! What was it?"

"We was a-talkin' of keel-hauling," answered Morgan.

"Keel-hauling, was you? And a mighty suitable thing, too, and you may lay to that. Get back to your place for a lubber, Tom."

And then, as Morgan rolled back to his seat, Silver added to me in a confidential whisper that was very flattering, as I thought, "He's quite an honest man, Tom Morgan, on'y stupid. And now," he ran on again, aloud, "let's see—Black Dog? No, I don't know the name, not I. Yet I kind of think I've—yes, I've seen the swab. He used to come here with a blind beggar, he used."

"That he did, you may be sure," said I. "I knew that blind man too. His name was Pew."

"It was!" cried Silver, now quite excited. "Pew! That were his name for certain. Ah, he looked a shark, he did! If we run down this Black Dog, now, there'll be news for Cap'n Trelawney! Ben's a good runner; few seamen run better than Ben. He should run him down, hand over hand, by the powers! He talked o' keel-hauling, did he? *I'll* keel-haul him!"

All the time he was jerking out these phrases he was stumping up and down the tavern on his crutch, slapping tables with his hand, and giving such a show of excitement as would have convinced an Old Bailey judge or a Bow Street runner. My suspicions had been thoroughly reawakened on finding Black Dog at the Spy-glass, and I watched the cook narrowly. But he was too deep, and too ready, and too clever for me, and by the time the two men had come back out of breath and confessed that they had lost the track in a crowd, and been scolded like thieves, I would have gone bail for the innocence of Long John Silver.

"See here, now, Hawkins," said he, "here's a blessed hard thing on a man like me, now, ain't it? There's Cap'n Trelawney—what's he to think? Here I have this confounded son of a Dutchman sitting in my own house drinking of my own rum! Here you comes and tells me of it plain; and here I let him give us all the slip before my blessed deadlights! Now, Hawkins, you do me justice with the cap'n. You're a lad, you are, but you're as smart as paint. I see that when you first come in. Now, here it is: What could I do, with this old timber I hobble on? When I was an A B master mariner I'd have come up alongside of him, hand over hand, and broached him to in a brace of old shakes, I would; but now—"

And then, all of a sudden, he stopped, and his jaw dropped as though he had remembered something.

"The score!" he burst out. "Three goes o' rum! Why, shiver my timbers, if I hadn't forgotten my score!"

And falling on a bench, he laughed until the tears ran down his cheeks. I could not help joining, and we laughed together, peal after peal, until the tavern rang again.

"Why, what a precious old sea-calf I am!" he said at last, wiping his cheeks. "You and me should get on well, Hawkins, for I'll take my davy I should be rated ship's boy. But come now, stand by to go about. This won't do. Dooty is dooty, messmates. I'll put on my old cockerel hat, and step along of you to Cap'n Trelawney, and report this here affair. For mind you, it's serious, young Hawkins; and neither you nor me's come out of it with what I should make so bold as to call credit. Nor you neither, says you; not smart—none of the pair of us smart. But dash my buttons! That was a good un about my score."

And he began to laugh again, and that so heartily, that though I did not see the joke as he did, I was again obliged to join him in his mirth.

On our little walk along the quays, he made himself the most interesting companion, telling me about the different ships that we passed by, their rig, tonnage, and nationality, explaining the work that was going forward—how one was discharging, another taking in cargo, and a third making ready for sea—and every now and then telling me some little anecdote of ships or seamen or repeating a nautical phrase till I had learned it perfectly. I began to see that here was one of the best of possible shipmates.

When we got to the inn, the squire and Dr Livesey were seated together, finishing a quart of ale with a toast in it, before they should go aboard the schooner on a visit of inspection.

Long John told the story from first to last, with a great deal of spirit and the most perfect truth. "That was how it were, now, weren't it, Hawkins?" he would say, now and again, and I could always bear him entirely out.

The two gentlemen regretted that Black Dog had got away, but we all agreed there was nothing to be done, and after he had been complimented, Long John took up his crutch and departed.

"All hands aboard by four this afternoon," shouted the squire after him.

"Aye, aye, sir," cried the cook, in the passage.

"Well, squire," said Dr Livesey, "I don't put much faith in your discoveries, as a general thing; but I will say this, John Silver suits me."

"The man's a perfect trump," declared the squire.

"And now," added the doctor, "Jim may come on board with us, may he not?"

"To be sure he may," says squire. "Take your hat, Hawkins, and we'll see the ship."

~

Robert Louis Stevenson (1850–1894) was a Scottish novelist, poet, essayist, and travel writer. His best-known books include *Treasure Island, Kidnapped, The Master of Ballantrae* and *Dr Jekyll and Mr Hyde*.

The Elephant's Child

Rudyard Kipling

In the High and Far-Off Times the Elephant, O Best Beloved, had no trunk. He had only a blackish, bulgy nose, as big as a boot, that he could wriggle about from side to side; but he couldn't pick up things with it. But there was one Elephant—a new Elephant—an Elephant's Child—who was full of 'satiable curtiosity, and that means he asked ever so many questions. *And* he lived in Africa, and he filled all Africa with his 'satiable curtiosities. He asked his tall aunt, the Ostrich, why her tail-feathers grew just so, and his tall aunt the Ostrich spanked him with her hard, hard claw. He asked his tall uncle, the Giraffe, what made his skin spotty, and his tall uncle, the Giraffe, spanked him with his hard, hard hoof. And still he was full of 'satiable curtiosity! He asked his broad aunt, the Hippopotamus, why her eyes were red, and his broad aunt, the Hippopotamus, spanked him with her broad, broad hoof; and he asked his hairy uncle, the Baboon, why melons tasted just so, and his hairy uncle, the Baboon, spanked him with his hairy, hairy paw. And *still* he was full of 'satiable curtiosity! He asked questions about everything that he saw, or heard, or felt, or smelt, or touched, and all his uncles and his aunts spanked him. And still he was full of 'satiable curtiosity!

One fine morning in the middle of the Precession of the Equinoxes this 'satiable Elephant's Child asked a new fine question that he had never asked before. He asked, "What does the Crocodile have for dinner?" Then everybody said, "Hush!" in a loud and dretful tone, and they spanked him immediately and directly, without stopping, for a long time.

By and by, when that was finished, he came upon Kolokolo Bird sitting in the middle of a wait-a-bit thorn-bush, and he said, "My father has spanked me, and my mother has spanked me; all my aunts and uncles have spanked me for my 'satiable curtiosity; and *still* I want to know what the Crocodile has for dinner!"

Then Kolokolo Bird said, with a mournful cry, "Go to the banks of the great grey-green, greasy Limpopo River, all set about with fever-trees, and find out."

That very next morning, when there was nothing left of the Equinoxes, because the Precession had preceded according to precedent, this 'satiable Elephant's Child took a hundred pounds of bananas (the little short red kind), and a hundred pounds of sugar-cane (the long purple kind), and seventeen melons (the greeny-crackly kind), and said to all his dear families, "Good-bye. I am going to the great grey-green, greasy Limpopo River, all set about with fever-trees, to find out what the Crocodile has for dinner." And they all spanked him once more for luck, though he asked them most politely to stop.

Then he went away, a little warm, but not at all astonished, eating melons, and throwing the rind about, because he could not pick it up.

He went from Graham's Town to Kimberley, and from Kimberley to Khama's Country, and from Khama's Country he went east by north, eating melons all the time, till at last he came to the banks of the great grey-green, greasy Limpopo River, all set about with fever-trees, precisely as Kolokolo Bird had said.

Now you must know and understand, O Best Beloved, that till that very week, and day, and hour, and minute, this 'satiable Elephant's Child had never seen a Crocodile, and did not know what one was like. It was all his 'satiable curtiosity.

The first thing that he found was a Bi-Coloured-Python-Rock-Snake curled round a rock.

"'Scuse me," said the Elephant's Child most politely, "but have you seen such a thing as a Crocodile in these promiscuous parts?"

"*Have* I seen a Crocodile?" said the Bi-Coloured-Python-Rock-Snake, in a voice of dretful scorn. "What will you ask me next?"

"'Scuse me," said the Elephant's Child, "but could you kindly tell me what he has for dinner?"

Then the Bi-Coloured-Python-Rock-Snake uncoiled himself very quickly from the rock, and spanked the Elephant's Child with his scalesome, flailsome tail.

"That is odd," said the Elephant's Child, "because my father and my mother, and my uncle and my aunt, not to mention my other aunt, the Hippopotamus, and my other uncle, the Baboon, have all spanked me for my 'satiable curtiosity—and I suppose this is the same thing."

So he said good-bye very politely to the Bi-Coloured-Python-Rock-Snake, and helped to coil him up on the rock again, and went on, a little warm, but not at all astonished, eating melons, and throwing the rind about, because he could not pick it up, till he trod on what he thought was a log of wood at the very edge of the great grey-green, greasy Limpopo River, all set about with fever-trees.

But it was really the Crocodile, O Best Beloved, and the Crocodile winked one eye—like this!

"'Scuse me," said the Elephant's Child most politely, "but do you happen to have seen a Crocodile in these promiscuous parts?"

Then the Crocodile winked the other eye, and lifted half his tail out of the mud; and the Elephant's Child stepped back most politely, because he did not wish to be spanked again.

"Come hither, Little One," said the Crocodile. "Why do you ask such things?"

"'Scuse me," said the Elephant's Child most politely, "but my father has spanked me, my mother has spanked me, not to mention my tall aunt, the Ostrich, and my tall uncle, the Giraffe, who can kick ever so hard, as well as my broad aunt, the Hippopotamus, and my hairy uncle, the Baboon, *and* including the Bi-Coloured-Python-Rock-Snake, with the scalesome, flailsome tail, just up the bank, who spanks harder than any of them; and *so*, if it's quite all the same to you, I don't want to be spanked any more."

"Come hither, Little One," said the Crocodile, "for I am the Crocodile," and he wept crocodile-tears to show it was quite true.

Then the Elephant's Child grew all breathless, and panted, and kneeled down on the bank and said, "You are the very person I have been looking for all these long days. Will you please tell me what you have for dinner?"

"Come hither, Little One," said the Crocodile, "and I'll whisper."

Then the Elephant's Child put his head down close to the Crocodile's musky, tusky mouth, and the Crocodile caught him by his little nose, which up to that very week, day, hour, and minute, had been no bigger than a boot, though much more useful.

"I think," said the Crocodile—and he said it between his teeth, like this—"I think to-day I will begin with Elephant's Child!"

At this, O Best Beloved, the Elephant's Child was much annoyed, and he said, speaking through his nose, like this, "Led go! You are hurtig be!"

Then the Bi-Coloured-Python-Rock-Snake scuffled down from the bank and said, "My young friend, if you do not now, immediately and instantly, pull as hard as ever you can, it is my opinion that your acquaintance in the large-pattern leather ulster" (and by this he meant the Crocodile) "will jerk you into yonder limpid stream before you can say Jack Robinson."

This is the way Bi-Coloured-Python-Rock-Snakes always talk.

Then the Elephant's Child sat back on his little haunches, and pulled, and pulled, and pulled, and his nose began to stretch. And the Crocodile floundered into the water, making it all creamy with great sweeps of his tail, and *he* pulled, and pulled, and pulled.

And the Elephant's Child's nose kept on stretching; and the Elephant's Child spread all his little four legs and pulled, and pulled, and pulled, and his nose kept on stretching; and the Crocodile threshed his tail like an oar, and *he* pulled, and pulled, and pulled, and at each pull the Elephant's Child's nose grew longer and longer—and it hurt him hijjus!

Then the Elephant's Child felt his legs slipping, and he said through his nose, which was now nearly five feet long, "This is too butch for be!"

Then the Bi-Coloured-Python-Rock-Snake came down from the bank, and knotted himself in a double-clove-hitch round the Elephant's Child's hind legs, and said, "Rash and inexperienced traveller, we will now seriously devote ourselves to a little high tension, because if we do not, it is my impression that yonder self-propelling man-of-war with the armour-plated upper deck" (and by this, O Best Beloved, he meant the Crocodile), "will permanently vitiate your future career."

That is the way all Bi-Coloured-Python-Rock-Snakes always talk.

So he pulled, and the Elephant's Child pulled, and the Crocodile pulled; but the Elephant's Child and the Bi-Coloured-Python-Rock-Snake pulled hardest; and at last the Crocodile let go of the Elephant's Child's nose with a plop that you could hear all up and down the Limpopo.

Then the Elephant's Child sat down most hard and sudden; but first he was careful to say "Thank you" to the Bi-Coloured-Python-Rock-Snake; and next he was kind to his poor pulled nose, and wrapped it all up in cool banana leaves, and hung it in the great grey-green, greasy Limpopo to cool.

"What are you doing that for?" said the Bi-Coloured-Python-Rock-Snake.

"'Scuse me," said the Elephant's Child, "but my nose is badly out of shape, and I am waiting for it to shrink."

"Then you will have to wait a long time," said the Bi-Coloured-Python-Rock-Snake. "Some people do not know what is good for them."

The Elephant's Child sat there for three days waiting for his nose to shrink. But it never grew any shorter, and, besides, it made him squint. For, O Best Beloved, you will see and understand that the Crocodile had pulled it out into a really truly trunk same as all Elephants have to-day.

At the end of the third day a fly came and stung him on the shoulder, and before he knew what he was doing he lifted up his trunk and hit that fly dead with the end of it.

"'Vantage number one!" said the Bi-Coloured-Python-Rock-Snake. "You couldn't have done that with a mere-smear nose. Try and eat a little now."

Before he thought what he was doing the Elephant's Child put out his trunk and plucked a large bundle of grass, dusted it clean against his fore-legs, and stuffed it into his own mouth.

"'Vantage number two!" said the Bi-Coloured-Python-Rock-Snake. "You couldn't have done that with a mear-smear nose. Don't you think the sun is very hot here?"

"It is," said the Elephant's Child, and before he thought what he was doing he schlooped up a schloop of mud from the banks of the great grey-green, greasy Limpopo, and slapped it on his head, where it made a cool schloopy-sloshy mud-cap all trickly behind his ears.

"'Vantage number three!" said the Bi-Coloured-Python-Rock-Snake. "You couldn't have done that with a mere-smear nose. Now how do you feel about being spanked again?"

"'Scuse me," said the Elephant's Child, "but I should not like it at all."

"How would you like to spank somebody?" said the Bi-Coloured-Python-Rock-Snake.

"I should like it very much indeed," said the Elephant's Child.

"Well," said the Bi-Coloured-Python-Rock-Snake, "you will find that new nose of yours very useful to spank people with."

"Thank you," said the Elephant's Child, "I'll remember that; and now I think I'll go home to all my dear families and try."

So the Elephant's Child went home across Africa frisking and whisking his trunk. When he wanted fruit to eat he pulled fruit down from a tree, instead of waiting for it to fall as he used to do. When he wanted grass he plucked grass up from the ground, instead of going on his knees as he used to do. When the flies bit him he broke off the branch of a tree and used it as a fly-whisk; and he made himself a new, cool, slushy-squshy mud-cap whenever the sun was hot. When he felt lonely walking through Africa he sang to himself down his trunk, and the noise was louder than several brass bands. He went especially out of his way to find a broad Hippopotamus (she was no relation of his), and he spanked her very hard, to make sure that the Bi-Coloured-Python-Rock-Snake had spoken the truth about his new trunk. The rest of the time he picked up the melon rinds that he had dropped on his way to the Limpopo—for he was a Tidy Pachyderm.

One dark evening he came back to all his dear families, and he coiled up his trunk and said, "How do you do?" They were very glad to see him, and immediately said, "Come here and be spanked for your 'satiable curtiosity."

"Pooh," said the Elephant's Child. "I don't think you peoples know anything about spanking; but *I* do, and I'll show you."

Then he uncurled his trunk and knocked two of his dear brothers head over heels.

"O Bananas!" said they, "where did you learn that trick, and what have you done to your nose?"

"I got a new one from the Crocodile on the banks of the great grey-green, greasy Limpopo River," said the Elephant's Child. "I asked him what he had for dinner, and he gave me this to keep."

"It looks very ugly," said his hairy uncle, the Baboon.

"It does," said the Elephant's Child. "But it's very useful," and he picked up his hairy uncle, the Baboon, by one hairy leg, and hove him into a hornet's nest.

Then that bad Elephant's Child spanked all his dear families for a long time, till they were very warm and greatly astonished. He pulled out his tall Ostrich aunt's tail-feathers; and he caught his tall uncle, the Giraffe, by the hind-leg, and dragged him through a thorn-bush; and he shouted at his broad aunt, the Hippopotamus, and blew bubbles into her ear when she was sleeping in the water after meals; but he never let any one touch Kolokolo Bird.

At last things grew so exciting that his dear families went off one by one in a hurry to the banks of the great grey-green, greasy Limpopo River, all set about with fever-trees, to borrow new noses from the Crocodile. When they came back nobody spanked anybody any more; and ever since that day, O Best Beloved, all the Elephants you will ever see, besides all those that you won't, have trunks precisely like the trunk of the 'satiable Elephant's Child.

I keep six honest serving-men;
(They taught me all I knew)
Their names are What and Where and When
And How and Where and Who.
I send them over land and sea,
I send them east and west;
But after they have worked for me,
I give them all a rest.

I let them rest from nine till five.
For I am busy then,
As well as breakfast, lunch, and tea,
For they are hungry men:
But different folk have different views;
I know a person small—
She keeps ten million serving-men,
Who get no rest at all!
She sends 'em abroad on her own affairs,
From the second she opens her eyes—
One million Hows, two million Wheres,
And seven million Whys!

~

Rudyard Kipling (1865–1936) was one of the most popular British writers. Many of his works are set in India, where he was born. His famous short story collections for children include *Just So Stories* and *The Jungle Book*, from which this story is taken. He was the first English-language writer to win the Nobel Prize in Literature.

Mrs Packletide's Tiger

Saki

It was Mrs Packletide's pleasure and intention that she should shoot a tiger. Not that the lust to kill had suddenly descended on her, or that she felt that she would leave India safer and more wholesome than she had found it, with one fraction less of wild beast per million of inhabitants. The compelling motive for her sudden deviation towards the footsteps of Nimrod was the fact that Loona Bimberton had recently been carried eleven miles in an aeroplane by an Algerian aviator, and talked of nothing else; only a personally procured tiger-skin and a heavy harvest of Press photographs could successfully counter that sort of thing. Mrs Packletide had already arranged in her mind the lunch she would give at her house in Curzon Street, ostensibly in Loona Bimberton's honour, with a tiger-skin rug occupying most of the foreground and all of the conversation. She had also already designed in her mind the tiger-claw brooch that she was going to give Loona Bimberton on her next birthday. In a world that is supposed to be chiefly swayed by hunger and by love Mrs Packletide was an exception; her movements and motives were largely governed by dislike of Loona Bimberton.

Circumstances proved propitious. Mrs Packletide had offered a thousand rupees for the opportunity of shooting a tiger without overmuch risk or exertion, and it so happened that a neighbouring village could boast of being the favoured rendezvous of an animal of respectable antecedents, which had been driven by the increasing infirmities of age to abandon game-killing and confine its appetite to the smaller domestic animals. The prospect of earning the thousand rupees had stimulated the sporting and commercial instinct of the villagers; children were posted night and day on the outskirts of the local jungle to head the tiger back in the unlikely event of his attempting to roam away to fresh hunting-grounds, and the cheaper kinds of goats were left about with elaborate carelessness to keep him satisfied with his present quarters. The one great anxiety was lest he should die of old age before the date appointed for the memsahib's shoot. Mothers carrying their babies home through the jungle after the day's work in the fields hushed their singing lest they might curtail the restful sleep of the venerable herd-robber.

The great night duly arrived, moonlit and cloudless. A platform had been constructed in a comfortable and conveniently placed tree, and thereon crouched Mrs Packletide and her paid companion, Miss Mebbin. A goat, gifted with a particularly persistent bleat, such as even a partially deaf tiger might be reasonably expected to hear on a still night, was tethered at the correct distance. With an accurately sighted rifle and a thumbnail pack of patience cards the sportswoman awaited the coming of the quarry.

"I suppose we are in some danger?" said Miss Mebbin.

She was not actually nervous about the wild beast, but she had a morbid dread of performing an atom more service than she had been paid for.

"Nonsense," said Mrs Packletide; "it's a very old tiger. It couldn't spring up here even if it wanted to."

"If it's an old tiger I think you ought to get it cheaper. A thousand rupees is a lot of money."

Louisa Mebbin adopted a protective elder-sister attitude towards money in general, irrespective of nationality or denomination. Her energetic intervention had saved many a rouble from dissipating itself in tips in some Moscow hotel, and francs and centimes clung to her instinctively under circumstances which would have driven them headlong from less sympathetic hands. Her speculations as to the market depreciation of tiger remnants were cut short by the appearance on the scene of the animal itself. As soon as it caught sight of the tethered goat it lay flat on the earth, seemingly less from a desire to take advantage of all available cover than for the purpose of snatching a short rest before commencing the grand attack.

"I believe it's ill," said Louisa Mebbin, loudly in Hindustani, for the benefit of the village headman, who was in ambush in a neighbouring tree.

"Hush!" said Mrs Packletide, and at that moment the tiger commenced ambling towards his victim.

"Now, now!" urged Miss Mebbin with some excitement; "if he doesn't touch the goat we needn't pay for it." (The bait was an extra.)

The rifle flashed out with a loud report, and the great tawny beast sprang to one side and then rolled over in the stillness of death. In a moment a crowd of excited natives had swarmed on to the scene, and their shouting speedily carried the glad news to the village, where a thumping of tom-toms took up the chorus of triumph. And their triumph and rejoicing found a ready echo in the heart of Mrs Packletide; already that luncheon-party in Curzon Street seemed immeasurably nearer.

It was Louisa Mebbin who drew attention to the fact that the goat was in death-throes from a mortal bullet-wound, while no trace of the rifle's deadly work could be found on the tiger. Evidently the wrong animal had been hit, and the beast of prey had succumbed to heart-failure, caused by the sudden report of the rifle, accelerated by senile decay. Mrs Packletide was pardonably annoyed at the discovery; but, at any rate, she was the possessor of a dead tiger, and the villagers, anxious for their thousand rupees, gladly connived at the fiction that she had shot the beast. And Miss Mebbin was a paid companion. Therefore did Mrs Packletide face the cameras with a light heart, and her pictured fame reached from the pages of the TEXAS WEEKLY SNAPSHOT to the illustrated Monday supplement of the NOVOE VREMYA. As for Loona Bimberton, she refused to look at an illustrated paper for weeks, and her letter of thanks for the gift of a tiger-claw brooch was a model of repressed emotions. The luncheon-party she declined; there are limits beyond which repressed emotions become dangerous.

From Curzon Street the tiger-skin rug travelled down to the Manor House, and was duly inspected and admired by the county, and it seemed a fitting and appropriate thing when Mrs Packletide went to the County Costume Ball in the character of Diana. She refused to fall in, however, with Clovis's tempting suggestion of a primeval dance party, at which every one should wear the skins of beasts they had recently slain. "I should be in rather a Baby

Bunting condition," confessed Clovis, "with a miserable rabbit-skin or two to wrap up in, but then," he added, with a rather malicious glance at Diana's proportions, "my figure is quite as good as that Russian dancing boy's."

"How amused every one would be if they knew what really happened," said Louisa Mebbin a few days after the ball.

"What do you mean?" asked Mrs Packletide quickly.

"How you shot the goat and frightened the tiger to death," said Miss Mebbin, with her disagreeably pleasant laugh.

"No one would believe it," said Mrs Packletide, her face changing colour as rapidly as though it were going through a book of patterns before post-time.

"Loona Bimberton would," said Miss Mebbin. Mrs Packletide's face settled on an unbecoming shade of greenish white.

"You surely wouldn't give me away?" she asked.

"I've seen a week-end cottage near Dorking that I should rather like to buy," said Miss Mebbin with seeming irrelevance. "Six hundred and eighty, freehold. Quite a bargain, only I don't happen to have the money."

***

Louisa Mebbin's pretty week-end cottage, christened by her "Les Fauves," and gay in summertime with its garden borders of tiger-lilies, is the wonder and admiration of her friends.

"It is a marvel how Louisa manages to do it," is the general verdict.

Mrs Packletide indulges in no more big-game shooting.

"The incidental expenses are so heavy," she confides to inquiring friends.

~

Saki is the pen name of Hector Hugh Munro (1870–1916), a British writer of humorous, often satirical short stories. He is said to have influenced writers such as P.G. Wodehouse and Roald Dahl. Many of his stories, such as "The Storyteller", "Sredni Vashtar" and "The Lumber Room", have children as protagonists. Saki died in the First World War.

From Mrs Dalloway

Virginia Woolf

Mrs Dalloway said she would buy the flowers herself.

For Lucy had her work cut out for her. The doors would be taken off their hinges; Rumpelmayer's men were coming. And then, thought Clarissa Dalloway, what a morning—fresh as if issued to children on a beach.

What a lark! What a plunge! For so it had always seemed to her, when, with a little squeak of the hinges, which she could hear now, she had burst open the French windows and plunged at Bourton into the open air. How fresh, how calm, stiller than this of course, the air was in the early morning; like the flap of a wave; the kiss of a wave; chill and sharp and yet (for a girl of eighteen as she then was) solemn, feeling as she did, standing there at the open window, that something awful was about to happen; looking at the flowers, at the trees with the smoke winding off them and the rooks rising, falling; standing and looking until

Peter Walsh said, "Musing among the vegetables?"—was that it?—"I prefer men to cauliflowers"—was that it? He must have said it at breakfast one morning when she had gone out on to the terrace—Peter Walsh. He would be back from India one of these days, June or July, she forgot which, for his letters were awfully dull; it was his sayings one remembered; his eyes, his pocket-knife, his smile, his grumpiness and, when millions of things had utterly vanished—how strange it was!—a few sayings like this about cabbages.

She stiffened a little on the kerb, waiting for Durtnall's van to pass. A charming woman, Scrope Purvis thought her (knowing her as one does know people who live next door to one in Westminster); a touch of the bird about her, of the jay, blue-green, light, vivacious, though she was over fifty, and grown very white since her illness. There she perched, never seeing him, waiting to cross, very upright.

For having lived in Westminster—how many years now? over twenty,—one feels even in the midst of the traffic, or waking at night, Clarissa was positive, a particular hush, or solemnity; an indescribable pause; a suspense (but that might be her heart, affected, they said, by influenza) before Big Ben strikes. There! Out it boomed. First a warning, musical; then the hour, irrevocable. The leaden circles dissolved in the air. Such fools we are, she thought, crossing Victoria Street. For Heaven only knows why one loves it so, how one sees it so, making it up, building it round one, tumbling it, creating it every moment afresh; but the veriest frumps, the most dejected of miseries sitting on doorsteps (drink their downfall) do the same; can't be dealt with, she felt positive, by Acts of Parliament for that very reason: they love life. In people's eyes, in the swing, tramp, and trudge; in the bellow and the uproar; the carriages, motor cars, omnibuses, vans, sandwich men shuffling and swinging; brass bands; barrel organs; in the triumph and the jingle and the strange high singing of some aeroplane overhead was what she loved; life; London; this moment of June.

For it was the middle of June. The War was over, except for some one like Mrs Foxcroft at the Embassy last night eating her heart out because that nice boy was killed and now the old Manor House must go to a cousin; or Lady Bexborough who opened a bazaar, they said, with the telegram in her hand, John, her favourite, killed; but it was over; thank Heaven—over. It was June. The King and Queen were at the Palace. And everywhere, though it was still so early, there was a beating, a stirring of galloping ponies, tapping of cricket bats; Lords, Ascot, Ranelagh and all the rest of it; wrapped in the soft mesh of the grey-blue morning air, which, as the day wore on, would unwind them, and set down on their lawns and pitches the bouncing ponies, whose forefeet just struck the ground and up they sprung, the whirling young men, and laughing girls in their transparent muslins who, even now, after dancing all night, were taking their absurd woolly dogs for a run; and even now, at this hour, discreet old dowagers were shooting out in their motor cars on errands of mystery; and the shopkeepers were fidgeting in their windows with their paste and diamonds, their lovely old sea-green brooches in eighteenth-century settings to tempt Americans (but one must economise, not buy things rashly for Elizabeth), and she, too, loving it as she did with an absurd and faithful passion, being part of it, since her people were courtiers once in the time of the Georges, she, too, was going that very night to kindle and illuminate; to give her party. But how strange, on entering the Park, the silence; the mist; the hum; the slow-swimming happy ducks; the pouched birds waddling; and who should be coming along with his back against the Government buildings, most appropriately, carrying a despatch box stamped with the Royal Arms, who but Hugh Whitbread; her old friend Hugh—the admirable Hugh!

"Good morning to you, Clarissa!" said Hugh, rather extravagantly, for they had known each other as children. "Where are you off to?"

"I love walking in London," said Mrs Dalloway. "Really it's better than walking in the country."

They had just come up—unfortunately—to see doctors. Other people came to see pictures; go to the opera; take their daughters out; the Whitbreads came "to see doctors." Times without number Clarissa had visited Evelyn Whitbread in a nursing home. Was Evelyn ill again? Evelyn was a good deal out of sorts, said Hugh, intimating by a kind of pout or swell of his very well-covered, manly, extremely handsome, perfectly upholstered body (he was almost too well dressed always, but presumably had to be, with his little job at Court) that his wife had some internal ailment, nothing serious, which, as an old friend, Clarissa Dalloway would quite understand without requiring him to specify. Ah yes, she did of course; what a nuisance; and felt very sisterly and oddly conscious at the same time of her hat. Not the right hat for the early morning, was that it? For Hugh always made her feel, as he bustled on, raising his hat rather extravagantly and assuring her that she might be a girl of eighteen, and of course he was coming to her party to-night, Evelyn absolutely insisted, only a little late he might be after the party at the Palace to which he had to take one of Jim's boys,—she always felt a little skimpy beside Hugh; schoolgirlish; but attached to him, partly from having known him always, but she did think him a good sort in his own way, though Richard was nearly driven mad by him, and as for Peter Walsh, he had never to this day forgiven her for liking him.

She could remember scene after scene at Bourton—Peter furious; Hugh not, of course, his match in any way, but still not a positive imbecile as Peter made out; not a mere barber's block. When his old mother wanted him to give up shooting or to take her to Bath he did it, without a word; he was really unselfish, and as for saying, as Peter did, that he had no heart, no brain, nothing but the manners and breeding of an English gentleman, that was only her dear Peter at his worst; and he could be intolerable; he could be impossible; but adorable to walk with on a morning like this.

(June had drawn out every leaf on the trees. The mothers of Pimlico gave suck to their young. Messages were passing from the Fleet to the Admiralty. Arlington Street and Piccadilly seemed to chafe the very air in the Park and lift its leaves hotly, brilliantly, on waves of that divine vitality which Clarissa loved. To dance, to ride, she had adored all that.)

For they might be parted for hundreds of years, she and Peter; she never wrote a letter and his were dry sticks; but suddenly it would come over her, If he were with me now what would he say?—some days, some sights bringing him back to her calmly, without the old bitterness; which perhaps was the reward of having cared for people; they came back in the middle of St. James's Park on a fine morning—indeed they did. But Peter—however beautiful the day might be, and the trees and the grass, and the little girl in pink—Peter never saw a thing of all that. He would put on his spectacles, if she told him to; he would look. It was the state of the world that interested him; Wagner, Pope's poetry, people's characters eternally, and the defects of her own soul. How he scolded her! How they argued! She would marry a Prime Minister and stand at the top of a staircase; the perfect hostess he called her (she had cried over it in her bedroom), she had the makings of the perfect hostess, he said.

So she would still find herself arguing in St. James's Park, still making out that she had been right—and she had too—not to marry him. For in marriage a little licence, a little independence there must be between people living together day in day out in the same house; which Richard gave her, and she him. (Where was he this morning for instance? Some committee, she never asked what.) But with Peter everything had to be shared; everything gone into. And it was intolerable, and when it came to that scene in the little garden by the fountain, she had to break with him or they would have been destroyed, both of them ruined, she was convinced; though she had borne about with her for years like an arrow sticking in her heart the grief, the anguish; and then the horror of the moment when some one told her at a concert that he had married a woman met on the boat going to India! Never should she forget all that! Cold, heartless, a prude, he called her. Never could she understand how he cared. But those Indian women did presumably—silly, pretty, flimsy nincompoops. And she wasted her pity. For he was quite happy, he assured her—perfectly happy, though he had never done a thing that they talked of; his whole life had been a failure. It made her angry still.

She had reached the Park gates. She stood for a moment, looking at the omnibuses in Piccadilly.

She would not say of any one in the world now that they were this or were that. She felt very young; at the same time unspeakably aged. She sliced like a knife through everything; at the same time was outside, looking on. She had a perpetual sense, as she watched the taxi cabs, of being out, out, far out to sea and alone; she always had the feeling that it was very, very dangerous to live even one day. Not that she thought herself clever, or much out of the ordinary. How she had got through life on the few twigs of knowledge Fräulein Daniels gave them she could not think. She knew nothing; no language, no history; she scarcely read a book now, except memoirs in bed; and yet to her it was absolutely absorbing; all this; the cabs passing; and she would not say of Peter, she would not say of herself, I am this, I am that.

Her only gift was knowing people almost by instinct, she thought, walking on. If you put her in a room with some one, up went her back like a cat's; or she purred. Devonshire House, Bath House, the house with the china cockatoo, she had seen them all lit up once; and remembered Sylvia, Fred, Sally Seton—such hosts of people; and dancing all night; and the wagons plodding past to market; and driving home across the Park. She remembered once throwing a shilling into the Serpentine. But every one remembered; what she loved was this, here, now, in front of her; the fat lady in the cab. Did it matter then, she asked herself, walking towards Bond Street, did it matter that she must inevitably cease completely; all this must go on without her; did she resent it; or did it not become consoling to believe that death ended absolutely? but that somehow in the streets of London, on the ebb and flow of things, here, there, she survived, Peter survived, lived in each other, she being part, she was positive, of the trees at home; of the house there, ugly, rambling all to bits and pieces as it was; part of people she had never met; being laid out like a mist between the people she knew best, who lifted her on their branches as she had seen the trees lift the mist, but it spread ever so far, her life, herself. But what was she dreaming as she looked into Hatchards' shop window? What was she trying to recover? What image of white dawn in the country, as she read in the book spread open:

Fear no more the heat o' the sun
Nor the furious winter's rages.

This late age of the world's experience had bred in them all, all men and women, a well of tears. Tears and sorrows; courage and endurance; a perfectly upright and stoical bearing. Think, for example, of the woman she admired most, Lady Bexborough, opening the bazaar.

There were Jorrocks' *Jaunts and Jollities*; there were *Soapy Sponge* and Mrs Asquith's *Memoirs* and *Big Game Shooting in Nigeria*, all spread open. Ever so many books there were; but none that seemed exactly right to take to Evelyn Whitbread in her nursing home. Nothing that would serve to amuse her and make that indescribably dried-up little woman look, as Clarissa came in, just for a moment cordial; before they settled down for the usual interminable talk of women's ailments. How much she wanted it—that people should look pleased as she came in, Clarissa thought and turned and walked back towards Bond Street, annoyed, because it was silly to have other reasons for doing things. Much rather would she have been one of those people like Richard who did things for themselves, whereas, she thought, waiting to cross, half the time she did things not simply, not for themselves; but to make people think this or that; perfect idiocy she knew (and now the policeman held up his hand) for no one was ever for a second taken in. Oh if she could have had her life over again! she thought, stepping on to the pavement, could have looked even differently!

She would have been, in the first place, dark like Lady Bexborough, with a skin of crumpled leather and beautiful eyes. She would have been, like Lady Bexborough, slow and stately; rather large; interested in politics like a man; with a country house; very dignified, very sincere. Instead of which she had a narrow pea-stick figure; a ridiculous little face, beaked like a bird's. That she held herself well was true; and had nice hands and feet; and dressed well, considering that she spent little. But often now this body she wore (she stopped to look at a Dutch picture), this body, with all its capacities, seemed nothing—nothing at all. She had the oddest sense of being herself invisible; unseen; unknown; there being no more marrying, no more having of children now, but only this astonishing and rather solemn progress with the rest of them, up Bond Street, this being Mrs Dalloway; not even Clarissa any more; this being Mrs Richard Dalloway.

Bond Street fascinated her; Bond Street early in the morning in the season; its flags flying; its shops; no splash; no glitter; one roll of tweed in the shop where her father had bought his suits for fifty years; a few pearls; salmon on an iceblock.

"That is all," she said, looking at the fishmonger's. "That is all," she repeated, pausing for a moment at the window of a glove shop where, before the War, you could buy almost perfect gloves. And her old Uncle William used to say a lady is known by her shoes and her gloves. He had turned on his bed one morning in the middle of the War. He had said, "I have had enough." Gloves and shoes; she had a passion for gloves; but her own daughter, her Elizabeth, cared not a straw for either of them.

Not a straw, she thought, going on up Bond Street to a shop where they kept flowers for her when she gave a party. Elizabeth really cared for her dog most of all. The whole house this morning smelt of tar. Still, better poor Grizzle than Miss Kilman; better distemper and tar and all the rest of it than sitting mewed in a stuffy bedroom with a prayer book! Better anything, she was inclined to say. But it might be only a phase, as Richard said, such as all girls go through. It might be falling in love. But why with Miss Kilman? who had been badly treated of course; one must make allowances for that, and Richard said she was very able, had a really historical mind. Anyhow they were inseparable, and Elizabeth, her own daughter, went to Communion; and how she dressed, how she treated people who came to lunch she did not care a bit, it being her experience that the religious ecstasy made people callous (so did causes); dulled their feelings, for Miss Kilman would do anything for the Russians, starved herself for the Austrians, but in private inflicted positive torture, so insensitive was she, dressed in a green mackintosh coat. Year in year out she wore that coat; she perspired; she was never in the room five minutes without making you feel her superiority, your inferiority; how poor she was; how rich you were; how she lived in a slum without a cushion or a bed or a rug or whatever it might be, all her soul rusted with that grievance sticking in it, her dismissal from school during the War—poor embittered unfortunate creature! For it was not her one hated but the idea of her, which undoubtedly had gathered in to itself a great deal that was not Miss Kilman; had become one of those spectres with which one battles in the night; one of those spectres who stand astride us and suck up half our life-blood, dominators and tyrants; for no doubt with another throw of the dice, had the black been uppermost and not the white, she would have loved Miss Kilman! But not in this world. No.

It rasped her, though, to have stirring about in her this brutal monster! to hear twigs cracking and feel hooves planted down in the depths of that leaf-encumbered forest, the soul; never to be content quite, or quite secure, for at any moment the brute would be stirring, this hatred, which, especially since her illness, had power to make her feel scraped, hurt in her spine; gave her physical pain, and made all pleasure in beauty, in friendship, in being well, in being loved and making her home delightful rock, quiver, and bend as if indeed there were a monster grubbing at the roots, as if the whole panoply of content were nothing but self love! this hatred!

Nonsense, nonsense! she cried to herself, pushing through the swing doors of Mulberry's the florists.

She advanced, light, tall, very upright, to be greeted at once by button-faced Miss Pym, whose hands were always bright red, as if they had been stood in cold water with the flowers.

There were flowers: delphiniums, sweet peas, bunches of lilac; and carnations, masses of carnations. There were roses; there were irises. Ah yes—so she breathed in the earthy garden sweet smell as she stood talking to Miss Pym who owed her help, and thought her kind, for kind she had been years ago; very kind, but she looked older, this year, turning her head from side to side among the irises and roses and nodding tufts of lilac with her eyes half closed, snuffing in, after the street uproar, the delicious scent, the exquisite coolness. And then, opening her eyes, how fresh like frilled linen clean from a laundry laid in wicker trays the roses looked; and dark and prim the red carnations, holding their heads up; and all the sweet peas spreading in their bowls, tinged violet, snow white, pale—as if it were the evening and girls in muslin frocks came out to pick sweet peas and roses after the superb summer's day, with its almost blue-black sky, its delphiniums, its carnations, its arum lilies was over; and it was the moment between six and seven when every flower—roses, carnations, irises, lilac—glows; white, violet, red, deep orange; every flower seems to burn by itself, softly, purely in the misty beds; and how she loved the grey-white moths spinning in and out, over the cherry pie, over the evening primroses!

And as she began to go with Miss Pym from jar to jar, choosing, nonsense, nonsense, she said to herself, more and more gently, as if this beauty, this scent, this colour, and Miss Pym liking her, trusting her, were a wave which she let flow over her and surmount that hatred, that monster, surmount it all; and it lifted her up and up when—oh! a pistol shot in the street outside!

"Dear, those motor cars," said Miss Pym, going to the window to look, and coming back and smiling apologetically with her hands full of sweet peas, as if those motor cars, those tyres of motor cars, were all *her* fault.

~

Virginia Woolf (1882–1941) was born in London. A pioneer in the narrative use of stream of consciousness, she published her first novel, ***The Voyage Out*****, in 1915. This was followed by literary criticism and essays, most notably** ***A Room of One's Own*****, and other acclaimed novels, including** ***Mrs Dalloway*****,** ***To the Lighthouse*** **and** ***Orlando*****.**

ALSO IN THE CLASSICS SERIES

Best Classic Short Stories for Children brings together some of the most well-known and beloved stories by authors like O. Henry, Oscar Wilde and Saki, and extracts from children's classics such as *The Railway Children* and *Little Women*. With a mix of genres including science fiction, mystery and ghost stories, and a host of popular characters such as Oliver Twist, Sherlock Holmes, Jane Eyre and Dracula, this is the perfect introduction to a range of classic literature.

Authors featured in this anthology include Charles Dickens, Charlotte Brontë, Rabindranath Tagore, Rudyard Kipling, Louisa May Alcott and Anton Chekhov among others.

Now available in hardback and paperback!

HARPERCOLLINS
CHILDREN'S
CLASSICS
The
Swiss
Family
Robinson
JOHANN DAVID WYSS

HARPERCOLLINS
CHILDREN'S
CLASSICS
The
Jungle
Book
RUDYARD
KIPLING

HARPERCOLLINS
CHILDREN'S
CLASSICS
Anne of
Green
Gables
L. M. MONTGOMERY

HARPERCOLLINS
CHILDREN'S
CLASSICS
Little
Women
LOUISA MAY
ALCOTT

HARPERCOLLINS
CHILDREN'S
CLASSICS
The
Wonderful
Wizard
of Oz
L. FRANK BAUM

HARPERCOLLINS
CHILDREN'S
CLASSICS
Peter Pan
J. M. BARRIE

HARPERCOLLINS
CHILDREN'S
CLASSICS
Pinocchio
CARLO COLLODI

HARPERCOLLINS
CHILDREN'S
CLASSICS
The Secret Garden
FRANCES HODGSON BURNETT